Healing Falls

Faith Eidse

Faitheyes Books
Tallahassee

Faitheyes Books published by Faitheyes Press
5210 Pimlico Drive, Tallahassee FL 32309
Email: faithleap7@gmail.com https://www.facebook.com/EidseFaith/

Healing Falls is a work of fiction drawn from the author's imagination.
Where real people, events, places appear, they are used fictitiously.

By permission:
Econfina Creek waterfall, by David Moynahan Photography, p. 111.
"Tubs" photo courtesy of Kathy Burgess, breeder of Comfort Retrievers. p. 128.
"Good Good Father," Anthony Brown, Pat Baret © 2014 Housefires Sounds
(ASCAP) Tony Brown Publishing Designee(NS) Common Hymnal Digital
(BMI) worshiptogether.com Songs (ASCAP) sixsteps Music (ASCAP) Vamos
Publishing (ASCAP) Capitol CMG Paragon (BMI) (adm. at
CapitalCMGPublishing.com). All rights reserved. Used by permission, p. 209
"I'm Going Free (Jailbreak)," Vertical Worship ©2013 Provident Label Group,
LLC, (Tyler Miller, Jacob Sooter, Benji Coward), p. 91.
"Abide with Me," Henry Francis Lyte lyrics, 1847; William Henry Monk tune
1861, in the public domain, p. 232.
"Praise You in This Storm," ©2005 My Refuge Music (BMI) (adm. At
CapitolCMGPUblishing.com) / Be Essential Songs (BMI) / Dayspring Music
(BMI) All rights reserved. Used by permission, p. 270. "The River," Brian
Doerksen, Brian Thiessen, Michael Hanson ©2004 Integrity's Hosanna! Music.
Used by permission, p. 292-3.
Unless otherwise noted, scripture is from the *Holy Bible*, New International
Version © 1973, 1978, 1984, by International Bible Society. Used by permission
of Zondervan. All rights reserved worldwide. Hosea 2:15 is from the New
Living Translation © 1996. Used by permission of Tyndale House Publishers,
Inc., Carol Stream, Illinois 60188. All rights reserved.
Every effort made to obtain permission:
"Welcome Into This Place," Unknown Writer, p. 9.
"Poke Salad Annie," Tony Joe White ©1968, BMI Music, p. 30.
"I dance for my father," Harley Osbourne, ©2010, p. 204.

Cover art ©2018 Tracy Leigh Foutz

ISBN: 978-1-7320254-0-0
First printing, March 30, 2018, printed in the United States

For the women inside

Leon County Detention Facility (Faith Eidse photo)

I needed clothes and you clothed me,
I was sick and you looked after me,
I was in prison and you came to visit me.
Matthew 25:36

Healing Falls
Fiction Shortlist - Word Alive Press 2017

What readers are saying:

The novel explores critical issues facing the American justice system, as well as the power of faith and artistic expression to transform lives.   -   Donna Meredith, *Fraccidental Death*

What a vision you have with this new book!
  -   Nina Sichel, *Unrooted Childhood, Writing Out of Limbo*

I started reading and could hardly pull myself away.
  -   Camy Keele, greatbuys4less.com

Healing Falls is a real page-turner... I couldn't stop reading and read it in two evenings. I loved the characters and their stories. Their names, the surprising originality of their words and wisdom. The way the narrative voice shifts from person to person and we get to see events and relationships from different perspectives. The redemptive experiences—the healing falls—of even the less likeable characters. At the same time, the book lays bare injustice and abuse of power in the current US prison system, and suggests ways to transform the system. I would say that reading this book has been a transformative experience. It has left me with more hope.
  -   Grace Eidse, Executive Director, Altered Minds, Inc.

Your writing is beautiful, ... a strong novel with a solid plot.
  -    WordServe Literary

A fantastic, life-changing, mind-changing book, ground-breaking, inspirational.
  -   Babette de Jongh, *Angel Falls Romance Series*

Contents

Hope's Prologue

Across sweltering Tallahassee, far from the women's prison, Chaplain Hope kicked off her covers, freeing her legs. The need to run ambushed her sometimes, twitching her muscles and tendons. At times, it was an older man on the Congo mission where she grew up, chasing her. At others, it was her mother suggesting she could marry him. At sixteen.

One day, Mom had rushed on. Was she pregnant?

No, and no, she would not be. Yes, she'd been cornered by him while down on her knees, pulling sand, trying to free the van from a sand pit. And yes, he'd descended breathing nonsense about her tiny waist. *Oops, she sprayed sand in his face. Sorry.*

But no, she would not let a man, mom or mission trap her that way. She wanted college, career, a path of her own. Like her mother, a doctor; or father, a pilot.

How was it now, Hope went inside every chance she got? Let the metal gates clang shut behind her, razor wire etch the sky. She spent her days, confined, listening to other women like herself, seeking a path of their own.

Hope turned up the fan, settling into restless dreams. The propeller whirred. They were flying over green mountains of Congo, her father at the controls, when it veered toward the moon and out into the Milky Way.

This was all wrong. Her father slumped over, unconscious. Hope reached past him, grabbed the controls and steered the plane to ground. There were too many problems on earth for the rapture just now. She set the plane down in a tropical storm, rain shaking the palms and drumming the dusty macadam.

Besides. She woke up, murmuring. *I've always prayed for God's kingdom to come on earth.*

Cinnamon's Prelude

The organ played "Steal Away" when a shadow filled the center aisle. The floor boards creaked, smelling of dusty pine. A stocky brown man in a gleaming white suit eased onto our pew. Shades, braids, gold tooth, lemon-musk scent.

"Daddy?"

"Cinnamon!" He rubbed my hair, nodded to Mama and Kita, and picked up my three-year-old Annie, snuggling her on his lap.

My dream of making a home for her seemed so close, I was floating. The preacher called on him to lead us in worship.

And Daddy, in his white suit, Air Jordans, chains and ice, started soft and low, walking the bass, guitar and drums slowly into his old favorite. Eyes closed, beard trembling, moisture beading his forehead and running down his face. The drug dealer repenting.

He motioned us to rise, "Please join in. You don't have to be perfect."

His voice rose, soft as a dove's wing. "Welcome into this place, welcome into this broken vessel."

He built to a soaring tenor, African-Seminole face creased. "You desire to abide in the praises of your people."

In measured steps across stage, "So we lift our hearts, and we lift our hands and we offer up this praise unto your name."

I pulled Annie close, though she was still a little stiff with me. I had disappeared too many times in her short life, lost in my own addiction, and prison. I closed my eyes, wanting to live in that harmony forever.

Part 1

Cinnamon Falls

Tallahassee station (en.wikipedia.org)

1
Broken Vessel

Hello, my name is Cinnamon, Cinny for short. I'm a
grateful, recovering addict.   - Cinnamon's 12-step greeting

On Tuesday, I hit a man.

I squealed the brakes but the tires skidded, leaving tread marks.

How long he'd been lying in the street, I didn't know. I backed up and leaped from the van.

My sister Kita rushed from the passenger's side where she'd been letting me drive—helping me get my license back after prison. Fat chance, after this. The guy looked a wreck.

He lay there rasping, blood pooling in his mouth, running down into the gutter. It soaked his black beard, Seminole shirt, gold chains, braids.

Just like Dad's.

"Dad! Daddy?" What was he doing back here, just blocks from Mama's? Had our tires done this? "It's Daddy!"

"He's been shot!" Kita fell to her knees in her nurse-assistant scrubs, sweat purling her forehead.

"Duck!" I crouched and peered into dark alleys around the old train station, keeping watch while Kita pressed his chest, one hand on top of the other. Applying pressure, trying to stop the flow. Listening for another gasp. Pressing harder. Hard and fast, hard and fast.

"One, two, three, four…" Hard and fast, hard and fast. But all that bubbled up was blood. She leaned over him, listening, and kept at it, hard and fast, hard and fast, "…ninety-nine, one hundred." She bent close, again, ear to his mouth. "That was his last gasp."

She circled 'round and peered beneath him, careful not to turn his head. "Oh no, he's been shot in the head. The bullet cut right into his crown and through his brain. He's gone."

I crawled to see the small, black hole, my vision blurred, unfocused, dripping sweat and tears. It was a muggy 90 degrees, July in northwest Florida.

"There's a lump on his head, too, and—" she pointed to his fingers, "his knuckles are bruised. Oh, and look, at this."

His suit ripped at the shoulder, blood-stained. Another bullet?

From the haint-mossed oaks and warehouses of Railroad Square, an owl screamed, red fox screeched, twig cracked and a dog growled. I backed under the van bumper. "Duck!"

We hit the pavement, scraping knees and palms, fingers raw, searching black shadows for men with guns. My pulse beat a staccato in my throat, my hands stuck to the pebbled pavement, blood like glue gleaming in the street light. A hard, round object touched my finger—shell casing. No, getaway!

Kita crept up beside me, kneeling over him, listening. "He's bled out. His heart stopped pumping."

I reached to touch him but she brushed my arm away. "No! Don't add your DNA. This is a crime scene. He's been shot from behind, executed. The bullet went through the back and cracked his teeth. See how shattered they are?"

Yes, teeth shards floating in glinting blood.

Dad was gone. Shot while we drove out for milk, blocks from Kita's trailer.

"Nooo. Daddy, come back." I moaned, wanting to shake and wake him. "You can't die now, Daddy! Just when you were getting your life together."

Sunday in church, his hands raised in blue-green stained-glass light, tears streaming down bronzed cheeks, the grieving drug-dealer led us in worship.

There in the street, I was so blinded by loss, all I could see was darkness. I'd never seen a real bullet hole through a head. Exactly how my big brother Denzel—Dex—died, only by his own hand. And Mama had slammed the door so I couldn't look. Now there were two blasts blowing us to pain and rubble.

If only— If only we'd come sooner, if only we'd reached him somehow—

Bullets made it all so final.

Kita was dialing 9-1-1.

I knocked the phone from her hand. "Kita, nooo! What if the police did this?"

"The police wouldn't leave him this way." She scrambled after her flip phone, blood-smeared in the gutter. "Only hoodlums."

"The hel—" But I caught myself. Her husband was military police in Iraq and I lived in dread every day. But she, calm as ever, picked her phone out of Daddy's blood, and wipe it on her scrubs.

She opened her phone again and read the light display. "Time of death, 8:38 p.m."

How could she be so cool? "Kita, Daddy's dead!"

"This is what they teach us in CPR. It's never your emergency. Never—" Rubbing the phone on her scrubs again, full lips drawn. "—your emergency."

How can you lose all the men in your life to bullets—and not crack? After Dex died, I couldn't draw, not even a black line. Finally, I drew a dot, a hole through a brain, a bullet tearing through it, trailing blood. Mama took me to a doctor who gave me Xanax and Oxies. But I couldn't take just one or the darkness closed in again. I was sent to prison for popping—and then selling—roxies.

Squinting and blinking in the dark, Kita dialed again and got a dispatcher. Gripping the phone and wobbling on her knees, she spoke low and controlled. "I'm Nikita Johnson here with my sister Cinnamon Rose. Calling from Railroad Avenue near Gaines."

She waited, then answered, her voice pinched. "Yes, Tallahassee."

Where else would Railroad and Gaines be? Tallahassee was in the middle of nowhere surrounded by prisons, twenty-eight in an hour's drive. Some counties had more prisoners than residents.

And I'd done too much time in them away from my family—away from Daddy. I swallowed against a rock in my throat.

"We drove up on—" Kita's strong voice cracked.

My feet jolted at the sensation of tires scorching him.

"We drove up on our father, DeAndre Harris, shot in the street." She paused, controlling the snag in her voice. "Please hurry. We'll stay here, by the car. Yes, yes, her name is really Cinnamon." She cut the phone and wiped her face on her sleeve.

My real name is Keisha but Dex called me Cinnamon after that spoonful I choked on. It stuck. Even Daddy called me Cinnamon in that smooth baritone I wouldn't hear again. Except on his YouTube recordings.

Daddy didn't live with us but I always tried to pull him in, my first crayoned words inviting him to my third birthday party. He came late, held me in strong brown arms and colored with me.

After that, I never stopped inviting him to things. Sometimes he came and twirled me, sometimes he didn't and Mama tried to make it up with buckets of colored pencils, markers, chalk. I drew my little heart out; Daddy sailing up high, holding a microphone, and Mama, Dex, Kita and me on the ground looking up.

Daddy never was steady, Mama said, and he never married her. Still, she kept praying for him and inviting him to Sunday dinner.

"I can't believe it." Kita's cheeks glistened in the streetlight. "All those times we didn't spend together, all those years missed and gone." Her shoulders shook and she gave in at last to shuddering sobs. She cradled herself in strong arms tears welling and spilling over. "He was so alive on Sunday."

The offering plates came around and Daddy kept singing. The man who'd slammed preachers for just wanting your money, kept singing for the offertory. "Dig deep folks," he said. "The Lord can do more with your gifts—his gifts really—than you can."

There under the streetlight, with Daddy's teeth shards flowing away, I trembled 'til my teeth rattled. Would the shooters come after me next? Who were they?

"You're in shock." Kita took off her lab coat and wrapped it around me, each nerve a wounded fiber. She opened the passenger door and lifted me in. I tucked my feet under me away from the chilled milk jug. Would we be next? Who were these monsters, cutting down my daddy, just when he was shining his light like a city on a hill? I moaned and bawled.

Kita handed me some fresh napkins and we dabbed our faces. She was the grownup to my child, the coffee to my cocoa, the high school grad to my dropout.

But there was something she seemed to be forgetting. Worship was not the last we'd seen him.

2
Cinnamon's Sight

In the dark van, I gripped Kita's sleeve. "Sissy, remember? We saw him after church, at Mama's."

Kita rubbed her temples with both hands. "Yes, he got to Mama's ahead of us, but he didn't stay."

"Right? He was in a hurry. Remember, that strange thing that happened?"

"What strange thing?" Her neat braids began to unravel, crimped hair silhouetted in the street light.

"He came from around back with some dirty plastic bags in one hand, church mug—the stained-glass kind—in the other." Did he hide stuff in the crawl space under Mama's house?

Kita's chiseled cheeks gleamed in the streetlight, her black eyes blazed. "Oh yes, the kids raced for Big Daddy, begging for popsicles. He reached into his plastic sacks and pulled out some bills—the man who wouldn't pay five cents to see Jesus ride a bicycle."

"Kita." It hurt too much to grin, or groan.

"Just sayin'. He never did remember my birthday. Remembered yours."

"Always. I wouldn't let him forget. Well, on Sunday he said something important. Did you hear?"

She shook her head. "Really, Cinny, I was racing after the kids again. The neighbors nearly backed over them."

"He said something and Mama stepped in front of me. He set his mug on the car roof and searched the trees by the railroad." Did he see something out there?

Kita wrinkled her forehead.

"Mama's eyes flashed and her nostrils flared, doing her Cleopatra act. She said, 'Who? Who's after you, Andre?'

Kita turned in the van and faced me. "Yeah, she was fuming. Arms crossed, whipping her tail."

"The 12:45 for Pensacola blared and clattered through then. I couldn't hear."

Kita raised her eyebrows. "Oh, yes, I hung onto Annie's hand extra tight then."

"I had to move closer. Daddy was saying, 'Someone broke in my house. Could be some 'my homeboys—out of prison, worse than ever.'"

Kita napkin-blotted my forehead. "Go on."

"Mama tore off her hat and paced like a caged panther. Daddy said something about his boys 'trying to drag him down again.'"

There in Mama's yard with the tankers and box cars rolling by, I had ducked, not meeting Daddy's eyes. His friend Doobie, Annie's daddy, had just been sprung. He was the Officer in Charge when I went to prison, and at first, I thought he would protect me. The way he spread his jackboot in my path, when he recognized me. Muscled arm cocked, so I had to step around him. He was Daddy's buddy after all, used to hunting doves and wild turkeys together.

In the van near Daddy's body, Doobie's scowl loomed over me. It took him no time to get me alone when I was cleaning prison bathrooms.

A few weeks later I found myself pregnant in prison. At first I thought I'd die, or the baby would. I waited until Annie started doing flips and growing. Then I got some legal help and, over the next months, we sued the prison. They let me out, and locked Doobie up.

I was not his favorite person anymore.

After the train passed, Daddy had tossed his shopping bags into his garnet-n-gold Lexis and slid behind the wheel.

"You better change your ways," Mama said. "Stop selling drugs and start recording your music. Use the gift God gave you."

He nodded. "I was at the recording studio when they broke in. I gotta find me a new hiding place." He backed out and drove away, his church mug sliding off the roof and shattering on the ground. The stained-glass glory crashed around us.

16

In the van, Kita stirred in the driver's seat. "Cinny, you with your artistic sight, catch things the rest of us miss. You're like our own private eye."

I gripped Kita's arm. "But why? Why would he come get his stash from Mama's house?"

Kita frowned. "What do you mean?"

"Doobie wouldn't know about that. It must've been someone closer, someone he hung out with and told all his secrets to."

"You mean like Cuz?" Her voice strained.

"I know." I was miserable. Our cousin Rocky was like a big brother to us. He was slow and trusting. But he was also easily led.

"He's family." Kita peered down the railroad tracks into darkness. "Why would he sell Dad out?"

"Maybe not. Maybe it was one of Daddy's other buddies, someone we don't know." I leaned across the console into Kita's encircling arm.

She squeezed me tight. "I do remember Daddy and Mama being upset, but I was so distracted. I wished Daddy had stayed for dinner."

"Me too. I can't believe I didn't even offer to help him."

Kita rubbed my shoulder. "That was not your place, Cinny. There's nothing you could've done."

She was often my defender, believing I'd been too caught up in Daddy's drug scene. She even got me a temp job cleaning instruments at the hospital for a while. I pulled her lab coat tighter, wiping my nose on her sleeve.

"Did his friends do this?" He'd grown up in small-town Quincy with a bunch of them always talkin' 'bout "hittin' a lick," trying to get lucky in love or money.

"Don't know." She'd been raped by one of them, years ago. Had a baby too, her oldest, Ruby.

Kita released me and bent over her phone again. "Guess I have to call Mama." She kept Mama on speed dial one, but she hesitated before pressing the key and raising it to her chiseled cheek.

Mama had such high hopes for Daddy. This would crush her.

Several rings later, Kita hung up. "I sure hate to wake her like this. Should we wait and go over there?"

I flashed on Annie, sleeping in a nest at Kita's trailer. Was she stirring, calling me? "What about the kids? When're we going to get back to them?"

"Yes, I thought about that. The police will want to take us in, get our statements. We have to call Mama to babysit."

I stirred and bristled, surprised at the edge in my tone. "What was Daddy doing down here anyway?" He had escaped to the leafy hills north of Interstate 10, while all around us shotgun houses were falling to decay and gangs. And state offices and cheap rentals for Florida A & M students took over.

"Coming to see Mama?" Kita blew her nose, hung up and pressed one again. She let it ring a few times until Mama finally answered.

"Sorry to wake you." Kita paused and put the phone on speaker. "But I have some sad news. Cinny and I are on Railroad Ave near the train station with Dad's body. He's been shot dead."

On the phone, Mama screamed so loud I hit the floorboard, scared the guys with guns would hear. A cold, wet skull rolled around my ankle and I screamed, too.

3
Hittin' a Lick

I pulled my feet up on the van seat and peered into the foot well.

The skull was cube-like and had no eye sockets, nose or mouth. Shaken and mute, I pointed at the creepy thing.

"What? Hang on Mama." Kita followed my shaking finger. "Cinny. That is the milk we just bought. Sorry Mama. Cinny just freaked out over a bottle of milk."

Mama groaned.

"I guess you should swing by and give us some hugs. We could use you right now."

Kita closed the phone and ruffled my hair. "She'll be here in a moment."

We watched the street. In the rearview mirror, a rusty truck pulled into the gas station behind us. Guys in ball caps smoking cigarettes. Then out of the shadows, headlights lit the street. Kita opened her door and we moved toward Mama, wrapped in a blanket, hair sticking out all over, so unlike her usual polish. She trudged to Daddy's body, and stood over him, shoulders heaving, the scars on her wrists purple in the street light.

"What's she gonna do?" I whispered. Bile rose in my throat and I clutched Kita's arm, wretched all over again at how Mama had slit her wrists after I went back to the street.

Kita understood perfectly. "You didn't do this, Cinny." She moved me toward Mama. "It's not your fault." She pulled the three of us together, closing the circle, and we huddled over Daddy's body—still as night.

Mama wiped her face on her blanket. "First my baby boy and now my Andre—." She broke off, choking and coughing. I thought she would throw up and then I knew I would. I tumbled to the ground and retched in the dirt.

Kita knelt over me, holding my head until dry heaves racked me. I seemed to be trying to expel a monster.

"You okay?" Kita asked.

I retched again. How could I tell her I was pregnant? It was all wrong, bringing life into this darkness.

Sirens rose in the distance and she lifted me on trembling legs.

"Mama, the police are probably going to take us in for questioning." Kita's voice was gentle but strong. "Can you please go to my place and sit with the kids?"

"Thank you, Mama." I leaned into her, wanting more than ever to get back to Annie.

"I better go before they get here." Mama stumbled to her car and pulled a u-turn in front of Bread and Roses. Her headlights lit the hill to FAMU and turned east, sweeping along the railroad tracks past her yellow clapboard on cinderblocks, and beyond that, across South Adams, to Kita's trailer in Smokey Hollow.

Blue and red lights strobed into the street, bouncing off the ivy-draped All Saints Café, old train station turned indy-movie-house, warehouse art galleries I once loved, live oaks trailing scaly Spanish moss. *Dust to dust, ashes to ashes.*

Police cruisers and ambulance spilled people in uniform. Kita stood ready, sinewed hand on the driver's door, steadying herself. A medic hurried to Daddy, pulling on blue-gloves, setting down his kit and crouching over him. A woman in brown lit the ground with her flashlight and placed some yellow markers.

"Shell casings." Kita's voice, calm and low, reached me through the open driver's window. She'd slipped back into not-my-emergency mode. "Three, looks like."

A man in brown uniform came over with a notebook. Kita gave Daddy's name and age. "39." She told him what Daddy said about the burglary and his homeboys, just out of prison.

"Who would that be?"

She hesitated and so did I. There were several running loose.

"Names, we need names." The investigator tapped his pen on his notebook. "You want these guys to go free?"

I flinched. "Billie Hutchinson goes by Doobie." My voice quavered. I used to sleep behind the sofa with Annie, so afraid he'd send someone from prison to shoot me in my bed by the window. When even the nest behind the sofa seemed too dangerous, I'd sleep at friends' houses, leaving Annie with Mama.

"Pardon? Slowly please." The man held his pen ready.

Kita straightened and spelled it slowly, "B-i-l-l-i-e Williams. Lives right over there in those apartments on stilts." She pointed her chin. "First one, back row."

How had I ever caved in to him? I was still trying to heal that little girl in a Red Riding Hood play, looking for Daddy in the audience. I was that beaming blue-ribbon winner at the art show hoping for Daddy's crooked grin and strong, warm hug.

The medics slid Daddy's cold body onto a stretcher, zipped him into a gray bag and rolled him into the ambulance. The doors clanged shut, opening a deep wound in me like a burst appendix or cut artery. The ambulance drove off silently, carrying Daddy away without sirens or lights.

"We'll need to take you in for a complete statement."

Kita got in and we buckled our seatbelts. "We'll follow you."

At the police station on Seventh Avenue, we sat on hard chairs in the brightly-lit station while first one officer and then another pieced together our family history and worked out all possible leads on suspects. They lingered on the summer Mama went to jail on false charges, and the years Daddy spent behind bars.

The officers ran background checks and discovered I was on probation, sentenced to outpatient drug rehab. A round-faced officer in ponytail and bangs asked how that was going.

"We got past the hard stuff." I read her warm smile and kept going. "And we're writing dream journals. I have dreams again." My voice caught. "Or had."

"Yes?" She pushed back her long bangs.

"I wanted my Daddy clean—I guess he is now. And I want to use my art to get my life on track and make a home for my daughter."

Kita reached over and squeezed my wrist. "You can do it."

They typed up our statements and I used Kita's phone to text my boyfriend Tony. I waited, but there was no reply. That was not like him. Still, I didn't want to wake him just to break the bad news.

Finally, as midnight rolled into pre-dawn, we signed our testimonies and they let us go. We swung around Lake Ella with its splashing fountain and paddling ducks, St. Paul's steeple reflected in its ripples.

Lake Ella (Faith Eidse photo)

"You know what I hate?" Kita turned off the radio. "This is going to hit the news today, with all the buzz about black-on-black crime."

"He's a victim for real." I quoted Tupac, heat pricking my brittle eyes.

"Yeah but it wasn't the police this time. Cinny, we have to respect each other before others will respect us."

We dipped into a deep pothole and rolled up over sharp lime rock, a sinkhole yawning, threatening to swallow us whole.

We passed the old capitol with its little dome on top the big one, and red-striped awnings. The new capitol soared behind it, a stark, twenty-two-story concrete block tower. Then we turned south toward her trailer, clinging to the edge of historic Smokey Hollow. The railroad had cut the first slice through its heart, knocking down our shotgun houses, and trains blaring horns and covering us in soot. State office building followed until only fringes were left on Marvin and Seaboard streets.

Those ghosts lingered as we parked and went inside Kita's cramped but orderly mobile home. My chubby, pig-tailed Annie was still nestled between her string bean cousins. We huddled in the front room, Kita moving stacked laundry so I could sit beside Mama on the sofa.

"He's probably leading Dex in the heavenly choir." Kita always said the calming thing, cool water on our burning eyes. "What a mercy that he left us one shining hour of love and devotion."

That soulful man had given his last performance and he would not be back on this earth again to guide us.

"Who would do this?" I kept asking. Would his homeboys get me next? I curled tighter into the sofa, wrapping myself deep in Kita's lab coat.

But Kita wouldn't believe it. "They grew up together. Why would his friends do this?"

Mama pulled me to her soft self and sighed. "You're beautiful, Cinny, you know that? I'm so glad you came off the street."

"Mmm. Me too, Mama." Spanish moss coils brushed the screen, filtering light from Florida's high-rise capitol.

"You come from strong people who worked hard to get us where we are today—and that's a good thing." Her voice was low and soothing.

My dry eyelids grew heavy.

"But it's also a hard thing. Others can be jealous of us." She hugged me tighter, her razor-scarred wrists scraping my soft arms. She had nearly killed herself over me.

Kita had found Mama passed out in a crimson tub and tied off her flowing veins. Mama recovered and fought back, too, studying until she was promoted to fingerprint analyst. She knew the stories, the miniscule chance of addicts like me making it out alive.

"But this," Mama said. "Your daddy rolled by his homeboys—if he was—Lord, preserve us.

4
Gateway of Hope

Hello, my name is Hope. I'm a grateful, recovering addict and codependent. My higher power is Jesus Christ.

Chaplain Hope entered the prison chapel to an echoing din. Women in blue scrubs shouted, clapped and bounced along to the "Jailbreak Song."

"Right when the gavel fell, I heard the freedom bell,
Ring through the heart of hell, I'm going free."

Hope joined the raucous chaos, twirling down the aisle, slapping high fives, and shouting along. "I'm going free!"

Up front, Julie was out-singing them all. She would be released in the morning, and she had veered wildly in recent days. From saying she could resist anything—her family on meth—to fearing she could resist nothing.

Hope knew the memory pathways of drugs and alcohol, the chemical changes in her youthful brain. Shattering glass, crunching metal, her convertible sliding under a semi nearly severing her head. Sirens blared, lights strobed and she was rushed to emergency with multiple fractures. The pain in her chest, her shaking limbs, the lives she had risked, flipped a switch in her that day.

She entered AA and gradually gave up mornings with Tom Collins, evenings with Baileys and coffee. In small groups, she recalled grabbing her father's pilot hat on his way out to fly another mission. *You trying to ground me?* He growled and chased her 'til she fell, laughing on the sofa. How could she let him go? And yet she'd had to, every mission he flew, and the day he'd never returned. After that she'd needed a boyfriend like some people need air and water.

She had married a college classmate, a scientist who could calm her down. And had clung hard to their twin girls when they were born. She wanted to parent them completely, and in the process, finish parenting herself. They were her pride and joy now, finishing college and starting careers.

And though it had been a long time coming, she'd wept and pleaded when her husband moved out last year, taking his hat, the same as her father. Yet she soon saw the futility of chasing a fleeing man.

The night he left, she curled in grief and heard an inward audible command, *Hope*. And she had, not in a man but in the creator of the universe, that he would restore the family.

She saw herself, a bird with feathers, perched on a sun-warmed branch over an eternal spring.

At the podium, an inmate chapel monitor, Lexis, read from II Chronicles where Solomon's son had listened to his lousy friends and divided the kingdom. Lexis closed the Bible, placed a paper crown on her gray curls and climbed on a chair. She held out a hand to Hope. "Come up here, peasant. Let me pull you up to my level."

Hope tried to get on the chair, but instead easily pulled Lexis down.

The women hooted and hollered, clapping at their performance.

Hope took the podium. "Like Lexis on that chair, Solomon's son was pulled down to the level of his foolish friends. Though his subjects begged for tax breaks, he doubled them, leading to revolt and breakaway of ten tribes. Do you know that ended the united kingdom?

"As a woman, I was raised to please others. And yet I did myself serious harm by pleasing the wrong people." She paused and gazed into a sea of somber faces. "I even left my husband for a time, and was raped while traveling abroad."

Murmurs rose from the crowd. "Thank you, Chaplain. Thank you for sharing."

"Yes, and yet we have this hope." Her chapel monitors joined her in the benediction. "Now to him who is able to keep you from falling, and to present you faultless before the only wise God, our father...."

Afterward, she took Julie's hands. "Your family and community need you. Go in God's power and light. And don't let them drag you down."

Tallahassee's hanging tree at the old Leon County Jail.
(Faith Eidse photo)

5
Mama's Cross

The window air conditioner kicked on and Kita brought us her favorite quilt. She'd pieced it from camo fatigues—Dex's and her husband's—and lined it with Mama's old prison scrubs.

Mama had been thrown in jail on false charges in the eighties, accused of embezzling while keeping books for an insurance agency. She worked with several bleach-blonde women who clacked around in red heels and sent her for coffee.

Daddy said they'd got the wrong woman. Mama could out-game anyone. In fact, she logged all the checks she cut, even the ones they told her not to. She kept that log separate, locked in her desk.

I was only four and I cried every night she was gone, missing her like my heart had gone out of my rib cage and was roaming the city, searching for her. When we saw her on Sundays, she always said she needed me to cheer up, so she could remember my dimples all week. She was young and big-eyed then, smooth-faced with her hair up in braids, wrapped in the yellow scarf we bought her.

We hung onto her, all of three of us at once. And she wouldn't let me go, even when the guard said visiting time was over. She hugged me hard and said, "Don't worry, Cinny. I will be home soon."

On Kita's trailer sofa, I pulled the camo quilt around Mama and me, breathing in her lilac scent. I had grown stiff with her in my addiction, echoing our broken bond in childhood. Yet her mothering was what I clung to and wanted to pass on to my kids.

The summer Mama was in jail, Daddy took us to his Seminole nana, his mama's mama in South Georgia, near Camilla.

He chased us through pecan orchards and we tumbled into pokeweed.

"Here's some good eatin'." He sniffed the plants. "It's like turnip greens."

I tore off a leaf and chomped it—bitter, tangy—and spat it out.

"Naw, don't eat it raw—it'll kill ya. We'll get Nana Mama to cook it up."

He pulled out his pocket knife, cut the young stalks and we carried them home like babies' breath. Daddy's nana, always outside and barefoot, washed the greens in the rain barrel and spread them on her work table. On the outdoor fire pit in a big frying pan, she heated bacon grease and shooed us onto the porch.

Daddy strummed his guitar, Dex whittled an arrow, and Kita rocked me on the bench swing. The sweet salty scent watered my mouth; a pink-orange sun sank into the leafy orchards. We were all together except for Mama with her low laugh, lilting voice, wrapping arms.

In Kita's cozy living room, I stirred in Mama's arms. "Do you remember the recording we made for you when you were in jail? Daddy even sold them to get you out."

"Mmhm. He was an original, a great and generous musician." She stroked my hair. "Tell me about it."

"Daddy strummed his guitar and pressed the record button on his old cassette recorder. He sang, *Poke salad Annie...that's you, Cinny. Your mama ain't workin' on a chain gang. But she' sittin' in the pokey 'cause someone poked her in the eye.... You reckon there's some gators in that there pond?* I said in perfect rhythm, *Naw, I ain't seen no gators.*"

"Yes, you did." Mama squeezed my shoulder. "My cell mates called themselves gators, 'member? They fell in love with you when I played that recording."

"Dex and Kita joined in the chorus. *Poke Salad Annie, Gator got your Granny...chomp, chomp.* I squealed, *Nooo, Daddy! She right there cookin' poke salad!*

"Daddy kept strumming. *Cinny, you make the alligators look tame...that's you baby—*"

"Dex came chomping after me. *'Nooo I ain't. I make 'em look wild!'* I shrieked and ran, but Dex caught me and pretended to chomp me up."

Mama pulled the camo quilt tighter around us. "That recording helped me stay strong inside, Cinny. I gave the prosecutor and state's attorneys what they wanted, my hidden log book. They traced the checks not to my bank account, but to my accusers'."

After that, she came home more quiet and serious, hugged us and wouldn't let go. She jumped when the screen door slammed, checked under the bed before kneeling, and when she prayed, couldn't stop. She prayed Psalms and Proverbs, thanked God for being in control and prayed hedges of protection around us. That forcefield sometimes repelled me; sometimes pulled me in, bringing me back to myself.

Kita's phone rang in the trailer and we all jumped. It was the police and she put it on speaker.

"We found your father's Lexus south of town. It was charred from a fire started in the driver's seat. We suspect the perpetrators were trying to hide blood-splatter."

Mama groaned and Kita thanked them and cut the phone, joining us on the sofa under the camo blanket. The window air conditioner cycled again, blowing cold air on us and Mama finally fell into a leaden sleep.

Kita stirred and re-filled my iced tea, setting it on the table in front of me and paging through my sketchbook. I talked her through the graphic novel I was working on again. The cover was Tallahassee's hanging tree, a twisted grandfather oak, wide-eyed ghosts of a 1937 lynching rising from its trunk.

One Sunday when I was in high school, Mama had taken me across the tracks to the gnarly oak by the old white, art deco Leon County jail, with its nested-box windows and stylized cupolas. This was not the jail where they'd held her in the eighties but where they'd locked up her mama, a bus-boycotter in the fifties. That day, I ran my hand along the bumpy trunk that rippled with ridged knots like flailing, contorted bodies, arms covered in jagged brown ferns and gray Spanish moss.

"Four black men were lynched here, taken from the jail by white men and killed. Two may have hanged from this tree. Two were teenage boys driven out and shot in the woods. They were accused of stabbing a police officer who caught them robbing a store. The policeman recovered."

"Wasn't there a guard?" I couldn't understand why someone would break *into* a jail.

"Oh, the guard stepped aside—and was later elected city police chief."

Mama took my hand and ran it along the dusty, brown ferns. "Resurrection ferns," she whispered. "They turn glossy green after rain."

In the cooling trailer, Kita straightened in her kitchen chair and faced me, lifting the detailed graphic novel cover. "It won the art show, Cinny." Her voice was ragged, hushed. "I hope you don't give that up. Daddy would want you to continue."

I sighed, sliding out from under Mama's arm, and sipping the sweet lemony tea. "Even the story of his murder?"

"Oh, I know so." Kita gripped my knee. "Tell me about winning that show. Was that the year after your class painted a whole show in colorful, Florida Highwaymen styles?"

"Yes, you remember my blazing skies, reflected in the jungle swamp?" Mama still had that one hanging in her living room.

"Oh Cinny, yes! Those wild Florida scenes were so popular, you sold out and made enough to put on a serious contest the next year." Kita's nudged me under the table. "Go on. The contest."

"The judge came back to my drawing several times before putting a blue ribbon on it. He said, 'This is the first frame of your graphic novel. Keep going.' I didn't know what a graphic novel was, but my art teacher gave me *Maus* by Art Spiegelman, drawings of skeletal death camp survivors. They were all mice with sunken eyes and crepe paper skin, guarded by cats in Nazi uniforms. That's what gave me the idea to use southern foxes and armadillos."

Kita sat forward. "Yes, keep going."

"In *Maus*, Art's mother slit her wrists, too, years after Hitler's Germany. The artist ends up in a mental institute thinking, *Hitler did it, Mommy. Bitch.*"

Kita gasped and Mama shifted on the sofa. We waited until she'd settled again.

"I know, right? I understood how Hitler was responsible but I keep wondering, who was the bitch? Hitler or Mommy? Or how had Hitler turned Mommy into a bitch, and affected her children."

"And children's children, Cinny. It's self-betrayal to slam the ones we love, but we've faced that with Daddy, haven't we?"

"Yes, Kita, we slammed him ourselves sometimes when he didn't show up, and now he's slammed for good."

"Ah, Cinny. Remember the resurrection ferns you talked about? These dark, glossy ferns you drew on the lynching tree?"

I nodded. "Yes, Mama told me they gave our people hope."

Kita picked up another panel I had sketched that afternoon, studying it in the dim light. It was a fox waving a Confederate flag "x" over the snout of a startled armadillo. Above them, a razor wire fence cut the sky.

"We're still struggling," she said, and turned to my next panels of armadillos hand-cuffed for sitting with foxes in the front of the bus. In the next frames, armadillos refused to ride the bus, and instead walked to work on screaming hooves, buses passing empty. Armadillos driving cars picked them up, and Nana Mama sat in the back like royalty, gently crossing her hooves. The next panels showed foxes in white hoods burning crosses on armadillo lawns, and armadillo drivers herded into jail cells.

"What were the foxes so worried about?" I asked.

"Mixing foxes and armadillos on buses would lead to mixing them in schools, in love and marriage, making everyone equal. That might end up putting some armadillos on the tippy top."

"Oh, I need to draw armadillos teetering on foxes' shoulders! The one on top has Obama ears. Do you think…?" I hesitated.

"What?"

"Do you think people are still angry about that—enough to kill?"

"Of course, sweetie. Yes, of course."

If I kept drawing our stories, where would the images take us?

Mama was stretched on the sofa, so I crawled into bed with Kita.

"You still using?" Kita plumped an extra pillow and put it under my head.

I squirmed. Silver-threaded Spanish moss brushed the screen like ghost hair. "Nah, I'm quitting."

"You've said that before."

"Promise. May God strike me dead. Besides I think I'm pregnant."

"What? Who's is it?"

"Tony, a sweet boy I met in rehab." I closed heavy lids, missing his Latin dance moves, sturdy arms around me.

6
Cinny's Hell

In the morning, still no word from Tony. Had he od'd? Was he blacked out somewhere?

We gathered the children on the sofa, Annie holding her baby doll and Denny a Lamborghini.

"Your grandpa has gone to be with Dex." Kita pushed back Ruby's hair.

"He's gone?" Ruby gazed at her mama, tears welling. We knew they would hear the story somewhere and we wanted them to hear it from us—from Kita—first.

"Yes, princess. Cinny and I found him in the street last night and tried to save him." Her braids had loosened and come undone, her full lips turned down.

"Did a car hit him?" Five-year-old Denny studied his race car.

Kita gathered him closer. "No, a bullet, sweetie. We don't know whose, but we're going to be alright."

"Don't worry, Mama, I'm here for you." Ruby patted Kita's face, ever the caregiver's daughter. Denny hooked his arm around Mama, who was still wrapped in the camo quilt.

Annie echoed her cousins. "Me too, Mama." I buried my trembling lips in her soft curls. "I know, honey dew. Every little thing's gonna to be alright."

I wanted to believe that.

"Heaven is a beautiful place," Mama said, "glittering with rubies, cerulean, diamonds, and gold. And Jesus is there, walking with them beside the crystal sea."

I wanted to believe that too.

I hated to leave that tender moment but I had to get to rehab by nine and see Tony. In the cool, lemon dawn, I left Annie with

Mama, and Kita walked me to the bus stop. "Don't assume the worst. Maybe he's just helping someone out."

"I know. It's not my emergency, right?"

I caught the bus to Frenchtown. There, Tony might be skipping rehab to join the work pool for contractor jobs. The oldest black neighborhood in the state, it had started as a land grant from Lafayette. Its first residents from France in 1825, planted fields, built homes, schools, and churches. They were joined after the Civil War by freed slaves.

Still a low-rent, low-lying area of floods and runoff behind the capitol, century-old service stations, drugstores and barbershops struggled to fend off the city's redevelopment.

But once Ray Charles, Nat and Cannonball Adderly drew crowds to the Red Bird and Café DuLuxe. In the fifties, Civil Rights protesters filled the streets. But in the sixties, the glory faded and by the nineties, the feds called it a drug corridor.

I got off the bus, dodging mini-cars, students rushing to class at nearby Florida State University and crowded into the squat, yellow Labor Finders storefront.

"Working for beer?" A tanned guy in ragged shirt and jeans pulled himself off the wall, uncrossed his arms and reached for me.

I glared him down, and he sagged back against the wall. What gave me away? My open collar, honey-brown skin, unraveling poof? I closed my top button and pulled my hair tighter in the rubber band.

There was no Tony lounging along the wall or sitting in plastic chairs. Just a mix of sun-hardened, muscled workers, all colors and sizes. Even a long-haired girl in bandanna, work boots and jeans. But no Tony. I asked around. No one had seen him.

The clock on the wall read 8:38. Dad's time of death the night before, and my time to hustle to rehab. I left, pausing at the light on Old Bainbridge and Brevard, a familiar haunt from my old life. A BMW slowed, but I crossed, head-down, ignoring the tinted window rolling down, the smirking dog whistle. I hurried toward Tony's mama's apartment, past the restored Frenchtown park and policeman statue, past the new brick three-story, clock-towered Renaissance Center. Property values were shooting up and barbershops and hair salons were shutting down. Caked in paint, powdered in dust, the promise of redevelopment had faded and they were boarding up instead.

Work trucks roared past, stench of soot and urine. I ducked behind the homeless shelter, closed for the day, and kept to the shade along Virginia Ave. Under the trees, several rehab friends nodded, but Tony was not among them. I fingered the roxies in my pocket, I'd sworn off for the baby. They were just a backup, in case, my psychiatrist said. In case I didn't make it to my next appointment.

In case I found Tony lying motionless in these bushes. I kept close to the wall past the gold-and-pink derby-hat car with Louisiana plates, and the van with flat screen TV plugged into the dashboard.

The city was building a new shelter west of town far from this homeless city beneath the trees; this block of cheap rooms, rescue missions and rehab centers. Big shots with hands in cookie jars were clearing the way for high-rises and hotels.

I dodged behind trees, searching the underbrush. When a car slowed in the street, I crouched, sure I'd seen a pointing gun. I rounded a grandfather oak and smelled espresso before I knocked on Tony's mom's door. Isabella, dark hair loose and floating, dropped an egg on the floor, and rushed to the door, fuzzy robe flying.

"Cinny! Have you seen Tony?"

"No! No texts, nothing."

She pushed dark curls out of puffy eyes.

I struggled to speak. "Daddy was shot last night."

She reached up and pulled me close, fresh citrus scent, breath catching in her throat. "Do you think Tony's safe?"

"I don't know." I scanned the leaf-shaded street, a man in coveralls passed, but no Tony.

"Do you think I should call the police? Report a missing person?"

I nodded, handing her my cell with trembling fingers.

"No it's okay, I have my own." She reached into her bathrobe pocket. "Want some huevos rancheros?"

"No thanks. Can't eat." I leaned against the wall, while she dialed 9-1-1.

"No one named Tony has been reported," the dispatcher said. "We'll keep looking."

"Yes, yes, please." Isabella hung up and we clung to each other until I extracted myself.

"Gotta go to rehab." I edged outside, feeling exposed, looking sharp and dodging traffic on Virginia Ave.

Across the street, sat the prison work release center—wide front porch, white rocking chairs bench swing, red door. It stretched a dozen rooms deep, alongside the so-called "crack house." A green-trimmed, white clapboard, the historic Tookes motel once welcomed African-Americans when white-only hotels wouldn't. In the forties and fifties, the Tookes's hosted bandleader Duke Ellington, singer Lou Rawls and author James Baldwin.

A lanky, tattooed, shock-haired white guy, planted sago palms in the front yard. He flashed a gap-toothed grin. "Good morning!"

"Is it?"

"Yes, yes. This is the day that the Lord hath ma—"

Before he could finish, I tripped over a big black brick.

"My Bible. Sorry, but this place is changing. You should join me and my roomies at Grace Mission."

My jaw dropped. "Diego is changing?"

"We're still working on him. He's around the side."

At the side entrance, a whirring surveillance camera followed me around a smoldering burn pile. Diego was Tony's cousin, a meth cooker. I called him Dayglo. Fire licked at leaves, Sudafed packets, coffee filters, plastic tubing, lithium battery bits and soda bottles. Crackles and pops filled the air and a sharp ammonia smell like cat pee drifted in the morning breeze. Tin-foiled window deflected bright morning sun.

Next door, at the work release center, the front door opened and two women in green uniforms left the shaded porch and headed up the sidewalk, shielding their faces against the morning sun.

Dayglo on his steps, brushed dreads out of a pock-marked face and drew on a cigarette—didn't dare smoke inside. He blew smoke away from me, and raised a hand at the uniformed women. Who ignored him. "Former clients."

"Have you seen Tony?"

"Nada."

"Da—agh—" I couldn't speak. "Daddy was shot. Dead. I want to know if they got Tony, too."

I wavered and Dayglo grabbed my arm.

He cupped my chin and searched my face. "What are you saying, Cinny? Someone shot Tony?"

"I don't know. We can't find him." With Daddy gone, all I wanted was to sink into Tony's strong arms. He was my high road to recovery, my promise that we'd steer clear of here and make a nest for our growing family.

My phone vibrated. *Kita.* "Yeah, sis?"

"Cinny, you were right. The police picked up Doobie, our cousin Rocky and some other ex-cons." I crumpled to the steps.

A car slowed at the curb, waving Dayglo over, and I crept behind a porch rail.

"Rocky could've led him straight to Daddy. Straight to Tony. Straight to me."

"Yes, Cinny, our own cousin played along for his cut of five grand."

"That's all Daddy's life was worth?"

"The cash Dad had stashed in those grocery bags."

My hair stood on end.

"Cinny are you sitting down? Rocky told the cops they were 'hittin' a lick' for Dad's flashy cars and money; they didn't want to kill him. But Dad fought back, pissed off that his own boys were rolling him—in ski masks."

My mouth was cotton.

"Cinny, still there?

"Yeah." My voice rasped.

"Stay safe, Cinny, please? Go to rehab like you said."

"Okay, Sissy." I closed the phone. Lava stung my raw cheeks. My limbs were liquid, making it impossible to stand. Rehab was a block away but it seemed like miles.

On the sidewalk, two more inmates passed in gray hotel cleaning scrubs. They had their shit together and I had— What?

Dayglo gave them a thumbs-up and returned to me. "More ex-clients. Nice to have them next door." But they ignored him, not missing a beat.

He ground out his cigarette, came up the steps and held out brown-stained fingers. "You look terrible, niña." He pulled me up the steps and I followed, stumbling over the threshold into his room, sinking into the rotten-egg smelling sofa. My throat burned, ribs ached. Had Tony taken a bullet too? I couldn't move. Doobie had warned me he wanted to be Annie's only daddy.

Dayglo paced the dirty carpet. "You're a mess, chica."

He put water in a microwave and sterilized a needle. I trembled, repulsed and needy. He pulled back the stopper, sucking up clear liquid from a distiller. "Ready?"

"No! The baby."

"Who're you kidding?" He grabbed my arm and tied it off. "Shh. Quiet."

I watched the needle glide in and moaned. I could not undo what I'd just done.

For a moment, I felt the familiar liftoff and fearless flight, the sheer speed. But then I was free-falling, tumbling down a dark pit—tongue in my throat—nothing to grab onto. I slammed into metal gates, inhaled the sulfur stench of demon breath. Bony fingers grabbed my arm, bloody knuckles pulled me in. Flames licked my feet. Hollow demon eyes drilled right through me, laser-sharp incisions tore my arms. Black mouths gaped and rasped with gurgling blood. I screamed, "Jesus! Help me!"

Strong arms reached down, scooped me up, and put me on a soft white cloud.

When I woke, my arm swelled with infection. Dayglo washed it with a soapy cloth. "Whose nail marks are these?" he asked.

"Those are demon prints. I was in hell."

He looked at me, his pupils jumpy.

"But Jesus yanked me outta there."

"Now you're calling me Jesus? You were jerking on the floor. I put you back on the couch." He tore a pillow case with his teeth and bandaged my arm. "Cinny, I'm dropping you at emergency."

He flipped his dreads out of an ashen face, stood me up, arm around my waist and half-dragged me to his old Corolla. "I have to drop you off and leave or they'll arrest me."

"They'll arrest *me*."

I struggled in his sinewed arms, but he hung on, shoving me into the passenger seat, slamming the door. He sped the few blocks to emergency, reached over, popped my door handle and pushed me out. I hit the pavement and crumpled. He raced away.

Tookes House (Wikimedia)

7

Healing Falls

A thick white fog covered me and distant voices wove in and out, "Faint pulse…, barely breathing…, ah there…., she's coming around."

I woke to lab coats, face masks, serious eyes.

"Okay?" Gentle hands untied the pillowcase strips and examined my arm.

"Hold still, this will only pinch a little." A pink-faced nurse inserted an intravenous line and hung a drip bag.

"Antibiotics," she said, flicking the line to get it flowing. "What happened to your arm?"

"I had a bad trip. And fell. Right into hell."

"What were you on?"

"Something nasty." I was pretty sure the toxicology report would find meth.

Even before my daddy was shot, I had a "reason" to do drugs. My brother came back from Iraq alive and shot himself. The bang from his bedroom woke me. That army cap he always wore was clear in the hall. I was only fifteen. Mama held me back and the ambulance men rolled him out under a sheet.

The house turned dark and depressing, so I took my grief outside. Out where the grandfather oak cracked the sidewalk, I climbed up and into its branches, watching buses and cars roll by; traffic rumbled on the overpass. About six, a train clattered through to Pensacola, Mobile, New Orleans. Sometimes it slowed so I could read the graffiti tags, and once it stopped. I crept up and sprayed "Dex," half-wavery as though the letters were rising out water. I placed it right next to the "Stone" tag with the upside "T" piercing the "O." Pure art riding the rails cross-country.

In my paintings at home that week, grays, sage, and mauve showed up. Finally, great arcs of colored chalk on the sidewalk brought the kids running. They wanted rainbows with dogs and kittens sliding down. The sun radiated from their glistening faces.

In the spotless hospital room, my EKG beeped steadily, the baby's heart echoing faintly behind it. The trauma team pulled off their gloves, turned down the lights and let us rest.

Hours later, a strong, warm presence sat on my bed. The mattress caved and I rolled against Kita's crisp nurse scrubs. She tucked my cold feet into her warm lap and sang, soft and low. "The Lord's my shepherd, I'll not want." Lids closed, full lips forming each syllable, lingering on *pastures green,* and *quiet waters by.*

"Oh Kita, you sing just like daddy."

She laughed. "Guess who taught me? We lullabied you when you were a baby."

I touched her sleeve. "I am so sorry. I never wanted to end up back here."

"I know, Cinny. I want you to make this your healing fall."

I let go her sleeve, my bandaged arm limp. "I want that."

Her face lit up. "Remember our pastor from Congo? He would start, 'Say yes and I'll tell you a story.'"

"Yes." I relaxed my aching arm and settled in for a tale.

"Our cousin David was diagnosed with hyperactivity disorder. Couldn't sit still, focus or learn; repeated grade four. He stayed on his skateboard whenever school let out. One day he got hit by a car, banged his head on the pavement, and the next day could concentrate like everyone else. He went on to college and became a math teacher."

My jaw dropped. "David repeated grade 4?"

"You didn't know? Bugged him all his life. And remember tall, bald Uncle Amos?"

"Yes! I used to sketch his shining round head in church!"

"Well he didn't always have a perfect face. A cold sore gave him Bell's palsy; half his face drooped from nerve inflammation. One day he did a face-plant off a curb and fixed his nerve.

"And Aunt Mabel, the praise dancer?" Kita twirled her hand in the air.

"Yes, with the feather dusters!"

"Cinny!" Kita laughed. "Those were peacock feathers— You must be feeling better!" She felt my forehead. "Hmm, low grade."

I nudged her with my knee. "Anyway, Aunt Mabel?"

"She got a hip replacement, and kept dancing. It slipped the ball and socket somehow. Made her limp. The doctors tried to manipulate it but couldn't fix it. One evening, she fell into her kitchen recycling and reset her hip."

"Crazy family." I squeezed her funny bone. It always made her flinch.

"Cinny!" She pulled away. "I see you getting up from here and never going back to drugs. This is it. Your time is now."

"Thank you, Sissy!" My belly growled and I clamped my hands on top to still it. "I hope so. I'm trying to have this baby."

"Oh, I brought you this." Kita pulled a granola bar from her pocket and ripped it open. I hadn't eaten since the night before, hot dogs with the kids. I finished the honey-oats bar in four bites.

Outside, the sky darkened, lightening strobed, thunder rolled. I gripped Kita's hand. "What about Tony? He would be here right now if he could. Do you think Doobie got him, too?"

Kita grimaced. "I don't know."

"If Doobie found out I was pregnant…." I shivered and Kita leaned over and smoothed my hair.

"Shh, it's gonna be all right. I can check hospital admissions and police records. What's Tony's last name?

"Garcia."

"Oh, your baby's Hispanic?"

"Puerto Rican."

Kita raised an eyebrow. "Goin' for high yella, then?"

We laughed and hugged before she went back on shift.

Supper trays arrived, turkey gravy, green beans, mashed potatoes. I cleaned the plate and dipped the dry cornbread in the canned peaches. The nursing assistant offered me seconds but I was exhausted, too tired to eat.

Kita popped in again as the sun rose, her face wreathed in a golden glow.

"The good news is, Tony has not turned up in ER or the city morgues. We've issued a missing persons' report." Yellow rays splashed lemon light around the room, glinting off white sheets. She folded my fingers in hers and bowed her pretty corn-rowed head, "Please, Jesus, watch over Tony, wherever he is, and keep Cinny safe too."

Breakfast trays arrived, and she pushed off "to look for Tony."

Scrambled eggs, bacon, toast, strawberry yogurt. I ate for me, for the baby and Tony.

I slept again until a brown-haired police woman arrived, the same one who had placed the yellow tags around Daddy's body.

"Hello Ms. Rose, we need to investigate your injuries and test you for DNA for evidence."

The room wavered as I tried to lift my weak, bandaged arm.

"Wait." I pressed the buzzer. My face burned, though I was shivering from head to toe. The officer shifted in her jack boots. Finally, a plump, red-faced nurse came and unwrapped my fresh bandages, revealing three deep grooves, bruised and swollen.

The officer adjusted her glasses, pulled on blue gloves and opened her test kit, taking out a queue tip and glass tube. "This may hurt a little." She swabbed the cuts and dropped the cotton swab in the tube.

The nurse stepped in front of her and wrapped my arm with fresh bandages.

The officer inserted herself again. "Who did this to you?" Her voice was firm but low.

"Demons, I gave my statement when I was admitted."

She scowled. "Was anyone with you?"

"In hell? Ma'am, I believe it was an afterlife experience and I don't intend to go back and find out." I'd said enough. If I told her about Dayglo's injection, she might charge me with fetal endangerment.

"May I check your pockets?"

"What pockets?" I patted my thin hospital gown. Before I could say more, she'd picked my jeans off the chair and shook them out. Pennies and roxies fell out.

"Ooops." She scrambled after them as though it were an accident.

I winced. "I have a prescription."

She pulled a plastic evidence bag from her kit and dropped them in.

I wanted out of this scene, free of all my hurts, habits and hang ups.

The officer closed her kit and stripped off her gloves, hand on her holster. "I'm taking these to the crime lab. Don't go anywhere."

I gestured at the IV-dripping antibiotics into my arm—*fat chance*—and pressed my buzzer. A nurse crashed into the officer taking a wide swath through the door.

"Can you please call my sister?"

This time Kita appeared in minutes, in black pantsuit and hand bag, breathless from running the halls.

"Cinny, what happened?"

"The officer dumped my jeans and found roxies. I'm screwed."

"I'll say, Cinny. Why? I thought you were giving that up. For the baby." Her lips turned down. She crossed her arms and faced the window.

I had cleaned out her savings several times with my legal troubles, but this should not be one of them. "Sissy, I have a prescription even if I wasn't carrying it."

"I know you do." Kita turned, her golden irises lit by inward fire. "Drug companies lied to us—nurses, doctors—" She unhooked my IV. "slow release roxies weren't addicting for pain."

I tried to laugh, but failed.

"Oh Cinny, this time is so hard for all of us." She reached into her bag, then stopped. "The doctor gave me permission to take you to Daddy's funeral. But now, with these new charges pending.... I don't know."

"Oh, please, get me out of here?" I begged.

She stood me up and pulled a lilac lace dress over my head. It was the one Daddy bought after his release—for my sweet sixteen birthday. I couldn't believe it still fit, barely showing my baby bump.

She set my tan heels on the gleaming tiles and I slipped them on.

"We're just going and coming right back." She grabbed my wrist and pulled me down the hall.

Annie and the others were waiting in the van and I snuggled right next to her car seat, getting wet sloppy kisses.

At True Communion Church, I held onto Annie on one side and Mama on the other. She could hardly stand and could not sing a note.

"Swing low, sweet chariot…" the organist wailed, channeling Ray Charles. Those who could, raised plaintive voices, "Comin' for to carry me home."

Kita pulled the hospital tissue box from her handbag and we soaked them all.

"If you get there before I do…" Our friends hemmed us in, propped us up and helped us stand. "…tell all our friends we're coming too."

The blue-robed choir sang, "Come and go with me to my father's house…" and "I'll fly away…" That anticipation was the most healing of all.

"We weren't put on this earth to stumble around in the dark," the pastor said, speaking straight to me. "The God of the Universe has made a path for you…. Even our brother DeAndre showed us which way his feet were turning last week…."

Hallelujah, the people chorused.

That music lingered, healing me through those painful days when nothing anyone could say softened losing daddy and Dex that way. And Tony. Where was Tony?

8
Caged

Gray-green light filtered through narrow, slat windows at the Leon County Jail. It was my second possession offense, so after my release from hospital, I sat in a cement block cell, doing time through all the motions and court judgments.

My first trimester was a long, tired walk, both a comfort and a worry that my baby might not be okay. My arm was healing to itchy scabs but I ached all over for Tony and Annie. And I longed to see and hold my baby.

I paced my little cell. How was Annie getting on without me again? And *where was Tony*? In an alley somewhere with a needle in his arm? What if he'd taken a bullet while hanging out in Frenchtown? A bullet that Doobie had intended for me when— if Cuz told him I was pregnant by Tony?

I spent days sleeping, waking to my growing baby—but Daddy, Dex and Tony—gone. I had been raised that God held our lives in his hands, but where was he? Had he gone too? I tried to focus on breathing, growing my baby, going to rec with other inmates, drinking in lacey mocking bird song, white clouds, green leaves, blue sky.

Long evenings, I sang to my baby, *Hush little baby, don't say a word, Papa's gonna buy you a mocking bird.* I loved extravagant mocking bird song, but where was Tony? I asked for pencil and paper and drew white-feathered mocking birds, trees planted by rivers, a sun-browned Tony carrying a wooly bundle; a little house with candles reflecting in the water.

In dreams, monsters swam just beneath the surface with small, piercing eyes. Monsters who knew where Tony was.... *Doobie, Rocky*? I woke and I asked God to keep his eye on Tony, my eyes on God and to guide us with his eye.

That evening, I opened my cell New Testament to Romans and stopped when I got to an old favorite. "For I am convinced that neither death nor life, neither angels nor demons, neither the present nor the future, nor any powers, neither height nor depth, nor anything else in all creation, will be able to separate us from the love of God that is ours in Christ Jesus our Lord."

The verse was Romans 8:38-39, the time of Daddy's death. It was like a special message from him that I would always be loved, no matter what or who was trying to hurt me.

The very next day, my cell door opened, letting in a cold draft and a tall blonde, chained and hand-cuffed.

"Ms. Rose, this is Cherise Flowers, your new bunkie." The officer unlocked her and released her into the narrow room.

Cherise held out a slender hand saying, "Hey," with a country twang. Her nose was dented, flat—a birth defect?

I took her hand slowly, my solitary nest invaded. "Hi, I'm Cinnamon, Cinny for short."

The officer eased out and locked the door.

"Do you go by Cher or Reese?"

"Oh, I like Reese!" She flashed me a crooked, green-eyed grin.

Part of me welcomed the company, the distraction. But her nasal twang rankled me and I filed a move request. But then I withdrew it. She used her country twang to make me laugh, stating the obvious and making dry observations. "You pregnant? Immaculate conception?"

She'd squint at those hand-width windows and say, "If I get any thinner, I could slip right out of here."

Meanwhile, I was gaining weight, growing a small baby bump, far enough along that the assistant warden loaded me in a van and took me for an ultrasound.

On the way, she let me call and invite Mama and Annie. By the time we were called in, they had arrived. I hugged my squirmy daughter until I had to get on the table. Together, we watched the baby's heartbeat. It turned our way, and we tried to sneak a peek. Boy or girl?

"Could be a boy." The tech snapped a picture.

"Named Tony," I whispered.

Mama squeezed my hand and Annie twirled, palms up. "Brother, brother, brother."

I clutched the photo all the way back to jail and when Reese saw it, she squealed. "It's an eggplant!"

Later that week, after a day of cleaning toilets, I lay on my top bunk gazing at my eggplant baby. Reese paced the cell and pivoted, like a model on a runway. The orange sunset hit her like a spotlight.

"Hey, you remind me of a movie star," I said.

"Yeah, which one?" Reese swept her long straight hair out of sage green eyes.

"That Uma girl."

"Thurman?" She cocked her hip. "My favorite actress named Uma."

I laughed out loud—a deep, resonant sound, echoing in our cinderblock fortress.

She paced a bit more. "You remind me of Sasha Obama— without the wardrobe."

I flew off the top bunk in my baggy scrubs, pretending outrage. "Are you saying my wardrobe stinks?"

We kept each other laughing and, at meals and recreation, drew people to us. We even got chosen to clean the warden's office. In that safe, secure space, on long, pent-up nights, Reese began telling her story.

9
Reese's Story

It was another long fall evening in our tiny cell, fourth floor of the Leon County Jail. The sun had set behind the narrow, dimpled glass of our single window slat. We'd been discussing baby names. Names to love, names to avoid. Morty, Hector, Attila, Rummy, Tyrone.

"That was my pimp's name," Reese said.

"No way! That's the name of a dinosaur, t-rex in Annie's picture book."

"He was a t-rex alright."

She stopped pacing and sat on the bunk. "I first met Tyrone when I was 14, a freshman at Leon High. It was the start of spring break 2008 and I was walking with a friend, my arms full of science books. I was going to ace my project on Florida's springs, and win the prize."

She paused and laughed a sharp, two-note, *Ha-ha*.

I patted her back and leaned against my pillow. "Go on."

She gazed beyond the palm fronds scraping the blurry window.

"He roared through campus on his Harley with some other bikers. One stopped to pick up my friend and I screamed, 'Bring her back or I'll kill you.'

Tyrone turned and circled back. 'You better come along and keep an eye on her.'

I kept walking. My strays would be mewing under the porch.

'She needs you.'

So did my cats, scratching at their bowls.

'You better.' His chrome pipes gleamed, his diamond studs scattered the evening sun.

I stuffed my books in my backpack, and hitched it over my shoulders, ignoring him.

'Think of your friend.' He waited.

I snaked my leg over the seat and set my feet on the studs.

'Hold on tight.' He wrapped my arm around his solid, narrow waist. He cranked the throttle and his muscles rippled. He was Adonis.

We ended up at a big old house in an empty field. There was booze and pizza and rap and guys in do-rags laughing and cutting up. Before the night was over, Tyrone had put his diamond stud in my ear, kissed me deep and wouldn't let go.

Mom called, sounding drunk, as usual. I told her I was spring-breaking with friends, and could she put out some scraps for my cats?

The guys passed a joint and it smelled like burnt rope, not sour, stinky alcohol. It made me laugh-y and light-headed. Then Tyrone lit a crack pipe and when I puffed it, I felt so alive, nothing else mattered. I just wanted to be flying that way forever.

Sometime that night, the police came, but we escaped on our motorbikes through the woods. We ended up hiding at Tyrone's apartment, blinds closed, lights off. I heard my girlfriend crying in the next bedroom. But he wouldn't let me go to her. In the morning, I noticed the crack pipe in his pocket and tried to sneak it out.

'You want that, girlfriend? You'll have to work for it.' I laughed, but he wasn't kidding." Reese stopped and couldn't go on.

I didn't press her. Some things were too hard to talk about. She was in for prostitution and DUI manslaughter, awaiting trial and sentencing. But she wouldn't say much about that either.

I took out the paper supply the prison had given me and gave her a few sheets. I sketched my graphic novel panels. She sat beside me drawing a floor plan with open courtyard, play structure and fountain-pool in the middle.

I leaned over and added a few splashes. "Is that your dream home—with splashes all over the place?"

She laughed so hard, she couldn't hold her pen. "It's my animal shelter." She gasped. "A theme park for animals."

I added armadillos in swimsuits holding a sign, *Wet'n'Wild.*

"Wet'n'Wild! Perfect." She snorted through her flat nose, wiping tears.

I added snakes in stilettos and boas. It was easier to laugh with a friend in the present, than be trapped alone in the past.

She grabbed her side and doubled over.

"Liver?" I knew the gesture. I'd seen Daddy doing it. Cirrhosis. A twinge under the ribs, low grade fevers. I felt her forehead. Dank, hot.

"Reese, may I pray for you?" I had never done this before, but Kita and Mama did it like it was just part of the conversation.

"Yes, please, Cinny. Do you think it will help?"

"Definitely, especially if you believe it." We clasped hands and bowed right there on the bottom bunk.

"Daddy—Father, please forgive our sins and heal Reese from the inside out. Place your healing hand on her and bring her the medical help she needs."

I looked up, knowing the next step. "Let's file a medical request for you."

She hugged me. "Of course. I needed to meet a friend like you."

Kita, Mama and Annie came to visit Saturdays, usually after lunch when the visiting lines thinned. I'd inhale my mushy pole beans, macaroni and salty brown meat gravy, and wait my turn for the phone receiver at the wire mesh windows on the visitor's mezzanine. Reese brought a broom and dustpan up the stairs overlooking our common area, so she could catch a glimpse and wave at them.

We talked over the phone receivers through the crisscross glass. There was no contact, but sometimes Kita held an encouraging verse to the glass, "I will restore the years the locust has eaten." Joel 2:25.

Annie jumped up and down and said. "Mama, when can I come inside with you?"

I ached for her squirmy self, deepening dimples, clamping arms. "I'd rather come outside with you. Soon, I hope."

Within minutes my family had to give the phone to someone else coming to visit their mama, sister, wife or friend.

One day it was Tony's mom, Isabella, girlish in t-shirt, yoga pants and tennis shoes, curly hair wet and stringy from running through the rain. She looked shrunken from the last time I'd seen her in a pink bathrobe, the day Tony disappeared. Her dark eyes glowed at seeing me, just like they had on Mother's Day at St Thomas More Co-Cathedral. She'd taken my hand from Tony's, kissed me on both cheeks and stage-whispered, "Tony tells me you're keeping him in line." That was just months, but seemed like years ago.

Kita held out the phone for her.

"Oh, sweet Cinny, how are you and the baby?" She spoke in soft, lilting tones and smiled when I patted my growing belly.

"We're good, Isabella. Maybe Mama told you. The warden took me for an ultrasound—we think it's a boy!"

"Yes, your mama said."

Mama beamed, her white teeth gleaming.

"And Kita helped me issue a lookout for Tony," Isabella said.

"A BOLO? Have you heard anything?"

"Nothing." She dabbed her nose, her hands red and peeling from hotel-cleaning solutions. "Do you have any idea where we can look?"

Kita wrapped an arm around Isabella and spoke into the mouthpiece. "Yes, Cinny, you always have such great instincts."

"Can the police pump Rocky? Or Doo— Doobie?" I could hardly speak his name. But I couldn't shake the idea that he was gunning for me and the baby the night he killed Daddy.

10
Patterns

The day of my court hearing, the wind shook the giant oaks around the prison, dark clouds descended and the guard held a large black umbrella against a drenching downpour. I shuffled in shackles to the prison van, scanning the bushes for men with guns. After weeks unchained inside, I was a hobbled target, my belly protruding, unprotected. Doobie was behind bars but that didn't stop him sending someone to kill me and my baby, to get even for reporting him raping me in prison.

The radio crackled and the guard helped me in and buckled my seatbelt. The driver turned up the volume against the pounding rain. *A warm el Nino combined with hurricane season is causing flooding throughout the Big Bend.* Water swirled around our tires on Franklin Boulevard and I hoped Mama's house on cinderblocks was above water.

We entered Leon County Courthouse through the back door and took the infamous service elevator to the second floor. It was once used to transport Ted Bundy, away from flashing cameras. But the tiny space creeped me out. I pulled in my elbows and sucked in my belly, avoiding any skin cell DNA Bundy may have left on the walls.

Mama, Kita and Isabella, already in the gallery, lifted their hands and smiled. The bailiff called *Order* and the judge entered in flowing black robes, her hair pulled into a severe ponytail.

Have mercy on me, Lord, please, I breathed. *Forgiveness, strength and healing.*

The prosecutor wanted to charge me with possession with intent to distribute, and serve up to ten years. It was my second charge, he said.

I cringed. I'd done the crime, but I hadn't wanted to. And with a baby on the way, I sure didn't want to do that much time.

Kita handed out tissues and blew her nose.

My defense attorney took the podium, produced my pain med script and pled for me to serve out the unserved portion of my first sentence. Eighteen months for violating parole and carrying pain killers without a prescription.

That would still mean giving birth in shackles and giving up the baby.

Mama was called to the stand for the sentencing phase. She stood unsteadily, opened the wooden gate and circled the prosecutor's table, heading to the stand in a crisp, navy-blue suit with matching pumps and hat. I held my breath. She had used some tough love on me in the past.

"We love Cinny." She paused, her jaw set as she looked at the judge, as though daring her to argue.

"She was born on May 5, 1990, a darling slip of a girl. Soft buttery curls, cinnamon skin and rosebud lips. She stole everyone's hearts." Mama smiled as my attorney projected a baby on the big screen. Me on my tummy, big forehead, raised brows, pink silk ribbons. Mama had chosen the best from our family albums.

"But with three kids under five, I was busy." The screen flashed three children on Mama's bench swing, Dex strumming guitar, me in a jade dress on Kita's lap. "That was the summer I spent in jail on false charges." She lifted her chin.

"I was exonerated, but it cost Cinny six critical months without me when she was four. And made it hard to get a better job."

"I got my accounting job back, but had to take in laundry and mending while her daddy worked long hours as a valet at the new civic center. He got to take in concerts and meet his idols, Prince on his "Purple Rain" tour. Our lives took different directions.

"Finally, Andre and me separated and I had to find a better job. I was hired by FDLE and worked hard, studying to be a fingerprint analyst. So Cinny sometimes missed her parents growing up." Mama dabbed her forehead and neck.

"She loved to draw; it helped calm her whenever she was upset. I gave her crayons, chalk, paints, and she loved them all. She painted everything—family, trains, dogs, whales—in every style. 3-D, tricks of the eye. She could turn a solid walkway into a sky with clouds and rainbows. That's what she did to win a blue ribbon in Springtime Tallahassee. And got her picture in the paper.

"Cinny grew strong and expressive and made sure I invited Daddy to her school play—" The screen showed me in red riding hood and basket of bread. "Her middle school graduation." Daddy chest-puffed in white suit beside me in blue gown and mortar board. "And her high school art exhibits. She won those contests, too." Me on the front page, with my blazing sunset in a jungle river, and the lynching tree ghosts, holding a blue ribbon.

"But then her big brother came back from Iraq, and couldn't sleep or function much. He loved his little sister and she had grown very attached to him. But one night he shot himself... ."

Mama slumped and hid her face. I dipped my head, wishing she wouldn't do this for me, expose us this way. But when she looked up, she was still and calm. Out the second-floor window, sun filtered through the dripping clouds.

"We were all in shock and went through some dark days. Cinny's art turned alarming for a while—exploding heads and bodies. I was concerned, so I took her to a psychiatrist who put Cinny on Xanax and Oxycodone." Mama faced the judge and raised her chin. "And doubled the meds.

"Cinny got to the point where she couldn't concentrate on homework and began skipping school. Her psychiatrist advised me to remove her allowance and put her on restrictions.

"Instead, she moved in with friends. It was hard to see her go, and I always wondered if I had done the right thing." Mama trailed off. But my attorney flashed a picture of us in white lace and pink-flowered hats at Easter. Mama brightened. "Sometimes, though, she let me pick her up for church." Her face glowed in the underwater light from the window, sun rays through the rain.

"Her first arrest for pain pills, I didn't bail her out. I was told she needed to suffer her consequences. She was sentenced to prison. But there she was raped by a guard, once a family friend.

"She had her baby, sued the prison, and came home. She gave me child support from the settlement, and we found Annie a preschool so Cinny could go back to school and look for a job. Do you know how hard it is for a felon to find work?" She turned from the prosecutor to the judge. They nodded, motioned her to go on.

"Annie's father had threatened Cinny from jail, and she wouldn't sleep in her bed by the window anymore. Cinny took Annie out of her crib and made them sleeping nests behind the sofa. She started hiding out at friends' houses. Her sister Kita and I were looking after Annie more and more."

I hung my head; a big clock ticked and echoed in the nearly empty courtroom. In those days, I'd see Mama's beige Camry cruising Frenchtown, my Little Orphan Annie crying or singing in the back, aqua ribbons bobbing in her springy curls. I shifted in my handcuffs; my baby somersaulting inside me.

Kita had found me on the street, and admitted me to detox. I was ready and wanted to stay sober, but the house rules were impossible and the place was falling apart. I ran, and was next rounded up with my friends in a drug bust. We were sentenced to drug court and outpatient rehab. I hung out more with people who were trying to stay clean. I moved back home and played with Annie.

The courtroom clock ticked past 4:30. Mama leaned forward. "It took several rehabs, but she straightened out, came back home and devoted herself to a job in her sister's lab. After work, she was always down on the floor, playing with Annie. Please be lenient with her. She just lost her father to murder and she's expecting a baby." Mama's voice snagged. "Also, the baby's father has disappeared. We worry he may have been killed, too."

Mama stumbled while stepping down, and the bailiff caught her arm and helped her back to her seat.

The late afternoon sun streamed into the courtroom and the clock ticked five. My attorney stood and buttoned his suit jacket. "Your Honor, as you just heard, Ms. Rose's psychiatrist pushed extra doses on her.

"Objection!" The prosecutor stormed from his seat. "Her psychiatrist is not on trial here."

"Sustained." The judge nodded to my attorney. "Continue."

"Ms. Rose has just lost her father to murder and her boyfriend to a mystery disappearance. She will miss her daughter's preschool years, and give birth in prison, having to give up her baby, and miss the child's most critical first year. Your honor, that's punishment enough."

I squinted out the window. My kids were four-year-old me, clinging to a cold chain link fence, waiting to visit my mama inside.

I would miss hours holding and nursing my new baby, and playing *Lion King* with Annie. She loved holding up her stuffed lion cub, perching on the sofa back, blasting, "Baaahsowhenyaaah!" Jumping down and crawling through blanket tunnels and sofa cushion caves, Simba chasing Timon through savannah woodlands. Her snuggled warmth bonded us to each other and Africa while reading, *Bringing the Rain to Kapiti Plain*. Her bobble head and tiny shoes cheered me, climbing the steps on Mama's back porch, one at a time and counting by ones. Then, stretching her chubby legs, climbing again, and counting by twos.

The prosecutor summed up, wanting to charge me with fetal endangerment for using while pregnant. But the sharp-nosed judge swung her pony tail, and chewed into him. "Not in my courtroom. Not until you charge a white woman for drinking while pregnant."

She sentenced me to eighteen months in prison, and tears welled when I told Reese. But she twanged, "Aw, that's okay. You can do it." She hooked arms and swung me around the cell.

11
Thanksgiving

Six of us shackled in pairs hit the crisp morning air, shuffling toward the prison transport bus, yellow leaves showering us. A mockingbird stitched her intricate melody in the orange-leafed crepe myrtles overhead. Sounds of Eden, my Father singing over me. We were headed to the Lowell Reception Center in central Florida to get prison assignments. It was Thanksgiving week, and I was making progress in my sentence.

Clanging metal doors opened and closed behind us. Segregation cages held prisoners from other facilities. They shifted and called above the diesel rumble. "Please bring us water. Snacks, we're starving."

"My legs are swelling. They're turning purple, officer." A large man, head down, stuffed in a seat far too small, lifted his pants leg. I couldn't see him, but his raspy voice sounded familiar.

Guards often said their duty was to protect us. This was not that. We were locked inside cages on a moving bus. What if we plunged off an overpass into a lake, or got hit by a train and burned alive at crossing? We all knew stories like that, and they cranked our nerves.

Here was a prisoner in pain, legs swelling, and we were pulling out on a five-hour drive. What law said they couldn't call a medic?

Lord, save us. "Sir!" I was surprised at the strength of my own voice.

"Sir!" Another inmate cried out and another, so the guards couldn't single us out. Our strength depended on unity. "Please, sir! We've got a guy swelling up, could die in here."

"Sit down. Shut up! We're taking him to medical in Lake Butler."

We banged our cages. That guy needed off, or he'd die in here.

The transport security officer touched his holster.

A lot more of us could die if we didn't shut up.

These guards were contractors. Corrections officers didn't carry guns. Too risky. As we trundled through the city and headed east on I-10, the large fellow in front of me moaned, struggling to move his shackled feet, caged legs.

The distance stretched from home; Annie holding her lion cub, singing "Baaahsowhenyaaah!" from the sofa back. We turned south on I-75, the grass dry and brittle as my aching heart.

My own legs swelled and itched and I couldn't forget the large guy's aching legs. I shifted my weight, my round belly squished. My shoes pinched my swollen ankles, but I couldn't reach them to loosen the laces.

At our next prisoner pickup, Taylor Correctional in Perry, security officers handed out water and permitted a rest stop. I was off the bus, ankle chained to my shackle-buddy, before the large prisoner managed to stand, with help from the guard.

In the restroom, no paper products. "Typical. At least there's running water to wash our hands." My shackle-buddy was bittersweet, like Reese. *Reese*. I missed her.

We passed the large guy on our way back. He ducked his head. There was something familiar about him. He looked a bit like... *Rocky*? If so, he had swollen up in the few months since Daddy's murder. Had his kidneys shut down? Was he going in for dialysis?

"Rocky?"

He didn't turn, didn't look at me.

"Where's Tony?" My voice shook.

Rocky crumpled against the guard, taking him down. The driver rushed to pull him off and together the driver and guard hobbled Rocky toward the bus.

"Rocky, where's Tony?" I shouted.

Rocky groaned. "Don' know."

"Shut up, bitch!" The guard heaved him up the stairs. "Can't you see he's sick?"

They pushed Rocky up and laid him across two seats at the front, locking him in a cage.

I gritted my teeth, resisting the urge to scream. Everything was wrong. The guard calling me bitch, locking us into cages, rolling us down the interstate in a bus bomb. Tony missing. Rocky too sick to talk.

I laid my cold hands on my warm belly and hunched deeper into my prison-issued sweatshirt. *Tony, Tony. Annie. Daddy. Dex. It hurts so bad, Lord.* Finally, I nodded off, and slept.

I woke to screeching brakes, a dull thud, crunching metal, shattering glass, my face hitting the metal cage. Silence. *What, what?* Wet sticky blood ran down my face. A moan, a scream. I wiped my gashed forehead, nose and lips, pressed my sweatshirt sleeve against it. Pressure. "You okay?" I asked my shackle buddy, crumpled on the floor. She struggled to get up and I was glad we'd worn double socks against the bite of the shackles.

A large bump rose on her forehead, shock in her eyes. "I need ice."

Smoke filled the bus from the exploded airbags. The driver stumbled off the bus toward a small white car crunched on our bumper. The guard surveyed us. "Is everyone okay?" He called our names and checked off the list on his clipboard, waiting to hear from each of us. Now and then he glanced at Rocky, on the floor, unmoving.

"Crystal Smith?"

"Bleeding, cut forehead."

"Wesson Lewis?"

"Slammed hand."

"Misty Creel?"

"Cut lip."

Sirens closed in, and he continued down the list.

"Okay, sit tight. Help is on the way. Don't move if you can help it. Use pressure if you're bleeding." The guard frowned at Rocky's cage, unlocked it and crouched over him. Ambulance and squad cars surrounded us, EMTs and police boarded and the guard let them in. They filed down the aisle with ice, bandages, splints, water.

Rocky was rolled onto a gurney and off the bus. Would he be leaving prison in a pine box?

Wait, what happened to Tony? I wanted to scream.

The driver pulled out the spent air bags, sweeping out windshield glass.

"What's he doing?" My shackle-buddy snorted.

"Right? Looks like he's planning to keep driving this wreck."

"We should be going to a clinic, getting medical help. They're treating us like dangerous criminals."

"Some of us are. That's my cousin Rocky they rolled off, serving time for murdering my father. And maybe my boyfriend, Tony. He's missing."

My shackle-buddy gaped, lowering the ice pack from her head. "I am so sorry, Cinny. You okay?"

I nodded. My tongue wooden, my mouth dry.

She offered the ice pack.

"Okay, thanks." I pressed it to my forehead cut, and yielded to its numbing chill.

A mobile glass unit arrived and removed the jagged windshield, replacing it while we waited. The guard let in a uniformed med tech who swabbed my cut, applied a gauze bandage and head bandage.

The driver started the engine and we rumbled back to the interstate. Every time he turned right, hanging metal scraped the tire. Great. We'd be arriving in style. My head throbbed and I laid it on my shackle-buddy's shoulder. She cradled it like a baby.

At Lowell Reception, chain-link fences and razor wire surrounded dry grass stretching between cement block buildings. The gate opened and we filed off, ankles-chained, hands-cuffed, helpless against the flies pinging our eyeballs. In the large, chilly barracks women from all over Florida—all races, ages, and abilities—sprawled on dozens of bunks lining the walls. You could tell the wheeler-dealers from Miami, clustered at one end, gold front teeth gleaming, carved with hearts and diamonds.

I wrapped myself in a blanket and laid my throbbing head on a flat pillow. Finally, a guard filed us out to chow as the sun set into a cold prairie scrubland, filled with the harsh scratchy rattle of scrub jays.

The next morning, after oatmeal and brown bananas, the staff met with us in classrooms, one-on-one, and evaluated us for mental illness. I had been sentenced to residential drug rehab, so I would be headed to a prison rehab dorm, substance abuse classes, counseling and group therapy.

A pale counselor in periwinkle shawl-neck sweater asked what else I wanted to do with my life.

"Draw, paint, create." My forehead throbbed and itched under the bandage and I struggled to concentrate. I wanted my Annie, close. I wanted a pen and paper to draw the crazy bus accident.

"Successful re-entry starts the day you're sentenced to prison." The counselor's pale irises reflected her blue sweater, her white hands stroked her long, ash-blonde hair. She seemed so calm and flawless. Had she ever lost someone close? A father, brother, boyfriend?

"That's what I want for each of you." She seated us at desks in a classroom and handed out paper and pens. I sketched at my desk, a cage-bus crunching a small car, me bleeding inside. Guard foxes bared their teeth, training guns on us. The next frame, a broken bus driving down the interstate. The next, chained and bleeding armadillos crossing dry grass, leaping with bugs and grasshoppers.

I drew prisoners—a teen, a young mother, a grandma—crowded behind barbed wire. Foxes in uniform, snapped at us, though we all belonged in rehab or psych wards. Beneath it, the verse Kita gave me through crisscross glass. *I will restore the years the locust has eaten.*

Most of all, I wanted to get back and pick up where I'd left off with Annie, Kita and Mama. Would time permit that?

When it came to picking our prisons, I chose Rocky Comfort Correctional Facility, a half hour west of Tallahassee, a crow's fly from Daddy's mama in Quincy. Daddy used to hunt wild turkey and doves on Rocky Comfort Creek before the prison was built. You could tell by the name *Facility* that it was run by a private corporation. State prisons were *Institutions.*

The newspapers in the library said the private prison company had laid off nurses and re-hired them for less, no benefits. And here I was pregnant, expecting in a few months.

But Rocky Comfort also had the drug rehab program I needed, courses I wanted to start my business, Computer-Aided Design (CAD) and faith-based programs. I could choose a faith-based dorm and that gave me some hope I could land on my feet—for the baby and for Annie.

The second week at Lowell, the guards shackled and cuffed us and put a dozen of us on a transport bus for Rocky Comfort, a six-hour ride in rattling cages.

I tried to ignore the incessant banging and set my face for Rocky Comfort. I had been sidelined so long, a program facility looked like university to me. I had never finished any program, had never started others.

With my shackle-mate, dark-eyed, olive-toned Melinda, I discussed getting my GED, learning a trade or technical skill and starting my own business.

"That's since so many won't hire felons. We won't even qualify for welfare with felonies, unless we can change the law."

"I want that, too," she said, tossing her head to get her long hair out of her face. "I want my own business, a flower nursery!"

"Cool, you can do it! May I call you Mindy?"

"Sure, my family does."

None of us was convicted of a violent crime, but we'd been caught in a crime worth over $1,000, stealing money, dealing or using drugs. Still, we longed for lenience and prayed for commuted sentences.

The months and years stretched like the solid, no-passing line, separating us from children and families. One gray-haired woman had an autistic son who'd depended on her night and day. A young, freckled red-head had a newborn, and a high-cheeked African-Seminole couldn't stop talking about her mother with dementia. They were the world to us, and we to them.

Yet most of us were traveling far from family, to the opposite end of the state, since most prisons were in the north, and most people in the South Florida.

I hated feeling down, and Mama always said the power of life and death is in the tongue. So I tried turning my dark thoughts upside down. "I'm going to be a better mom inside than I was out." I had to practically shout above the rattle.

"Pardon?" Mindy shook her thick brown hair out of her face.

I repeated it, and she nodded.

Prison would separate me from the people, places and things that had lured me too often from my daughter, kept me hooked, hooking or stealing.

Mindy looked at me frankly, her moist eyes reflecting the towering pines sailing by. "The crazy thing is, I was arrested for DWSL."

"Driving While Lip-Synching?" The women around us leaned in.

She laughed. "Not quite. Driving While License Suspended. Only in Florida is that a felony. And only here can they suspend your license for a non-driving offense." Mindy raised her expressive brown eyebrows. "My attorney is appealing, but he says it may take an act of legislature."

"Whoa! What happened?"

"On my birthday, I registered my car but didn't get insurance since my car was broken down in the shop. After that, I got a letter saying I owed $350 for registering an unlicensed vehicle. I called the number and told them what to do with their fine."

"I'll say." We passed a rest stop and I rattled the cage. "Sir, can you stop at the next rest stop, please?"

"Yes, please," Mindy chorused with several other women.

"Go on," I prompted her.

"The next week, I was driving my mama's old caddy to my new job when I ran a yellow light. The police ran my license and told me it was suspended for failing to pay the $350 insurance fine. Plus, he wrote me up, another $250 for running a red light. I couldn't get to work without a license and I couldn't pay the fines without work."

"Was there no one to help you?" I was surrounded by helpers, Kita, Mama and Isabella. If my boat started to sink, they could row over and pull me out.

"No. My Mama's disabled and my boyfriend's in jail. I had a drug possession prior, so they cuffed me and took me in. At the trial, the judge gave me a year and a day and told me to spend it improving myself.

"*Better I spend it improving my kids*,' I said in Spanish. The Judge cited me for contempt and demanded I translate.

"'*I'm pregnant*,' I said. 'I'm going to have this baby in prison—and I have more babies at home!'"

"Me too!" I said. "I'm pregnant too. We'll be pregnant together."

Mindy smiled. "Si! For sure!"

"What happened then?"

"The bailiff grabbed me but I kept talking. 'My crippled Mama has to watch my kids! They'll go on food stamps! You call this justice? This is debtor's prison!'"

The women around us in the bus cheered.

"The state and private companies are putting us in prison for their profit and our poverty." Mindy said aloud what we all felt deep down.

Cuffed, she couldn't reach her own sleeve so she wiped her face on my sleeve. I soaked in her snot and hot tears and shivered as it cooled. Prison was teaching me that true friendship was tested in the gutter.

12
Rocky Comfort

We crossed the Suwanee River under gray skies, rusty cypress reflected in tea-brown water. The sun glinted behind clouds above soaring pines along I-10 and reflected lilac in office windows of Tallahassee. My family was just ten miles south; so near, yet so far away. We entered Gadsden County and pulled off the interstate on Route 12, passing the Creek casino, dipping onto Rocky Comfort Creek bridge and rising on the other side into the correctional facility parking lot.

An ambulance screamed out as we pulled in and I tensed, thinking of my baby. Would that be us one day? Who was inside that speeding vehicle? Would she make it?

We were minimum-to-medium security prisoners, not the kind who'd neutralize fences, throw jackets over razor wire and escape. And yet we were closely guarded getting off the bus with our clanking chains. Several guards in brown uniforms pulled us along and a big one with gray eyes walked Mindy and me through security. Her nametag said G-r-e-t-a something. I shuffled faster, trying to keep up with my shackle-buddy, but leg irons only stretch eighteen-inches.

Inner and outer electric fences, topped with rolls of gleaming razor-wire, enclosed a dozen gray block dorms trimmed in burgundy. An endless beeping pierced the evening from a jersey barrier factory across Greensboro Highway.

"Come on, pick 'em up." Greta didn't seem unkind as she held the gate, her brown pixie-cut blowing in the wind. Just gruff, the way some guards think they have to be since there's one of them to forty of us. The metal gate clanged shut behind us, razor wire shadows etched the prison walk—a sight I had never wanted to see again. I tripped and went down, not seeing the raised sidewalk 'til it hit my face. I pulled Mindy with me, my shackled hands useless.

"Jesus!" Mindy hit the ground on her knees.

"Mama!" I cried as my shackled hands jabbed my pregnant belly.

A hot leak soaked my undies. "My baby," I screamed.

"Your baby?" Mindy was holding her belly too, but grabbed Greta's offered hand without another word.

"Are you pregnant?" Greta helped me up next, grasping my cuffed hands and pressing her foot against mine to help me stand. This time I read her name tag, Greta Green.

"Yes." A sharp pain shot from navel to groin.

Greta leaned over me, frowning. "Your face is a bit raw. You'll need to wash with soap and water." She placed her cold hand on my belly and I cringed. It wasn't public property. "Are you feeling anything here? Contractions?"

I shook my head, horrified at her pushing on me. "Just a leak in my undies. I should probably get checked."

"You look okay." She shoved me ahead and smiled at a passing officer.

"Officer," my voice seemed tiny. "Aren't we going to medical? What if I'm bleeding?"

"She's right," Mindy said, but Greta glared her down.

Really? I wanted to scream. *You can deny a prisoner medical care in here?*

"You'll be fine." Greta shoved me inside the yellow line on the walkway shoulder where prisoners had to walk single file, except we were shackled. It was a tight, jostling mess. "Keep to the right!"

She might not want my fall reported on her watch, but I knew my rights. I could file a complaint, and I would if I needed to. My groin and cheekbone screamed, the sky blurred into blue and white haze and the gray stone bunkhouses wavered. I was numb with fear and my knees wobbled. Still, she kept shoving us toward the nearest dorm.

The evening chow movement had started, and dozens of prisoners in baby blue scrubs moved along the walkway edge, while brown-uniformed officers trotted down the middle. All my movements would be guarded and restricted for well over a year. My stomach clenched and churned, and my grazed cheek burned. *Please Lord, don't let me miscarry.*

A purple-gilded pigeon flew into sharp focus from the bunkhouse roof. It landed smartly in the middle of the walkway, pigeon toeing and bobbing its head like some miniature officer. A second pigeon cooed from the eaves and my baby somersaulted inside me. My heart leaped to know he was alive.

I was always amazed that these winged creatures nested inside razor wire, though they could live anywhere. Shamed as I was to be pregnant in prison again, I was glad we were alive and nesting in this confined space together. Besides, if Daddy's homeboys were after us, we might be safer in here.

Listening to a crackle on her radio, Greta pulled on my arm. "Stop. Turn your back." Women in blue scrubs, coming and going on both sides of the walkway, stopped and turned their backs. A large woman was being led down the middle, blood running from a cut on her temple, soaking her prison scrubs.

"Sock-locked," Greta said coolly, as if announcing a play-by-play. "She's going to solitary; sent her girlfriend to the hospital for cheating."

So that's why the screaming ambulance; the tensed guards when we arrived. I nearly hurled my grits, my forehead still bruised by the bus cage accident. It hurt just like the cut and dizzying concussion of a padlock swung inside a gym sock.

Greta continued. "See you stay out of trouble, Ho, you hear?"

Who you calling ho? I wanted to scream, but zipped it. I would not stoop to her level.

She nudged me toward the first dorm and I nearly tripped over my shackles again.

"You giving that baby up for adoption?" She pushed me to the wall as several girls passed on their way to chow. "Studies show it's best."

Hush, I thought, biting my tongue.

"Well, you just let me know and I'll arrange it, okay?" She sounded chipper as she opened the door.

I studied my feet, lifting them carefully over the door jamb. *I'm keeping my baby.* My baby might have no daddy; I was his world. I knew women who'd given up their prison babies and were angry the rest of their lives.

Officers buzzed us through two sets of metal doors and we entered the windowed booth where uniforms watched from two posts over two gym-sized rooms, rows of bunks. One guard for forty women. The dorm and windowed booth were called "the bubble" because we were under constant watch.

From there, doors opened to the newcomers' dorm. I had to concentrate on shuffling my shackled feet over the next ledge, and the next.

Finally, we were buzzed into orientation dorm—where guards watched everything we did day and night. Women were queuing for chow. I should be home eating Mama's ham hocks and collard greens with my little Annie, double for the baby.

Little had changed since I was last here, except maybe the prisoners. I searched their faces for someone familiar, but women stared back with blank, somber faces. Some had missing teeth or pock-marked faces. Neck tattoos—Rick, Harry—exes long gone. One had a jig-sawed face, likely from a shattered windshield. They had lived two lifetimes in the span of one, flying on meth or crashing on sedatives.

I must've looked a mess, too, with my raw, scraped up face.

A prisoner in blue scrubs with a tanned angular face and wavy white shag met us, smiling so big her chipped tooth and dimples showed. "Welcome, Cinnamon Rose," she said, reading my nametag. "Oh, what happened to your face? Let me get something for that."

"Yes, thanks. She tripped," Greta said as an afterthought, though in the bubble with other guards looking on, her tone bordered on care and respect.

The long-haired woman ran to the open bathrooms, across from the guard window, came back with soapy paper towels and dabbed at the scrape and lump that swelled my cheek. "I have some ointment at my bunk. Come on."

She guided us away from the crowded door, down a row of neatly-made bunks, each flanked by two desks. She paused to dig in her footlocker for ointment.

With feather-soft fingers she dabbed my cheek, her dark brown eyes full of concern, her face almost too big for her small body. "They should have taken you to medical, Rose," she murmured.

"Cinny, call me Cinny please." That's all I said with Greta in earshot.

"You're welcome. I'm Lexis, the Resident Alien." She grinned with me.

"Assistant." I grinned back.

Lexis pointed me to B16 lower and I gasped. God knew my name! This was the same bunk I'd had last time. Here, I had fallen into Jesus's arms and felt him holding me the night I found out I was pregnant. Someone said that God always meets you at your deepest need. Like Daniel in the lion's den.

Lexis raised an eyebrow. "Cinny? Anything wrong?"

"It's the same bunk I had last time."

Greta unlocked my shackles and strode away, radio crackling.

"Home sweet home." Lexis handed me clean scrubs.

"Medium, you even know my size." I hugged her and she squeezed back. "The drug rehab program doesn't allow hugging," she whispered. She was looking at the bubble windows, nodding and giving an okay sign. "I'm here for you. You need anything, just let me know. But for now, hurry and change so you can join us for chow."

My stomach growled even recalling the slimy white mush they served. I was hungry enough to eat 'gator. I hurried to the doorless latrine. Thank God, no blood in my undies. Too late I realized there was no toilet paper, but Lexis was handing me a roll. "I guess you remember, it's one roll a week, free," she grinned.

And yes, I did. If I didn't hide that one-week roll like contraband, it would get stolen and I'd have to buy one on the prison black market.

I hurried to join the chow line leaving the building, turned the walkway corner and stopped short, facing the chapel wall. The art gang had turned the solid cinderblock wall into a fluid landscape. A splashing waterfall flowed over rocks into a palm-lined pool and, on the other shore, a wind-whipped lighthouse beamed into crashing waves.

I had learned during my first pregnancy inside, to keep a beautiful vision in front of me for the hard times. For this term, I pinned that to my mind, convinced we could create beauty anywhere.

In the yard, women in white scrubs walked the service dogs they were training—golden retrievers and black labs rescued from shelters; whippets and greyhounds rescued from the dog track. Along the walkway, women in blue planted yellow and orange daisies, a sulfur butterfly floating over them.

At the kitchen door, women slowed, trying to hold their ground in the crush. No rush, right? Yet salty mush was a highlight of our day. When I finally got my tray, it was fat noodles dotted with brown rubbery chunks and a helping of tinned mandarin oranges. Up in the corner was a small, red delicious apple. That was worth keeping.

My face still prickled and my hands and knees burned from the fall. An apple would be a rare treat if I made it to nightfall without going to the hospital. Or, if I made it 'til dawn, I could trade it for something—microwave coffee in the dorm. I slipped it into my scrub pants before sitting beside Lexis.

"We get chow mein tonight." She beamed as though she'd just announced steak and fries. Then I noticed her buddies scooping with their plastic forks, savoring the gruel, saying, "Mmhm."

"We try to do all things without murmuring or complaining." Lexis caught my eye and flashed a gap-toothed grin.

Their gallows humor reminded me of Reese. I knew right away I wanted to hang with Lexis and her friends. I laughed and scooped some soggy mandarin slices. "Fresh oranges—all the way from China!"

Everyone laughed and I felt like one of the family.

"You should join us in Lamp Steps," Lexis said. "We meet tomorrow night in the chapel."

"What's that?"

Another girl leaned in. "Chapel, a room where people worship God."

I groaned.

"No-oo." Lexis laughed. "It's a Christian 12-step program. We're all leaders."

Leaders? They could be leaders in prison? That was more than I'd ever imagined.

We picked up our trays and headed for the conveyor belt, and I felt the little apple slip and drop down my pants leg. It hit the floor and rolled. Lexis gave it a solid kick.

"Why'd you do that?" I hissed.

"Are you kidding? You could go to lock for that."

I sucked my breath. I hated lock, a solitary cell with a cot and toilet, no one to talk to and no movement except one hour for rec. In a separate, secluded pen.

13
Lamp Steps

Back in the dorm, voices rose and fell, echoing off the cinderblock walls. It was hard to hear or even think, so girls just raised their voices louder, drowning everyone out.

I found Lexis on her bunk reading a manual, her Bible open. She patted a plastic bin at her feet. "Sit here. We're not allowed to sit on each other's beds."

Her workbook was titled *Lamp Steps*. It was easier to hear her when I was facing her on the lower bunk. "What is that?"

"Yes, great program. I've seen women change from night to day. They come in worrying over things they can't change— kids, parents, boyfriends. They cry through the first few lessons, some for the first time. And then, after a few more lessons they get it: I can't, God can, I'm gonna let him. They're smiling, upbeat and praying circles around—"

A loud crash and thud landed nearby. Lexis whipped around and flew between two inmates. A large woman had dragged a smaller one from her top bunk and thrown her to the ground.

The smaller one, barely five feet, 100 pounds, stood up, wild-eyed, red-faced and flailing. "Moose pulled me off my bunk."

Lexis caught the thin girl's hands.

"Yeah, after you took a high tone with me." Moose stood, hands on hips like a mountain towering over an ant hill.

"You stole my Cheese Puffs." The thin, stringy-haired woman screeched.

"Cheese Puffs?" Lexis yelled. "This is about Cheese Puffs?"

"Yeah, they're special. Hand 'em over!"

"Hush." Moose reached into her scrubs top and handed over a small red bag. "I could get you in so much trouble."

"Both of you hush," Lexis said. "Stay in your own bunks now, hear?"

I looked down when Lexis passed and returned to my bunk. Later, when the din in the dorm had settled, I asked her for a pencil and paper. She rummaged in her shelf and found some used math sheets, blank on one side. I took them back to my bunk and tried to puzzle out her algebra proofs, only proving I needed my GED.

The paper seemed too precious to draw flying bullets, splattered brains. Instead, I drew large round, dark eyes— Annie's—reflecting Daddy's large hands, reaching for her. I drew waterfalls flowing over a large round bolder. Inside, a baby curled, tiny fingers clenched.

Lexis stared at my drawing, her hair brushing the page. She knelt in front of me on the linoleum tile. "That's beautiful!" she said. "You're an artist! Can you tell me about this?"

"Well, I miss my daughter, Annie, and that's my daddy reaching for her the Sunday before he was murdered. Annie's daddy was involved."

"What? Your daughter's daddy?"

"He was charged anyway. There was a gang—and Doobie was in it." I shifted on my thin mattress, blanket pilled from too many washes. "I still ache from it."

Lexis studied my face, then my drawing. "Cinny, why did you draw pig ears on your baby?"

"Armadillo ears. It's for my graphic novel where my people are armadillos. But also, I don't know if my baby's okay. I shot meth in his first month, right after we found Daddy shot in the street."

Lexis covered her mouth and chipped tooth. "Oh Cinny, that is too much tragedy for one life."

"The waterfalls are my forever memory of my big brother, 'cause he took me there right before he—shot himself."

"Oh dear, Cinny." She leaned her head against my leg. "Wait a minute! Where are these falls?"

"Right out the prison gate, turn south on Highway 12 to 20 West. You'll cross Econfina Creek just north of Panama City. From 231 and Scott Road, hike downstream."

"My daughter lives near there, in Fountain." Lexis paused.

Cinny nodded, "Yes, near Fountain."

"Or, lived there before she was sent to prison. Her baby still lives there."

The longing in her eyes stung me. "Lexis, it's a lovely, wild place. If your grandbaby is in good hands, you should be happy."

She nodded. "Yes, I think so. With her father."

"Lexis, I was floating that day. A real high—nothing cooked, dropped or swallowed."

Econfina Creek falls (David Moynahan Photography)

14
Steephead Falls

That morning, Dex filled his coffee mug and invited me on a drive to the strange falls he'd discovered. I bounded ahead of him to the rusted Ford 150, but he stumbled around a bit, splashed his coffee and tripped over the dog.

"Should I drive?" I stuck out my hand for the keys. I was only 14 and had no license.

Dex laughed, his high, infectious ripple. "No, I'll be okay."

We drove west under tall pines along Highway 20 toward Panama City and he dialed the radio trying to find a new song—not his girlfriend's after she dumped him right after he got back from Iraq.

I told him to *stop*. "*Stop* dialing. That's the station. The one that was playing the Civil Rights protest song, 'Oh healing river, send down your water…wash the blood off the sand.'"

We got to Gulf County and headed north on Route 231 to Scott Road, skidded through the red sand dirt, to Econfina Creek Water Management District. There we parked at the trailhead, and followed a wide, sand trail and markers for the Florida National Scenic trail—blue paint blazes, six feet high on tree trunks. He showed me how the blazes guided you from one sighting to the next, and on the map, how this trail connected with the Appalachian trail in Georgia and went all the up to White Mountain in New Hampshire.

Hand-set long leaf pine grew in the long grass like large green bottle brushes. He pointed out the restored native pine in early and mid-growth. "Candle and candelabra stage."

But with all his knowledge and experience, he still seemed to trip over roots and stumps so I grabbed his hand to hold him up.

Finally, there was the creek like iced tea running along a deep, sandy gully.

"Long ago, this was the beach and these were the dunes." Dex gazed at the woods. "The ocean came all the way up here, 20 miles from the coast."

A tree had fallen across the creek, making a solid foot bridge, and I held Dex's hand to cross—for his safety, not mine. I wasn't worried about me back then. On the other side, the woods were full of tree trunks cut waist high.

"Two-man crosscut saws did this." He measured the stump against his hip "Two men pulled it back and forth, and tooled the teeth for hard or soft wood. They carried saw tool kits just for that purpose. The woods were once cut so clean, you could see clear to the Gulf without a tree to break the view." He had a way of talking that made history visible.

We hiked up and down the trail, beneath pines, oaks and long-leafed magnolias. "Magnolia grandiflora." He picked up and handed me a foot-long waxy leaf, fuzzy brown on the back. A magnolia branch brushed us, offering a serving-bowl-sized, creamy blossom. We paused to inhale its honey-citrus fragrance.

We descended the bank closer to the creek, knocking into woody fans of palmetto leaves, until we heard the rush of a powerful waterfall. We dipped into a few more tributary channels and rounded a sandy bend before we saw a powerful waterfall shooting over the bank into the creek.

"Here, our Native American ancestors, on Daddy's side, stashed arrowhead scraper tool kits." Dex shucked his shoes and I copied him. "Early American pioneers brought their slaves—our great grandpa—and settled around its springs."

We rolled up our jeans, skidding down into the cold creek. I waded along its course bottom toward the rushing falls. My jeans, soaked to the knees, dragged at my waist and hips. I stepped over a large log, but Dex lunged right over it into the creek and came up sputtering. His dripping tee-shirt hung off solid muscles to his thighs.

"Like a dress," I laughed. "Here, give me your hand." I held it under the falls.

"Feels like icicles!"

"Yes, Dex, cool and sharp as glass."

"Right, Cinny, that's how you know it's a steephead, cold as underground caves, a constant 62 degrees. Steepheads are what the pioneers called them because these are steep-walled canyons cutting into Florida's ancient dunes."

He stood, dark and tall, wet tee-shirt dappled in forest light. He reached up and dug an ancient seashell from the clay. "A lion's paw."

A dark, winged creature swooped down, grazing his outstretched hand, scooping up the shell.

He ducked and stumbled around the creek. "Hey! What was that?"

I smirked. "Pterodactyl."

He laughed and pushed me into the cold stream, thighs, belly, breasts chilled through, blue jeans tight and tee-shirt soaked, hanging to my knees. I dragged Dex in, and he was laughing too.

He went down gulping air and came up sputtering and splashing me. "Silly girl. Never lose that crazy streak, promise?"

"Promise."

He showed me how to duck around behind the falls and see the world through the flowing curtain, hard forest edges blurred to soft, shimmering greens and browns. Reality dimmed to translucent hues.

He stooped and fished around under the pounding falls. "Sometimes springs and steephead streams dislodge sharks' teeth or arrowheads. This is what divers call a honey pot."

He scooped up a smooth dark oblong disc. "Dugong bone. This is our lucky day. Those were ancient sea animals—and today we're miles from the sea."

He handed it to me and I rubbed it between my thumb and forefingers.

"You are touching ancient history."

I smiled all the way home, rubbing the dugong bone and singing along with our new radio station. "By the River of Babylon where we sat down..."

"That's a city in Iraq," he said. "We could see the ruins from Saddam Hussein's palace." He clenched his jaw, dark eyes reflecting the pinks and purples of sunset behind the pines.

"Was it scary?"

"Oh yeah, coupla times I thought I'd been hit. Once the rocket fire came so close, the shockwave threw me to the ground and I lost my hearing for days. It was like cotton in my ears—so quiet and peaceful."

I flinched.

"Next morning, we got up and went back on patrol. Didn't even take a break, just kept humpin'." He cleared his throat.

"Your old girlfriend didn't deserve you," I said. "She was no good for you anyway."

"Ah well, she never understood me when I came back. I kept hearing grown men screaming, drowning in an overturned tank in the river…. We couldn't reach them…. I couldn't sleep and the slightest noise made me jump. My drinking didn't help either. So…, you're prob'ly right. She wasn't that good for me. I wanted to be back with my men."

I never forgot that day, especially after he was gone. I imagined him tripping and falling into the crystal sea and Jesus picking him up, handing him a dugong bone.

I could see how that day may have been his stepping stone to eternity. He was feeling just better enough to pull the trigger and shoot the pain away.

In my bunk, I sketched the water curtain from the steephead falls, faint light shining through. I heard a tin-like squeeling and realized Lexis was circling by with her ear buds blaring. I motioned her over and took them out. "What are you listening to?"

She placed a bud in my ear and the transistor radio in my hands. "Keep it tonight," she said. "It'll cheer you up."

I put down the pencil and paper, and tuned out the dorm noise. "You are God and we will bless you, even if the healing doesn't come." I leaned back, feeling my baby somersault inside me. *Thank you, God, my baby's alive.*

Still, I missed my family and boyfriend, wherever he was. Years ago, Mama had adopted Annie so the state wouldn't take her away. Kita worked nights so Mama could work days and they could watch her together. It was a lot to ask of them to keep my newborn, too.

I pulled up my thin covers and prayed the universal prayer of every prisoner, *Please, Lord, shorten my sentence*. I'd be a model inmate, apply to serve some time in work release, and take what was dished out, even if that meant shutting my mouth.

In my dream, I was drawing Tony's muscled brown arm when, from nowhere, a needle glided in, sucking a slurry of blood and plunging it in again, filling his veins with brown gunk. He slumped against a dumpster, and I woke with my hair standing on end.

15
Lexis Helps

Chilled and jittery, I padded across the cold tile floor, passing among bunks lit by the prison yard light that never went out. My bruised cheek pounded, my stomach rolled. I threw up and drank some tap water, then held a wet paper towel to my swollen cheek. In the blurred surface of the metal mirror, one eye was swollen and turning black.

Who could I tell with everyone sound asleep? Where could I get help? I headed back to bed, and noticed Lexis tossing off her blanket. I sat softly on her plastic bin, not wanting to wake her. I missed Mama, who used to take me under the covers when I was a scared.

Lexis stirred. "Cinny?" She squinted and groped for my hand in the dark.

"I'm so sick," I said, my skin screaming, my teeth chattering.

"Well I'm sweltering. Take this." She unzipped her jacket and threw it over me.

I wrapped it tight around my shaking shoulders. "I dreamt my boyfriend was drugged—and dying. Do you think it's real?"

"I don't know, Cinny. Are you asking if dreams can reveal truth?"

"Yeah, maybe?" My cheek stung.

"Tell you what. Tomorrow you can use my phone credit to call home."

"What's a good woman like you doing in here?" I burrowed into her soft warm knit jacket.

"Oh, I'm not good. I burned my son's arms in a meth explosion. It got me too." She turned her face, pulling back her hair. In the yard light, I saw for the first time, her burned ear and scarred neck. "His arm caught fire and I smothered it with my jacket. His skin was dripping like black candle wax. I grabbed him and ran. Neighbors drove us to the clinic where police called me out of his room and arrested me. My daughter was in school at the time, but she was old enough to take custody of him. That was my first conviction, and I swore it would be my last."

Tears soaked her lean face and I handed her the few squares of toilet paper I was holding.

"Just when all I wanted was to hold and comfort him. During those five years in jail, my daughter lost custody and I had to give him up for adoption. I sank so low, I didn't think anyone could reach me. But Jesus did. I felt him holding me right down there in that pit. I had no righteousness of my own, but he gave me his."

"I understand." I wiped my sore eyes, wishing I could hug Tony again, every moment of every day. I hauled out the wad of toilet paper I kept in my bra and unrolled some more for Lexis.

She mopped her face. "The blessing I'm claiming is that I will reunite with my son one day." She paused and smiled unevenly. "Do you know that he's a lawyer now?"

"That's great. You must be so proud of him."

"Yes, by giving him up, I may have given him a fighting chance. By giving up on my power completely, I gave myself a second chance."

I drew long and hard on that thought, though I still didn't want to give up my son.

Lexis sniffled again, fresh tears. "My girl was your age when she got hooked on pain killers. I was getting clean and sober in jail, and she turned to heroin."

I touched her knee. I was once that lost daughter.

"I couldn't reach her, but finally, after I got out, she came to me. Her dealer was going to kill her if she didn't pay up. At that time, she owed like $1,500. He had already killed her best friend. So, I sold some jewelry from the estate I was cleaning, and went to meet him."

"You're crazy. He coulda killed you."

"I know. And I didn't do it just once. After that, he had my number. I did it over and over again, trying to keep my daughter alive."

"You know what that's called?"

"Stupid?"

"Enabling."

"Textbook definition." She smiled and squeezed my hand. "I used to be a people pleaser, but now I'm a Jesus pleaser."

"I want to be, too," I whispered.

"That's why I'm in here. Fifteen years for grand larceny, $25,000 to keep her drug dealer paid off. It's hard to pay court costs, fines and restitution while I'm sitting in here. That's the crazy thing about prison. Unless you're locking away serial killers like Ted Bundy, why not let us work and save taxpayers some money? Or pay us for the work we do here?"

On the top bunk, a woman mumbled and tossed off her blanket. We froze until she lay still again.

Lexis sat up and looked hard at my swollen black eye. She turned my head toward the light from the window, "Are you going to be okay?"

"Yes, I feel like I could sleep for a month."

She kissed my scarred forehead, her lips cool on my burning brow.

16
Tony

Kita was breathless when she answered my call the next day.

"Cinny, listen, I just left the courtroom. I was at Doobie's arraignment."

"For Daddy's murder?"

"No, for Tony's. I'm so sorry."

I felt socked in the gut.

"How, Kita?"

She hesitated.

"Come on, Sissy. It can't be worse than my dream."

"What dream?" Kita's hard breathing stilled.

"That someone injected him with heroin." The dream image was full color.

"No Cinny, it was exactly like your dream."

I gasped and crumpled into a plastic chair.

"After Doobie robbed Daddy, he scored some black tar and went looking for Tony. They drank a case of beer, then Doobie cooked up the heroin and injected him. Cinny, that combination can stop an addict's heart."

"So, what happened to Tony?"

"I'm so sorry, Cinny. Tony was found in the city landfill. Doobie managed to lift his dead weight into the dumpster behind the homeless shelter."

I sobbed, not caring who heard me, especially not Lexis who rushed to my side and tried to anchor me to the chair. I was slipping, sliding, tossed under a crashing wave.

"You were right again, Cinny," Kita tried to cut through my sobs. "Listen, Mama, Isabella and I will come see you with

Annie on Sunday—and we want to hear all about how you and the baby are doing."

"Tony, I've decided to call him Tony." Lexis wrapped her arms around me.

"Oh, I like that, Cinny. Tony." Rising voices echoing around her muffled Kita's voice. "Court's out. Gotta run pick up the kids. See you soon."

Lexis hung up the phone and I leaned into her, cradling my round belly. "He's dead. He's gone. My baby daddy's never coming back."

"Oh Cinny, how sad." She walked me to the window facing the tree canopy shading Rocky Comfort Creek. "Even though I walk through the valley of the shadow of death, I will fear no evil, for you are with me."

The baby somersaulted and I gradually subsided.

She stroked my back. "We'll have a wake in the dorm tonight."

That evening, Chaplain Hope came to the dorm, looking serene and regal in a blue shift. Lexis announced the memorial service and a dozen women gathered around tables near the bubble. Some hung back, sitting in nearby bunks. I motioned Mindy over, but she shook her head. I sat facing Chaplain Hope, drawn to her lemon-honey skin, loose dark curls, sage green eyes and quiet smile.

"We are here to commemorate Cinny's boyfriend and father of her baby, Tony Garcia." Hope paused and looked at each of us deeply. "None of us were sentenced to lose a loved one in prison, and none of us wants to walk that road alone."

She began humming, eyes closed, swaying and singing. "Jesus walked this lonesome valley, he had to walk it by himself…." And we all joined in, "Oh, nobody else can walk it for him, he had to walk it by himself." We sang all the verses, and I clung to each note.

"Many of us have walked through this most distressing time, losing family while locked up and not allowed to attend the funeral. Does anyone else want to lead a song?"

"Someone's crying Lord," I wailed and everyone joined in the Gullah lament. "Kumbaya."

When we'd faded, Hope asked. "Is anyone else grieving a loved one?"

Lexis nodded. "My father, grandpa and uncle all died this year—all the older men in my life. Our ties snapped before I came here and I never had a chance to make it right." She looked down, arms wrapped tightly around her waist.

"I'm so sorry, Lexis," Chaplain Hope said. "My mother died recently, too, and I didn't make it home in time. I threw myself over her cold body in the funeral home. But some of you did not even get that. Don't bury it."

"My grandma who raised me." said the thin, straggle-haired woman who'd been fighting with Moose. I was surprised to see them sitting together.

"My uncle Luther died in prison and we still don't know how or why." A brown-haired woman straightened, chin up, looking around the caring circle.

"My cousin, Keniedra, a quadriplegic, was found hanged in her cell after reporting on a guard. She couldn't have hanged herself." Moose wiped her glasses and straightened, meeting the chaplain's gaze.

"My three-month-old, in my boyfriend's care." A chubby-cheeked child of a woman blurted out.

Chaplain Hope nodded, head bent, inviting us into silent remembrance. She looked up at the dozen women gathered, and passed around song sheets. Others in the dorm stopped moving around and sat still on their beds, reading or listening. "It's also important to find a purpose in the grieving. Let's try the 'Hymn of Promise,' my favorite." She had a strong rich voice and we all followed along. "In the bud there is a flower, in the seed an apple tree.'" I added my alto, recalling how grandma used to sing this very tune in her garden, "In cocoons, a hidden promise, butterflies will soon be free!"

Lexis, who played banjo on the outside, found her voice at last and led out on the last verse. "In our end is our beginning, in our time eternity, In our doubt, there is believing..."

I tunneled deep on that line. Tony was taken, yet my life and the baby's spared.

"Unrevealed until its season, something God alone can see."

Tony Jr. flutter kicked inside me.

The next morning, I hurried with Mindy, my cage-bus shackle-buddy, from a breakfast of gray oatmeal and thin coffee to master gardener class. We had joined together and Mindy helped me mix piles of smelly cow manure with rich brown peat, using shovels and pitchforks.

Mindy was covered in dirt and smelling of rich manure. "Dirt bunny!" I called her.

"Si, dirt bunny, yourself," she said.

We filled wheelbarrows and trundled them around campus to winter flower beds. Mine was near the security office breezeway. I dug with a trowel into the cool moist dirt and set a bright yellow pansy with black ribbon markings.

I took another from its seed pot, shook out its tangled roots and placed it gently in the soil. A pigeon swooped down from the eves, cocked its head and pecked beside me, expertly pulling a long worm from the soil and flying back to its nest in the eves.

I grinned and sat back, stroking my tummy. I was well into my second trimester, week 25, and the baby was growing. We would spend Christmas together before its due date of March 7. I sifted loose dirt around the yellow pansies, breathing in the woody scent of blossom and sun-warmed earth, keeping Tony's memory alive.

I placed a russet pansy next to the yellow, its little face nodding in the early December wind—a miniature bushy-eyed man with full beard and mustache, just like Daddy's. His coffin was lowered right beside Dex, the blue-robed choir singing, "I'll fly away."

Beside the russet, I placed a purple pansy. In it, I saw my mother's face, shocked and amazed. Her DeAndre had repented, led us in worship, and then was taken from us.

Gardening, like grief, required patience; and grief, like this garden, birthed art, formed in pain and loss. I was finding in my sorrow, the source of my passion, to create beauty and solace for hurting people all around, including me.

A line of inmates passed—controlled motion, enforced schedules. "Hey those colors pop!" One said, and several others agreed.

I grinned up at them. Planting striking pansies in contrasting colors was giving me back my sense of self.

I had just dug another hole when a Cheese Puffs bag landed in it. I looked up to see Tony in guard uniform, caramel skin, long legs and dark, curly hair. I caught my breath. What was Tony doing alive? Standing right in front of me?

17
Strange Flowers

"Tony?" I picked up the Cheese Puffs and handed them back, but he motioned me to put them back.

He glanced over his shoulder at Greta descending. "Bury it quick!"

I threw dirt over it and sat stalk still, shaken.

Greta paused and barked. "Get busy!"

I dug another hole and waited 'til her shadow receded.

"I know, I look like Tony. I'm his cousin, Mario, remember?"

"Oh right, Squeak." That's what I'd called him, playing cops and robbers with Annie, his sneakers squeaking across Tony's mom's polished floors. "Got yourself a real cop job, I see?"

He winced.

I squinted up at his starched uniform. "You got any more Cheese Puffs to grow?"

"Cinny, I need you to keep this secret. Remember the g-code."

I clapped my hands over my ears. "No more g-code!" No way was I ever going to be part of the gangsta "don't-tell" code again.

Squeak pulled my hands away.

"For stupid Cheese Puffs?" I exploded.

"Shh. There's smokes in there—since the governor's ban."

"I don't wanna know, Mario!"

"Officer Damon to you, Cinny. And now you do, so no telling!"

Petite, round Mindy was pushing a cart full of pansies toward us, brown hair flying in the morning breeze. Damon raised an eyebrow at her sunlit smile, and moved to intercept her and several others passing through the breezeway. He strutted around, unlaced boots flapping, yelling, "Tuck in your shirt; no talking in the Breezeway." Mindy and the other girls paused and tucked in their shirts.

I understood. He had to act tough or he'd look weak—like boyfriend material, or someone who'd do favors for inmates. Still he looked so boyish in his loose curls and smooth olive skin.

Mindy knelt heavily beside me with a flat of snapdragons. More of my favorites. She wiped sweat from her face—dirt streaked her rosy cheek. I reached over and added a dirt streak to her other cheek. "To match the other side."

She laughed and got me back—two streaks on my cheeks. She tottered and fell into me. "Is that a baby bump or are you just happy with the food in here?"

I laughed. "Yeah right. No, I'm having this baby—Tony, Jr.—after my boyfriend." I tried to keep it positive. "He's more alive now than ever."

She patted her own round belly, "I'm having a boy too—Jason. What do you mean more alive?"

"This baby feels like a visit from heaven." I exhaled, weighing whether to say more, and realized I was talking to my honesty partner. "Tony disappeared the same night my Daddy died, off-ed by my ex, once a guard in here. My ex was getting me back for reporting he raped me in prison."

A shadow stood over us. "Girls, get to work." It was Greta blocking the sun.

I didn't bother looking up, but reached for my trowel and dug several deep holes, until she moved on.

"Let's plant some snapdragons for our sons. You mind reaching me those pots?"

"Sure." She fell over again, comically, in the black dirt. "So off balance. *De verdad.*"

"Why what's wrong?"

"I can't keep him." Her full lips turned down.

"Why not?"

"His daddy's in prison, and my mom's crippled with arthritis."

"That's tough." I set a snap dragon, patted soil around it and looked at her. "Don't you have anyone else—granny or sister?"

She shook her head and wiped her nose on her gray tee-shirt sleeve, wiping more mud on her face. "I'm a wreck. I would so love to keep my baby— It's a crime the way they do us in here."

"Do what?" I loosened some snapdragon roots, set them in a hole and patted more rich, black soil around them.

"You didn't hear it from me, but they give you money for your baby."

"Who? Who gives you money?" I popped a white snapdragon from the flat.

"The adoptive parents, through the agency."

"What agency? Is that legal?" I set a pink snapdragon and patted it in place.

"Well, they're allowed to pay living expenses. We're not supposed to tell but it's about $10,000."

I dropped my trowel and sat back on my haunches.

"They paid my court costs, restitution, and child support. They're sending money home for my kids. They're paying me $50 a month for canteen—coffee, chocolates, shampoo, sneakers—for a healthy baby."

How many mornings had I craved coffee inside? And I could sure use help paying the child support I owed Mama and Kita, plus court costs and fees, not to mention buying shampoo, shoes, uniforms. Uniforms that cost us $14, though we made 'em for free. But Mama and Kita would never let me sell Tony. How could a mother even live with that?

"That's cheap," I speared the earth and dirt exploded all over Greta's boots. Oops, I thought she'd moved on. Had she overheard us?

Mindy gasped.

"Cinnamon Rose, on your feet!"

I stood and saluted, "Sir." Don't ask me where that came from. Without even thinking, I was acting like a grunt, making her my Commander in Chief. What had gotten into me? Mindy rose and stood, wavering beside me.

"That will be a DR, Rose."

"Sir. Ma'am." But this time, I sagged against Mindy. I didn't want any Disciplinary Report—didn't want to serve a day over my 85 percent.

"At ease." Greta turned her back on us. "Carry on."

"Just like slavery," Mindy mumbled.

"Slavery? Yes. And no. My grandparents were born to former slaves. Grandma remembers her papa coming in from picking cotton, weeping and bleeding. Those bolls tore up your skin and he filled a 50-pound bag for 50 cents a day, crawling along just picking that long bag full, sunup to sundown."

Mindy stopped digging, and pointed her trowel at me. "That happened to my family, too! In the tomato fields right here in Quincy, 50-pound boxes, 50 cents a day"

I clanked her trowel with mine. "Yes, and Grandpa worked in turpentine just south of here. Had to work all day, cutting cat-faces in pine trees. Four cuts a minute, hang a cup to catch the sap, run to the next tree, and keep going; 20,000 trees in two weeks or they'd dock his pay."

"At least they paid him."

"Right? Unlike us. But it was tin scrip he had to spend at the company store where prices were hiked."

"Oh *si*! My *abuelos* were illegals, hired by the state—through a contractor—to plant trees. They'd run through those clear-cuts. Digging, setting, covering as they ran. It crippled them. And they got no path to citizenship or Medicaid."

Several women from education passed for lunch, laughing at our smudged faces. We stuck out our tongues. They clutched net book bags, spiral notebooks and pens, their faces set with purpose. The guards stood aside, letting them pass.

My stomach churned and growled. "I am so ready for lunch. Let's take this back to the greenhouse and wash up."

We gathered the tools and flower flats, and wheeled them through the breezeway, back to the greenhouse, Mindy walking close behind me.

Under the trees near our gardens, two prisoners were coming from canteen, whispering to Officer Damon. Were they putting in their smoke orders? One held a Cheese Puff bag scrawled with $20 in black marker, another with $30. How many cigarettes? What was in them?

I hurried Mindy along, screening her from the sideshow.

"My grandparents had to study reading and math in secret." I said over my shoulder. "They kept count for everyone, and got so dangerous that the owners promoted Grandpa to the boiler room."

Mindy unloaded the flowers and trowels, and waved to our gray-bearded teacher in his office at the back. "That sounds dangerous."

"Right?" We soaped our hands at the work sink, doused our faces, and dried with paper towels. "He had to listen to the boiling turpentine and not let it blow, or they'd dock him for his time in the air."

"Is that *true?*" Mindy looked up, dark brows raised.

I laughed. "Naw, that's an old turpentine joke."

"Oh, you *comedian.*" She jabbed me in the ribs.

"Hey!" I batted her hands away and waved the teacher down on his way to lunch. "Can we go to lunch and finish our planting later?"

His eyes twinkled behind black-frame glasses. "I depend on it." He buttoned his red-and-white snowman cardigan and whistled, "Frosty, the snowman," out the door

I followed Mindy outside and stayed behind her, inside the yellow line. Mindy turned in the walkway. "Did your grandpa survive?" She twisted her hair so she could see better over her shoulder.

I stayed practically on her heels, making sure she could hear. "No, he was shot by the owner breaking up a card game. The owner kept saying, 'I shouldn'a had to kill those men.' My nana packed some things in a washtub and hitched a ride to Tallahassee with her three kids.'"

The scent of sweet, pungent tomato sauce, browned onions and hamburger wafted from the mess hall, and the line of women pushed hard from behind.

"*Espaguetis.*" Mindy said.

"Spanish, right?" Annie calls it, "Basghetti."

Mindy smiled and inhaled. "Ah tomatoes! We escaped the murdering drug cartels to work the tomato fields of Quincy—that's where I was born—"

"In the field?" I picked up a tray and plate filled with red-meat sauce. My mouth watered.

"*Si*, my dad was only sixteen. When he was old enough, he joined the army, so we could immigrate legally." Mindy followed me, setting her tray beside mine, and swinging her legs over the long bench. The dining room echoed with the din of women eager for their portioned meals. I savored each forkful, mindful of families bent and sweating in the blazing sun.

After lunch, we collected our snapdragons and returned to our flower beds. We worked steadily, filling the beds with red, yellow, pink and white snapdragons as the sun traced a slanting arc. Now and then, I found a cigarette butt in the beds and showed it to Mindy.

Her big brown eyes flew open. "How did that get here?"

"Smuggled." If I told her how, she'd be involved too, and I didn't want that for her. Perhaps I should tell our gardening teacher? But then they'd come for me and I'd have to rat out Tony's cousin. I set a few more flowers. Sweat dripped into my eyes and I was glad for a cooling afternoon breeze.

I picked up a fallen snapdragon blossom and put it under Mindy's nose. She sniffed its soft, sweet scent.

"Don't smell, watch." I squeezed the dragon cheeks and opened its mouth, making it talk like a TV Chipmunk. "Will you marry me?"

Mindy plucked a yellow blossom right off its stem and squeezed its cheeks at me, "Marry a silly snapdragon?"

"Sure, we can have lots of snapdragon babies. My grandma used to plant these along the railroad in Tallahassee. She said knights used to give snapdragons to ladies for proposals—and she wanted us to be ready."

"It's a little late for me." Mindy rose heavily, and I helped her to her feet. We wheeled the cart back to the greenhouse, walking single file, disciplining ourselves, until we'd cleared the security office. We passed the garden we'd planted from useless lawn, filled with winter lettuce leafing out. "Do you know my grandma used to put pansies and snapdragons in our salads?"

Mindy pulled up alongside me. "Eating your snapdragon babies?"

I shoved her playfully and caught her when she stumbled over a sidewalk crack. We reached the greenhouse, turned on the hoses and watered poinsettias, lemon grass, cucumber and eggplants. What a shame we weren't allowed to send this fresh produce to the kitchen.

"Do you know, this is my sixth child? I adopted out one of my babies while I was using. That's what crack did to me."

I nodded. I knew too well how drugs wear you down, steal your joy and hope, and make you wish you'd never been born—or given birth. My first drugs were when one of Daddy's friends, stoned and high, passed me the crack pipe. I was only 13 and when I took a hit, Daddy beat the tar out of him. But I had learned what a freeing, blissful high it was.

"What happened to your other kids?"

"Two are with my boyfriend's mother who can hardly pay rent. The oldest is just ten but taking care of my mother. One I aborted, even though I'm Catholic. The dad was a monster. The night he punched me in the stomach, I crawled out on my hands and knees, hemorrhaging and cramping. I went to a clinic and asked for an abortion, terrified he'd come after me or my baby."

I hugged Mindy, checking for guards, knowing we could be sent to lock.

Behind the greenhouse, a lanky blonde with flattened nose, ducked, lighting a cigarette. Was that Reese? In here? With Cheese Puff smokes? Mindy was following my gaze but I stepped in front of her. "Hey, are you going for your GED like you said on the bus?"

"Well, I'm signed up. After Master Gardening, I hope."

"Me too! I need my GED before CAD. We can study together and buddy up 'til we have our babies."

She frowned and stroked her belly, growing round in her third trimester.

"Aw Mindy, we need to keep that baby for you. You can still back out, you know."

"Too late, Cinny, I've already spent the money." She turned off her hose and wound it around the caddy.

"That's it then." I turned off my hose and wound it up too. "We have to expose this. Maybe Chaplain Hope can help you."

Mindy grabbed my shirt sleeve. "No Cinny, please. They'll know it's me."

"How? Listen, Chaplain has to keep this confidential. We can ask her to check into it without mentioning you." A pain tightened around my belly and I grabbed Mindy's shoulder.

"Cinny! Sit down. It's too early for you to have that baby!" She cleared a space on the potting bench. "Teacher? Help please!"

Our teacher took off his large, red cardigan, threw it over me and helped me lean back and put up my feet.

I gave into the tightening band of muscles, trying to relax. "I think it's false labor. 'Braxton Hicks,' the nurse called it."

"Cinny, take care of yourself." Mindy set a folded garden blanket behind me. "Don't worry about me."

The tightening loosened and I sat up. "Fine, I'm fine. It's passed."

But our teacher insisted I keep the blanket, and tied it around my shoulders before releasing us into the cooling, November evening.

Girls were lining up for chow when we left gardening. And then there, coming from the canteen, silhouetted by the orange setting sun, was tall, regal Chaplain Hope. Oddly, she was ripping open a bag of Cheese Puffs.

"Whatcha got there, Chaplain?" I nudged Mindy.

"Kid's snacks! Want some?"

"You mean for our offspring?" I patted my six months' pregnant belly. "No thank you, Chaplain. You have to watch those Cheese Puffs; some've been tampered with."

Mindy butted in. "We do want to talk to you, please?"

"Sure, but it's cold here, let's step into the greenhouse, if it's still open."

Students had grown a forest of red, white and pink poinsettias for our plant sale; lemon grass plugs filled the air with their tangy citrus scent.

Chaplain Hope paused, breathing deeply. "Mm, how lovely!" Then called to our teacher. "Do you mind if we talk in here out of the cold?"

Our teacher waved us over to the potting bench in the corner. "Go ahead, I have to finish my paperwork back here."

We settled close together and I wrapped his sweater around Mindy and Chaplain too.

"It's about my baby." Mindy bit her lip and swallowed hard. "I have to give it up but I don't want to. Yet I've already spent the money."

Chaplain frowned, "What money?"

"It's about $10,000, living expenses, I was told. It went to pay my court costs and restitution and I sent some home for child support."

I handed her some of the folded toilet paper from my bra. "She feels like she was pressured, Chaplain, please help her."

Chaplain looked her full in the face. "Where? When did this happen?"

"It was at the Reception Center. A guard asked if I'd done drugs when I was pregnant and said I could be charged with fetal endangerment; that I wasn't ready to mother, and should give up my baby."

I pulled the sweater tighter around us. "There's a guard saying the same thing to me in here, Chaplain. It feels like she's pushing me to sell my baby like they did to the slaves. Please help us."

The Chaplain's eyes glowed a fiery green-gold in the setting sun. "What about your husband, Mindy? Did he agree?"

"My boyfriend? He caught ten years inside, Miss Hope. I can't even talk to him while I'm in here. Not allowed."

"So, he didn't agree to the adoption—?" Her brows shot up.

I could see where Chaplain was going. Maybe the agreement wasn't legal if the baby's father didn't sign.

"How did you sign? Who made you?" Chaplain placed her hand on Mindy's.

"No one; the adoption papers came in the mail. And the letter said they'd send money to the courts, my mom, or anyone, as soon as I signed and returned the papers."

Hope shook her head. "This is what's happened since we've privatized adoptions in this country. The only law guarding the process is that mothers must have legal representation. Who's your lawyer, Mindy?"

She shrugged and shook her head. "I was told they retained a lawyer for me. That's a lie?"

A thunderstorm rose in Hope's eyes. "It's probably for them. No wonder. Do you know how many women back out after they sign their babies away?"

"A lot?" I knew the ache in my arms, the pain in my breast, after Annie was born while I was still in prison. I had just 24 hours to hold and nurse her. No chance to fill up on each other's scent, drink from each other's eyes and wake in each other's arms. No hours rocking, napping, cuddling; laughing, singing, waltzing.

Miss Hope squeezed our hands. "Half. Fully 50 percent of women who sign away their rights renege and refuse in the end to give up their babies. I often wonder how I could have survived such a thing."

"Chaplain, Mindy isn't even here on a real charge, Driving While Lip-Syncing or something."

"DWLS." Mindy pushed back her hair. "I didn't realize my license was suspended. That was because I didn't insure my car, which was in the shop. The fine seemed like nonsense so I didn't pay it, and didn't realize my license was suspended."

A judge had sentenced Mindy to give birth in prison, yes. But would he have done it knowing how minor her charge? Or how wrenching it would be? Would a judge with a human heart, even one who respected the law, have willed such theft of a child from its mother?

The prison chorus started practicing in education, and surrounded us in four-part harmony, then hit *The Messiah* so hard, we almost rose to our feet.

After Annie was born, and before I was freed, I had spent nights rocking my pillow in weakened arms; mornings longing to hear her cry. There was nothing so cold as a prison guard taking your baby from your arms and ordering you on the bus; nothing so heartless as a system believing it would do you any good to go back behind bars instead of raising your child. Even a community lockup would be better.

The chaplain brushed Mindy's hair from her eyes. "Is your attorney appealing?"

Mindy nodded.

"These failures of justice are even more destructive than lawmakers know."

Mindy shivered and I threw my blanket over her.

The chaplain took a butterfly clip from her hair and tightened the wrap under her chin. "And do you know how likely it is that the babies and children of prisoners end up in prison themselves?"

"I did," I blew my nose in my toilet paper. "My Mama was in prison when I was four."

"Well it's five times more likely if your mama was in prison." Chaplain Hope slipped her arm through mine and turned to Mindy. "I am so sorry. I can't give you legal advice, but I can pray the creator will help you."

Melissa straightened, brushing sun-bronzed hair off her round cheeks. "When I signed him away, Jason wasn't real to me yet. I hadn't felt him move; now I never want to let him go."

We both reached for her hands. "The adoption agency said I was giving someone else the satisfaction. HeavenSent, they were called. They said that I didn't have to feel guilty; I was helping fulfill someone else's dreams, answering someone else's prayers."

"That just seems tone-deaf." Chaplain Hope bowed with us. "Please help us, Father; guide us with your glorious light."

Our gardening teacher stirred in his office, hung up his apron and changed into his street shoes. "Okay, I'm ready to lock up here." He turned off the overhead lights.

We rose together. "I'll look into it." Chaplain Hope gripped our hands. "I'll start by calling my chaplain friend at Lowell." She looked up, lit by an inner fire.

18
Birth Pangs

Leg irons bit through my socks as contractions gripped my torso. I tried to shift in the hospital bed, but the shackles wouldn't stretch. Fluorescent lights stung my dry eyes and I tried to roll onto my side but the chains held fast. How was I going to have my baby?

Another contraction took hold, throttling me from the inside. A sour taste rose in my throat, choking me. The bathroom was just steps away—but I couldn't move, couldn't breathe, couldn't even scream.

I tried to sit, but firm arms in a brown uniform pushed me down.

"Rose! You're not going anywhere!" Greta's eyes drilled mine.

I was going under, flailing.

My stomach rolled and I heaved butter grits all over myself.

"Mutha—!" Greta ran for the bathroom, retching.

I sank into pillows, helpless. Shame, a fat blubbery imp, sat heavy on my chest. How had I let myself drink, smoke, use, steal—and sell my precious self—until I'd hurt everyone around me?

A freckled girl in lilac scrubs, pulled my hospital gown off and tied on another. She reached in her pocket and sprayed a rose scent, murmuring, "It's okay, Cinny. Relax, breathe."

Cinny? How did she know my name?

She plumped my pillows and gave me ice chips in a paper cup to cool my swollen lips. Shame slid off my chest and let me breathe again.

"Do you know my sister, Nikita?" I gasped between contractions.

"Yes! Nikita said to take good care of you. She's in neonate with a preemie. She'll be here as soon as she gets off."

Greta, back at the foot of the bed, frowned, checking my shackles. The clatter of chains on bed rails was like prison gates clanging shut.

Outside the hospital window, a cloud passed over the sun, throwing shadows on the wall. Pain piled on pain, and I cried out.

"Hush," said a second officer from his chair by the door.

I turned away, and the sun splashed waterfalls on white hospital curtains. My brother, tall and dark, gripped my hand, across a sandy stream. He stumbled and I picked him up. We stood behind the falls; greens and browns blurred, soft and shimmering. This baby was for him, and Daddy, and most of all, Tony.

"She's crowning," the nurse in lilac said. "You're having this baby now."

"Call the doctor!" Greta acted like she was in charge. "Wheel her to delivery."

The bed rolled and I dry-heaved. I wanted to dissolve into the pillows. But I also wanted my baby. As doors flew open in the operating room, fast hands ripped away soiled sheets and a man in white mask and cap stood over me, pulling on blue gloves. Then, to my surprise, he knelt, gloved hands massaging, loosening the birth canal.

Suddenly my sister Kita was there looking fierce in yellow-flowered scrubs. "Take off those shackles!" she ordered. "She can't even get her legs in stirrups! We can't break away the bed with her chained like that!"

But the officer with the shackle key was gone. He had disappeared down the hall.

"It's okay, we'll have to work like this," the doctor said. He sounded like a teenager.

"It's not okay. It's inhumane!" Kita rushed to the hall and called a passing nurse, "Go outside, get the guard!" She returned as I screamed through another contraction.

"Breathe." Kita leaned close, studying me. "Look at me, Sis! Breathe."

"Wait—" said the doctor, "You're her sister?"

The officer entered, looking alarmed and Kita motioned him over.

"Unlock these." She glared at him. "Now."

"It's the law…"

"A law that can kill this child!"

The officer took a key from his pocket. The doctor leaned back—gloved hands high—while the officer removed the shackles.

Kita gently placed my feet in stirrups as contractions bore down like semis ramming me on I-10.

"Push," the doctor said. "Push, now!"

I no longer controlled my body. I screamed as a second semi hit my tailbone—backed up and slammed it again. I was being ripped apart.

"Breathe, breathe." Kita leaned over me again and her caring face glowed through gauzy light. But it was pointless. Through muffled pain, a baby's cry rent the air.

"Now the shoulders," the doctor said. "There! It's a boy."

A shrill cry filled the room and the doc handed a waxy bundle to the nurse in lilac who took him away.

I watched him go, my hands outstretched.

"It's okay." Kita nudged me grinning. "They're just weighing him, clearing his airways."

"You, Rose!" Greta was taking charge again. "Push, there's still the afterbirth."

I had no more strength. It was only Kita massaged my belly that helped me expel it.

"Okay, got it." The doctor caught the afterbirth and put it in a cooler.

"What—what are you doing with that?" Kita seemed baffled. "That placenta belongs to us! If anyone gets it, we do."

The whole room went silent, and she went livid. "Wait a minute! Are you harvesting prisoner's stem cells? By what authority? Besides, that placenta's got to be worth thousands of dollars."

"It's okay." I touched her hand. "I agreed in the ambulance."

"Agreed to what?" Kita's brow furrowed.

"Your sister agreed to donate it for research." Greta pulled a form from her cargo pants.

"Well, are you paying for it?" Kita demanded.

"Reduced fees." My voice strained, soft and hollow.

"Sounds like a rip-off to me." Kita folded her arms and faced Greta. "When are you going to stop making money on prisoners—and paying them nothing for it?"

The lilac nurse returned from the scales, but Greta blocked her path.

"I want my baby!" I said, "Please—"

"Does everything check out?" The doctor asked, trying to intervene without confronting Greta. The nurse turned towards him, taking a different path around the bed. But Greta strode toward them, and the doctor rocked back on his heels. Blood drained from his face.

"Yes, 7 pounds, 4 ounces. Breathing fine; color, normal." The nurse swept around the foot of the bed, cradling my little Tony, swaddled in white flannel blanket and blue stocking cap. She had put a blue identity band on his wrist and was holding a matching one for me.

"Then give Mom her baby." The doctor straightened and went to the sink, stripping off his gloves.

"She needs to give it up for adoption." Greta waved some more papers from the opposite side of the bed. "It's best."

"Hush!" Kita ripped the papers from her hands and trampled them. "No more prison baby sales! He's coming home with me."

"Well, I never—" Greta glared.

I reached for my baby, calling, "Tony."

The nurse waved my id at me. "First this."

Kita nudged Greta aside, circled the head of my bed, and lifted Tony from the nurse's arms. Her lilac scrubs were lemon fresh and she winked at Kita while securing my blue band. It read, *Cinnamon Rose, mother of Tony, Jr.*

Kita grinned into Tony's moist, blue-black eyes, and placed him gently at my breast—a caramel cherub.

I smiled up at Kita, saved by an angel. Tony rooted blindly and found my nipple—then lost it until I clamped him to myself as though we were fused. I tightened his blue-knit cap and white blanket. He was my blue skies, white clouds, light, peace and joy.

I felt blessed in that cleansing moment; everything was new. For a moment, while the doctor and nurses scrubbed and cleaned up, I made him one with me, willing his buttery flesh to be mine forever. All my past seemed emptied out, my fortunes changed. I was a new creature with a new life, mother of Tony Garcia Rose.

The fluorescent lights blurred and I reminded myself to enjoy one moment at a time—to be happy now or never. The drug treatment programs had helped—they just hadn't turned out the way I planned. Tony's dad had loved me intensely, night and day for three clean months before Doobie murdered him.

The operating room doors opened and a draft filled the room, smelling of nicotine and mint. The second officer joined Greta who glared steadily at Kita and me. Then he squared his shoulders, planted his feet and nudged her.

"Time for your rest now, Rose." Greta stepped forward.

I swung away, releasing Tony's suck and eliciting a wail. I stood up, clutching him tightly, a moment of fear blocking me, then lunged toward the door.

The officer dove around the bed and grabbed us.

"Yes, rest while you can." He shoved us back in bed. "The bus leaves in the morning."

Greta reached for Tony.

"No, you don't!" Kita said. "I take him from here." She lifted him from my arms and waved them off.

"Give us a moment." She turned her back on them and placed Tony back in my arms, cradling us until the baby fell asleep, a milky droplet on his full, rosy lips.

So many people had given up on me—the way I'd go missing for days, leaving my growing daughter for Mama and Kita to raise. It was hard for them to give me a second chance. Yet Kita knew the shock of losing our brother—and now our Dad and Tony—so violently. The delayed anger and long road to healing.

We cradled Tony. "He's beautiful, Sissy. You did a good job. You should be proud." She leaned close and added, "I'll bring him to you early tomorrow—you'll see him again soon. Now rest."

"Will you bring him every Sunday to see me in prison?"

"I'll try," Kita said.

"Then I want to keep expressing milk so I can nurse him."

The officer cleared his throat and Greta stepped toward Kita holding out her hands.

Kita ignored her, lifting Tony gently, setting him in his bassinet and pushing him to the nursery.

I was hiding behind the waterfall in emerald light, the sun warm on my forehead. I rose to the surface in a dim hospital room. Kita still in yellow scrubs, eyes red-rimmed from her all-night vigil was tucking Tony against me.

I lifted my gown and snuggled him close against my warm, flowing breast. He rooted and latched on, sucking softly. "Let this moment last forever." I inhaled his clean scent, running my fingers through his soft, loose curls. Just like his daddy's. His best gift lived on.

Kita sat at my feet, warming them. "Heavenly Father, bless Tony and Cinny, and bring them together again soon."

"Amen." My throat constricted. Tony had fallen asleep at my breast again, and I imprinted his angel face above the waterfall.

19
Nikita Endures

Nikita woke to a wail from the crib beside her in the trailer living room. It was Tony rooting and hungry at one in the morning. She had planned to run out for gas and groceries after her check cleared in the morning, since there was not a penny in the account. In fact, she was in the red and racking up overdraft charges. At least she could warm some honey-water. She rolled out of bed and picked up tiny Tony, cuddling him close and stepping to the kitchen sink. "Poor baby," she murmured, holding his rooting mouth against her bare shoulder, praying he wouldn't wake the kids.

He reared back and wailed. "Strong neck muscles." she whispered, laying his soft, loose curls back on her shoulder. Tony's skin glowed creamy in the street light. She turned on the hot faucet and let it run warm on the back of her hand.

Tony whimpered

"Shut up." Her son's voice from the bedroom was thick with sleep.

"Oh, my poor dear." Nikita filled a bottle with warm water and added honey, rocking Tony gently while she shook it.

Last night Ruby had fallen asleep with Annie, talking like sisters about unicorns and rainbows. Kita had inserted herself in their fantasy world and soaked up their blueberry-toothpaste kisses. Yet there was nothing magical about making her monthly budget. It wasn't just the baby, but Annie, that was costing her more than she could earn.

The girls went to school miles apart, requiring after-school programs and precious gas. The hectic schedule ate into work and homework time, too. She had no choice but to give up extra shifts.

The doubled cost of groceries and diapers had made her late with rent, so she would have to pay a $35 late fee.

Also, at midnight, the bank had taken the van payment and charged a $30 overdraft fee—nothing she could do about that at 2 in the morning. It was an old van, a gas guzzler, bought with her tax refund. But she was glad for it with her two and Cinny's two. Not that she was playing favorites; she was mom to all four these days.

Daily, she longed for her husband's return from Iraq. During their weekly calls, he assured her that he was staying safe, and he'd be back in a few months—not to worry. She dared not tell him about the bills. Then there was Annie's father, locked up for killing her grandpa and step dad. Forget child support. So many men, lost. Such a big hole in the family. *God help us*, she breathed.

Nikita shook the honey-water again, tested it on her wrist— lukewarm—and placed it in Tony's eager mouth. *Help us, please*, she whispered, and realized in the same instant that *He had*. Cinny was off the streets again, safe behind razor wire—or so she hoped—if she could avoid beatings by cell mates or guards, viruses or chronic diseases, cirrhosis or AIDS.

Nikita crept back to the sofa, cuddling sweet, contented Tony and his bottle. A calming peace flooded her. She drifted off and was sailing down the interstate with a van full of sleeping children. Gradually she circled the capital, and cornered the van too far, too fast. The van was sliding downhill on its side, bodies flying through the air.

Nikita flung out her arm and realized she had pinned Tony to the sofa. He jerked and wailed and the other children called out. "Mama!"

"Shh, everything's okay." Nikita lifted Tony in weary arms, her eyes half closed. She placed him on his side in the crib, vowing not to fall asleep so nearly on top of him again.

All would be well, if she could keep everyone safe and her bills paid on time. Her husband's check would be deposited the first of the month, though she hated to draw on it. He needed it for his own welfare while policing the morgue where families came to identify bodies lined in a warehouse, no air-conditioning. Tens of thousands—men, women, children, bloated beyond recognition, loaded and dumped into trenches north of Baghdad. *Help them, Lord. Help us. I know you will.*

In the morning, Mama drove up in her vintage Cadillac, inherited from daddy, *but not a replacement for him*, she'd said. She opened the trailer door a crack and stepped inside, careful not to let in the morning chill. Tony chortled in his crib and she reached for him, her wrist scars fading. She sank onto the sofa and bounced Tony on her lap, his little fingers curled around hers.

Nikita stirred up another honey-water bottle, placing it in Mama's hands, "I have to run out for formula and cereal." She crawled over Annie and squeezed into the tiny bathroom, splashing cold water on her face, puffy from lack of sleep. She slipped into matching pink scrubs and pulled her hair into a rubber band.

"Mama, thank you for babysitting." She looked around the table for her keys and also picked up Cinny's sketchbook—just to keep it off the sticky table. "I'll be back in twenty minutes." She headed out the door, into the Saturday morning sun peeping through moss swags of the live oak.

She couldn't ask for more. With Mama off nights and weekends, she could at least work steady shifts. She cranked the engine of her old Dodge Caravan. The needle was on empty, but the money would be in the bank today. One day, she hoped, Cinny would qualify for work release, get a decent job and pay her own way.

Wait a minute. She had Cinny's sketchbook right there in the passenger seat beside her. She could ask Cinny. Maybe they could make copies and sell it. Well..., first see if she had new sketches to add.

Meanwhile, this morning there'd be bananas, cereal and milk for all. She turned and backed to the road, bumped down Seaboard and Marvin and turned north on Lafayette, humming, "I've got sunshine..."

20
Casting Stones

You never want to see your long-lost friend in prison. But, I had. I *had*!

Mindy and I were coming around the mess hall, exiting from the back, when I saw Reese entering chow. That *was* her smoking behind the greenhouse before Christmas. And there she was again, surrounded by laughing women, head thrown back, strawberry-blonde ripples down her back. She looked my way and waved, flashing a huge grin. With an Uma Thurman glide, glinting green eyes and, yes, flat nose, she strode toward me.

I hooted, driving towards her through the crowd while Mindy shielded me, blocking the officer's view. We clasped each other hard and rocked in rhythm, while other girls gathered around us, screening us from the officers' views.

I still adored her, so cool and resilient. "Tonight, come to Classroom A in education. We have Lamp Steps at six and you're welcome to join us."

"Okay, I have a puppy, though. I'm in service dog training!" Her eyes lit up as though she were announcing a baby.

"Bring him. Or her."

"Him, Tubs—and look at you! You had your boy too, I see!"

"Right? Tony, Jr., comes every Sunday to see me."

Reese turned back to the chow line, and Mindy and I hurried to education. She told me all about baby Joshua. He was a chubby eight pounds, twenty-one inches, "practically walking when he was born." And he was home with her mother and oldest daughter. "We have a lawsuit against the adoption agency for the same amount they paid for my baby."

I gaped and fist-bumped her. I was high as cumulous clouds over the compound, and didn't think I could get any higher.

We paused at our flower beds. Someone had been digging in it, pulling out snap dragons. Was some inmate digging flowers for her teacher? Was it an armadillo looking for grubs? Or was someone digging for that Cheese Puff bag? Who even knew about it besides Damon? I could go to security and report it, or would that get me in trouble?

Maybe I could just ask Officer Damon next time, and try to stay out of it. I swept it from my mind and kept going. But it darkened my white cloud feeling, while I set plastic chairs in a circle, pulled out Lamp Steps manuals and erased the whiteboard.

Women trickled in, and finally, Reese entered leading a sweet puppy, a fluffy golden retriever. The dog pulled back at the threshold and Reese reached in her net bag and held out a treat, coaxing him into the room. The dog eased down on his tummy and crept over the threshold, nosing the treat until she released it.

Reese laughed her familiar flat, two-note, "Ha-ha." And sighed in her nasal twang. "He won't step foot on polished linoleum. The glaring lights mess with his depth perception, I guess."

Her dry mirth brought back hours, days, weeks and months idled in county jail. Yet here Reese looked radiant in her white service dog scrubs. This woman who'd never had a child, now had a dog who loved her no matter what. Their bond had a purpose, to train for service to a disabled person. She had six months in the program and would do a lifetime of good. She lifted her chin, announcing her newcomer. "His name is Tubs."

Her cheeks glowed, and women in blue took turns scratching his ears and stroking his soft, silky fur.

Tubs leaned in and licked at the friendly hands, until Reese pulled at his lead and gathered him behind her long, slender legs.

I sat right beside her in a circle of forty women. She leaned over and draped a long arm over my chair back. We were so happy together again.

Chaplain Emily Bowman, Hope's new assistant, nodded at me. She was from Pennsylvania, and wore her reading glasses atop a mass of white curls. I went to the front to open the meeting, smiling at the open faces tilted up at me.

"Hello, my name is Cinnamon, Cinny for short. I'm, a grateful, recovering drug addict, and Jesus is my higher power."

"Hi Cinny." The women chorused—wide-eyed, large and small, tan and brown, Hispanic and Haitian. Some would name a different higher power, and I welcomed them all. "At Lamp Steps, we know that a lamp lights only one step at a time. And we are here to help each other take the next step." I paused, looking around and landing on Reese. "And to welcome the newcomer."

Reese raised her hand.

"No, we're not going to ask you to stand up and introduce yourself."

Reese put her hand down.

Off script, I added, "But we know who you are."

Several women chuckled, and I continued. "Let's make a circle and open with the Serenity Prayer, page 10."

Voices in all timbres, high and low, rose in unison. "God grant me the serenity to accept the things I cannot change... ."

I jumped when a hand grabbed my butt. It was our brash pro ball player and she grinned crookedly, but shuffled to her seat when I motioned her to sit. Perhaps it was a reflexive sports gesture, but it rattled me. I had not invited such touch, certainly not since Tony died. And even he, knowing my past, had treated me with more consideration.

After everyone had settled, I continued, my voice shaking. "I forgot the safe sharing guidelines on page 15. Please remember that what's said here, stays here."

"Hear, hear," several old-timers said.

"Also, keep your sharing focused on your own thoughts and feelings. This is not a place to date or pick up dates. That's known as step 13. And we'll send you back to step one." Some women chuckled. "Which is where we start today."

I had regained my calm, and asked for volunteers to help me act out a story.

Reese's hand shot up. I assigned her to be the woman caught in adultery, another woman to be her guard, and me to be Jesus.

The guard grabbed her arms, and threw her at my feet. Reese fell, spread-eagle on the tile floor. Tubs crept up beside her.

"What are you doing?" I stood over them, hands on hips, and Tubs nuzzled her.

"Yeah." Mindy was the self-appointed chief priest, handing out rocks—crumpled paper from the waste basket. "You're not being arrested."

Reese squinted up at me. "Oh, I thought it went like this. I've been arrested so many times."

"You're supposed to beg Jesus for mercy." I pointed at myself.

Laughter filled the room again.

"How do I do that?"

"On your knees, with your forehead to the floor."

Reese did this—but facing the wall.

"Facing Jesus." I pointed to myself again, and gaged the room, waiting. "Okay, anyone without sin cast the first stone."

Mindy raised her throwing arm, but hesitated. Some of the other women did too, stopping just short of pelting Reese.

"Without sin." I narrowed my eyes, daring anyone to hurl a rock.

I knelt beside Reese, writing on the white linoleum tiles in red chalk, *Pride, Lying, Cheating, Cursing, Envy, Stealing, Lust.*

Melissa and the other women dropped their paper balls one-by-one back into the waste can.

I stood up and touched Tubs and Reese's smooth heads. "Woman! Where are your accusers?"

Reese looked around, puzzled, "I don't know."

I helped her up and gestured around the room. "They're gone, and I don't condemn you either. Go free now, and don't sin again."

We actors bowed to crashing applause. I scratched Tubs under the chin and he stood, too, wobbly on the slippery linoleum. This was the first time I'd felt pure joy since giving up Tony, Jr.

Reese coaxed Tubs back to her seat and I fist-bumped her.

"That's how it feels to be healed with one touch." I beamed with pride. "You're a natural with that puppy."

She leaned over and announced, "Plus, I'm six months sober today."

I hugged her long neck.

"Ouch you broke it!" She rubbed it comically.

Round-faced Chaplain Emily strolled to the front in a lavender tailored dress with purple-red valentine scarf, blinding us in our muted environment. She bent to pet Tubs, who shied away.

"He doesn't like people in civvies." Reese explained. "Sorry."

"Well, thank you anyway, Reese and Cinny!" Miss Bowman said lightly, bouncing on her toes. "You are natural hams!"

She handed out paper and pencils and we set them on the manuals in our laps. "First, I want to commend you for dramatizing a story of Jesus that isn't in the early manuscripts."

I looked up sharply. I had never heard anyone question how the Bible was put together. Yet it seemed important, like the way I was drawing my graphic novel, sometimes sketching at the front, sometimes at the end, with all the stories threading together somehow.

"People kept telling this story until someone wrote it like a patch to John, about 300 years after Jesus walked the earth. Why do you think they did that?"

Lexis's voice rang out. "Because Jesus showed mercy to a shamed woman."

Reese stood, and we all fell silent. "I like how there was no one left to condemn me."

Mindy raised her hand. "All the priests condemned themselves by not throwing stones."

"A good thing too." Chaplain Bowman nodded. "Since they didn't bother bringing the man caught in adultery."

We exchanged glances, knowing the double standard.

"Yet the Bible promotes women, from Queen Esther saving her people, to the prostitute Rahab rescuing Israel's spies." In that moment, I let go some of the shame of my past.

I sketched a girl armadillo, hooves tied up, blood dripping from her nose, foxes surrounding her, baring their teeth.

The chaplain grinned at my doodling. "I know we can't keep that girl from drawing."

She walked over to the chalk list on the floor. "See here, like a true scholar, Cinny was trying to imagine what Jesus wrote in the dirt. Her artist's eye will not let a single detail escape. In fact, I think she would make a great detective."

I stopped drawing and looked up. That was exactly what Kita had said about me.

21
Cinny Too Close

Emily swiped at *anger* and *lust* with her soft-soled red shoe. "And yet, since they're written in 'dirt,' I can erase them, see."

"*Si*." Mindy said.

'So, maybe Jesus was writing their *names* in dirt, showing he knew them and could erase them from the *Book of Life*."

Someone gasped.

Miss Emily erased *pride*. "The priests would have known that they were being judged for rejecting God's son."

She passed Tubs, and he whimpered. She waited until he'd calmed down. "And yet Jesus would forgive them, too, if they asked. The key is the location of our hearts."

She went to the board and drew a straight line, with the words *Close* and *Far* at opposite ends. "Imagine the moment when the miserable woman was left alone with God's own son. He was without sin and could have cast the first stone. In fact, he seemed to know that she was guilty. But what did he do instead?"

Lexis raised her hand. "Forgave her."

Mindy pointed at Reese. "He let her go."

"What about your relationship with your earthly father? How close was it to Jesus's relationship with the woman? Put a point on the line between *close* and *far*.

I put a point near *close*.

Reese marked her own line, and whispered. "You're lying."

I nudged her, making her draw across her page.

"Next, did you know your father well, yes or no?"

I wrote *yes* but Reese mumbled, "Lying again."

 "Three, did you trust your father?"

I wrote, *not much*. Reese's realistic view was infecting me, improving my honesty and admission.

"Four, did you ever ask your father for things? Five, did you get them? Six, right away or did you have to wait? Seven, how did this affect your relationship with your heavenly father?"

She paused. "Eight, does your relationship with Jesus need healing?"

Emily divided us into small groups. Reese and Mindy pulled their chairs close and Lexis joined us. As usual, her paper was written full.

I covered up my page. "Want to start, Lexis?"

"Okay." Her lined face shone olive in the florescent light. "My father died last year, and tonight I realize how sorry I am that I didn't show him more mercy. I didn't speak to him for years; we were all punishing him for drinking and running around." Her nose dripped and I gave her some tissue.

Mindy put out her hand for some, too. "I barely knew my Dad. After serving in the army, he was still thrown in jail in Alabama for being illegal—while planting a million trees for the state. There, he said, he was starved on $2 a day because, by law, the sheriff could pocket what he saved in groceries, and buy a beach house. That made me so mad at God and the government, I didn't follow the laws myself."

She wiped her nose. "You guys smile and hug me all the time and I want to be happy and loving like you."

Reese swept her long hair off her face. "Trust me, you don't want to be as happy and loving as I am. My parents were both drunks, but my Dad was also bitter and mean. I couldn't even get a free puppy for Christmas. I had to hide my stray cats under the porch." She grinned and her scar dimpled. "Best gift I ever got was Tubs, right here at Gadsden."

Tubs lifted his head and she scratched him. "I'm training him for a cerebral palsy child."

"Thank you for sharing, Reese." I took my hand off my cartoon and passed it around. "I relate to this armadillo, taken in adultery."

Lexis frowned. "Who are the foxes?"

"Those are the rich lawyers who bought me when I walked the streets, but threw me out like trash when I landed in court.

I unwrapped the last few precious squares of tissue and blew my nose. "I think Daddy could have done better if he'd been able to get somewhere with his music. He started singing gospel in church like so many blues greats, but he also got involved in drugs.

"Worst Christmas, Mama and me at the mall; Daddy passed with another lady and baby. I called, *Daddy, Daddy!* Lady said, right in front of everybody, *Sorry girly. He's not your Daddy.*"

The girls gasped.

"Mama swept me away, sat me by the fountain and spoke right out loud. *Dear heavenly father, we know you and trust you. Please bring Daddy back to us.*"

Lexis sat forward. "Wow, your mother was a saint."

"Yes, and God did. In his last days, my father sang in our church, and sat with us and held my little Annie. So, Mama's faith helped heal my relationship with my father and with God."

"That was lovely, Cinnamon! See, we moms have great power, even in here, to pray for our families." Lexis handed back my drawing. "You'll have to draw another frame, with Jesus raising you up, and your father helping, while the foxes slink away, tails between their legs."

Miss Emily gathered us back together. "How many of you were *close* to your fathers?" Only four out of forty raised their hands, and I added, "Sometimes."

Another woman chimed in. "Yeah, too close. My Dad was an addict."

I nodded.

"Yes, it's important to be honest." Emily held up bright, dye-cut letters, tied together with yellow ribbon. D-E-N-I-A-L. "For me it stood for 'Don't Even Know I Am Lying.' Our lesson today.

She taped the letters to the white board. "I came to Lamp Steps when my marriage was bone dry and my son was re-arrested for selling drugs. I finally had to listen to my husband telling me to stop *helping* my son and let him sink.

She paced in front of the room. "I came to Lamp Steps looking for relationship help and got it, just learning the small group guidelines. Listen without interrupting. Don't try to fix or solve for someone else."

She paused, facing us. "I had been so left to myself growing up, I wanted the spotlight. I didn't want to look at the woman in the mirror."

She drew an oval mirror on the board, a short round woman reflected in it. "But that's where recovery started, with 'I' statements. And with forgetting myself, too, in acts of service."

"Isn't that contradictory?" I asked

"Yes, it is, Cinny! How can I both focus on my recovery and forget myself in service? Especially when I'm recovering from codependence—a need to feel needed?" She pointed her marker around the room. "Anyone?"

Lexis raised her hand. "I'm no expert." We laughed; she was our rock, a mom who mothered us all. "But I found the harm was in thinking I could fix others. It's a joy to serve if I'm not trying to control others or short-circuit my own growth. I have to take time for reading and prayer—step 11—conscious time with God, for strength."

Miss Emily clapped and some of us joined in. "Oye, Lexis. I can get unbalanced quickly, over-committing time and energy. I sometimes think I like busyness more than my family or myself. That comes from low self-worth, trying to raise my value in other people's eyes." She pointed to her letters-on-a-string. "Denial prolonged my pain and slowed my healing."

Back in small groups, we turned to our lessons. I was a group leader and started out, sharing how I was "sick as my secrets" and what areas of my life were out of control.

"I stress a lot and used to mask the pain with drugs. Now I walk the track at recreation, drinking in blue sky, white clouds and singing—sometimes aloud—to shut out the beep-beep from the jersey barrier factory."

Reese grinned. "I'm not in control of anything. My thoughts ambush me, telling me I'm no good. My uncle raped me when I was 10, and Mom said it was my fault."

Some of us nodded, knowing her story, and how telling it strengthened others and helped us find purpose in our pain.

"It's clear," I said when the next question came around. "My life seemed so out of control that I shut God out, but that made it worse. Without him, nothing is possible, with him nothing is impossible."

Mindy jumped in. "I'm suing to keep my baby, thanks to help from Cinny and Chaplain Hope."

I had stepped outside my grief and bonded with Mindy, Lexis, Reese, all these women.

When we closed with "Our Father," Tubs stood with us on wobbly legs.

I shared my book with Reese and her nasal voice rang out above the rest. "Forgive us our sins as we forgive those who sin against us."

Reese was a natural loudmouth and quickly picked up our closing cheer. "Keep coming back; it works if you work it; so work it, you're worth it."

An officer stepped into the room to usher us out but I lingered at the back with Mindy and Reese. Gently, I took a photo from my Bible. It was giggling Annie and baby Tony on my lap in the visitors' park last Sunday. "We played 'roll over' with Tony. He's just starting to get it. And guess what?"

Mindy gathered her things and shook her head.

Reese asked, "What?"

"My sister Kita is taking my new sketches and putting a book together to sell. We hope it can help pay my child support."

Mindy's dark eyes glowed, and we followed the line of women out the door.

Reese led Tubs and me through the door. "Do you think that kind of help could happen for me?"

I looked hard at Reese. "What kind of help do you need?"

"Like the woman who met Jesus. Being healed with a touch?"

The moon floated in a cloudy sea and I had just let go again the guilt and shame I carried from years in addiction and prostitution. "What do you want healing from?"

"Oh, it's horrible. I killed a girl—by accident—I'll never forgive myself."

"Never forgive yourself?" I paused on the walkway beneath a moon-laced crepe myrtle and Tubs dropped to the ground at our feet.

"I was coming off work at the strip club, high and stoned. I pulled into Waffle House and went inside. People were staring at me, pointing out the window. 'Arm, arm!' someone screamed. A bloody arm was stuck to my windshield." Reese crumpled on my shoulder.

"What do you mean?" I patted her boney back and Tubs stood and nudged her.

"I hit a runner and ripped off her arm," Reese moaned. "And I didn't even know it. Hit and run."

"Oh no, that's awful!" I couldn't imagine such trauma. "You didn't feel the bump?"

"Nooo," Reese moaned. "I can hardly sleep sometimes. I keep seeing what I didn't see that night—a woman in my headlights, running shoes flying through the air, her arm catching my windshield. I lie in agony and wish I could sleep. Only Tubs here is helping." She scratched his ears and straightened again. "See my smashed nose?"

Oh, not a birth defect, then, but a life scar?

"Tyrone did that with a metal lock in his fist when I refused to walk the streets. Then, while my eyes turned black and blue, he kept me in a darkened bedroom and shot me up. That stuff numbed the pain. I was hooked. When I come to, there were girls from Mexico bringing me soup and soda. He had several, paying him off for housing them."

Clouds scuttled across the moon. "It's okay, Reese,"

"I wish I could undo all those wasted years."

"I know." I murmured, squeezing her elbow. "It's going to be alright."

"But how, Cinny?"

"He makes beautiful things out of dust. He had plans for you before he created the world—and those plans are still unfolding. You can start new now, no matter what you've done—"

"Move it, girls!" Greta called. "None of that fraternizing now."

I straightened. "Come on, Reese, we've gotta move."

Greta looked angry, "Cinny, you?"

"Miss Greta, we're just talking—it's not the way it looks."

"Talking back to an officer, Cinny! No work release!"

I reeled. My babies waiting for me....

Reese started moving along behind me, but Greta's grabbed her shoulder and spun her around. "You're going to lock, Miss!"

Tubs barked.

I glared. How dare she send Reese to solitary for trying to straighten out her life?

"It's not just fraternizing," Greta said, twisting Reese's free arm behind her, and handing me Tubs's lead. "Take this dog to the dorm."

She grabbed Reese's other arm and snapped on handcuffs, pushing her down the walk.

Part II

Reese's Light

Tubs (Jeannie Francis photo, courtesy Kathy Burgess)

22

Solitary

Hello, my name is Reese, recovering addict and alcoholic.

Reese stumbled over cracks in the sidewalk. "Ms. Green, what's this for?"

But Greta kept pushing her to lock. "It's the hooch gang you joined."

Reese sagged. So, the hooch gang had ratted her out? That's how they thanked her for quitting—for not collecting her share of buns, sugar, fruit. "Is that what they told you?"

Greta dug her fingers deeper. "You'll sit in lock while we investigate."

"What about Tubs?"

"You're worried about a *dog*?"

"Not just any dog. My Tubs, my charge!" Her voice was pitched and strained. But she had just earned her service dog, her sweet Tubs, and now she was losing him.

"You need to worry about yourself," Greta said evenly.

She steered Reese into solitary with its bright lights, bright metal doors and stairs. Two floors of isolation cells—cold and echoing. Inmates, hearing their steps in the corridor, banged on locked doors calling, "Get me out of here."

"Someone help me please."

Reese gritted her teeth and planted her feet. Greta shoved her into an empty cell, held her face to the wall, removed the handcuffs and left, locking the door behind her.

"I want to see a chaplain," Reese shouted as the door clanged shut.

"Fine!" Greta's voice faded.

Fine, fine, fine, echoed around the dorm. Reese rocked herself, summoning Tubs's silky fur beneath her fingertips. She would ask the chaplain to plead her case and get her puppy back. He was special, a Comfort Retriever®, bred as a miniature to shed less, live longer and love more.

He was probably already getting handed off to someone else. Reese's stomach rolled and she dashed for a stainless-steel toilet with sink attached. Was it a sink-let or toi-sink? She retched until all that came up were dry heaves. She ran the water and drank from cupped hands. The tiny cinderblock room contained a platform bed, desk, chair and platform bed covered by a thin mattress and blanket. She crawled toward it, seeing beneath it, in the shadows, a black book. Holy Bible. Why not a romance or mystery novel, some light reading with a plot?

She hoisted the heavy, hardcover book onto the bed and set it on weak knees.

Where to start? She set the spine in her palm and let it fall open. Jeremiah, it said at the top. *Was a bullfrog,* her parents' moldy oldies.

A sentence was underlined in wavy pencil, "I know the plans I have for you, says the Lord.

"Me?" Reese spoke it out loud. She read on. "Plans to prosper you and not to harm you. Plans to give you a hope and a future."

That was too hard to believe in this place with Tubs gone. Was it possible she could get out of lock and get Tubs back? Dare she hope for it, and more? A pardon, commuted sentence?

She closed the book and let it fall open again. Again, it was Jeremiah 29:11, "I know the plans I have for you..." Was that a double promise or just a fluke?

She stood the book on its spine again. Again, the book opened to Jeremiah 29:11, "...Plans to give you hope and a future." Could be a crack in the spine.

She tried to get comfortable on the platform bed, thin mattress, linen blanket. Where did she want to land? Despair or hope? She tossed, and turned. *Hope,* and finally found sleep.

Jackboots thudded in the hall, calls of "Breakfast" echoed down the corridor, and a meal tray arrived on her door shelf. Plastic gloves opened the flap.

"You okay?"

"Yeah, thanks. Sweet!" She crossed to it and lifted the cover. Buttered grits, toast, bacon. Her stomach growled and she carried it to her bed, and wolfed it like a refugee. Even the greasy butter grits soothed and lifted her mood.

Maybe she *could* start new, tell the chaplain how she'd broken with the hooch gang, a group of prisoners who took turns collecting meal tray items for distilling alcohol. She'd win Hope's support and work to get Tubs back.

She turned back toward her window slot, searching for something missing. Tubs. Was he out there on the dog yard somewhere on his morning walk? She couldn't see, and yet she could yearn. Was he looking for her, too?

Breakfast brought the inmates to life, some stuck in solitary for weeks and months.

"Tell them I didn't do it!" cried one.

"All you rotten bastards rot in hell!" shouted another.

The voices drove Reese deep under her blanket, pulled up over her ears. Too short, it let in a slat of sunrise across the narrow, recessed room.

She slept again, and woke to lemon light glinting off the linoleum floor. A round doe grazed in the clearing outside the fence, while a buck raised its crowned head, testing the wind.

Beyond that, a forest dipped into Rocky Comfort Creek. The name puzzled her. Was it a deliberate disagreement or were rocks somehow comforting in this red clay country?

Her life was like that, rocky at times, giving way to periods of comfort. Most recently there was Tubs, and reuniting with Cinny. Before that, nurturing teachers who encouraged her to read, and now the heft of a comforting book. She pressed her back against the wall and opened the book again, another wavy pencil line under Psalm 42. "As the deer pants for streams of water, so my soul pants for you."

Reese read through the early morning, drinking deeply, then drifted off and rose to women in blue moving single-file toward chow. Officers paced the intersections, shouting orders. She knew the script. "No talking. Stay inside the yellow lines."

Every week they seemed to create a new rule. "Two shirts. Where's your t-shirt? Go back and get it. T-shirt and button up shirt."

Why was that necessary? Inmates complaining the prison cut the heat in winter?

Or the way you weren't allowed to wash your uniform in the dorm, even if you sweated it full at rec. They did dorm inspections just to enforce that. "No hanging laundry in the dorms."

To flex their authority, some guards sent inmates back to their dorms even if they were on program call-out lists.

This might look like a college campus, but it lacked basic freedoms. In the dorms, women took turns pressed against the window slots, blocking sunlight, watching case workers come, and teachers go.

Outside on their way to chow, several newcomers passed, shackled and haughty. Youngsters with long shiny hair—short-timers. She knew the type.

"Let me out, and I'll do it again," one said in newcomer's dorm.

Reese had shot back. "Really? You'll be back in three months. Sell drugs a third time and it's 15 years. Trust me, I was you. I'm not joking about mandatory minimums."

A break in the line, and there was toothless Edith, pushing her walking frame, gray hair pulled into a bun. Wasn't there a better place for her, a psych ward somewhere? Hooked on painkillers after a car crash, she'd shot her toes off to get more. She said it was an accident but Reese knew the impulse.

An officer knocked and called, "Rec. Showers" Reese rose, but her liver twinged, as it often did in the morning, the inflammation of Hepatitis C and cirrhosis. "Sorry I'm sick."

She lay on the hard bed and pulled up the white linen blanket, tucking her long legs to fit inside the mattress. The fevers had let up, thanks to the nurse who'd been injecting her with interferon. One day, she might be cured. Still, today she welcomed the opportunity to rest. The segregation cells hushed at last, murmurs faded and she found peace.

Headlights broke the night and a runner appeared—on her bumper. She screamed and stomped the brakes, but the girl was already airborne—horror in her eyes.

23

Reese's Nightmare

"Cherise!" An officer peered through the door slot. "Cherise! Are you okay?"

"Aaaagh!" Reese realized she was screaming. "Night—mare," she gasped.

"Nightmare? It's breakfast."

Breakfast? Had she slept that long? She felt rested and clear-headed for the first time in months. The sun rising over the compound seemed brighter than usual and the snapdragons along the walkway deeper coral and yellow.

"And you didn't even touch supper."

Reese picked up the hot breakfast tray.

"The chaplain's making her rounds."

Reese carried the plastic tray of grits and meatloaf to her bed. Her stomach felt hollow after throwing up the night before. She tucked her shivering feet up and hitched the blanket over her shoulders. *Thank you, Lord, for solitary.* She laughed. *For the rest and chaplain's visit I get this morning. And Tubs, bring back Tubs.*

She unwrapped a plastic fork and paper napkin. Under the plastic cover was something like meatloaf though it was hard to tell. She raised a bit and sniffed—not beef or pork. She nibbled – perhaps ground turkey, oatmeal, and butter? She was hungry enough to taste another bite, and another, while sunrise glinted on her linoleum floor. Tubs would be wobbling all over that slick surface—*sweetheart*!

Where was this joy coming from? Even the grits were edible, soaked in butter. *Thank you for the women who rose at four to cook these.*

Pure, sweet water rounded out the meal. So different from the tangy malt that once ruled her days. She had sometimes waited at the corner store before sunrise, counting down the minutes until six, when liquor went on sale. Those days were in the deep dark past when a six pack for breakfast could ease her looping thoughts, slow her down, even put her back to sleep until she had to walk the streets again, Tyrone at her heels.

She had begun blacking out, which made it easy for Tyrone to tell police that her bruises came from her attacking him—not the other way around. At least in prison she was getting nursing care. They had even suggested she might improve enough to get a liver transplant when she left. Perhaps, with *believing prayer*, as Cinny had said, she could recover completely and even get Tubs back.

Reese was six months sober. The pink cloud feeling come and gone since her arrest, being recruited in prison by the hooch gang and then breaking with them the morning she woke in agony—her liver screaming. She had seized her chance to quit. If not here, where? If not now, when?

Her very life was at risk smuggling the buns, sugar packs, apples, oranges and raisins to mash and ferment in gallon zip lock bags; keep warm in hot showers and strain through an old sock. A nasty sweet-sour, margarita-with-bread-crumbs taste, it worked to get them drunk for a few hours in the yard. Gang members had been discovered, sent to lock, lost gain time. She wanted to serve her time and crawl out of the wreckage.

Reese returned her empty tray to the door slot, slid her fingers along the floor and picked up the Bible. Was it possible to read it through in a week, while trying not to miss Tubs? Depending how long they kept her here. She skipped the Table of Contents and found Genesis chapter one. *In the beginning God created the heaven and the earth.* Sounded familiar. Pretty straight forward; not too complicated. Maybe she'd break some sort of jailhouse record if she just kept chugging, turning pages.

"Hello, Cherise?" An officer opened and announced Chaplain Hope Springs. Tall and willowy with shiny bronze skin and copper-streaked hair curling softly around her face. Her warm green eyes reflected her green dress. She shook Reese's hand with a warm, calloused grip.

"Hi Cherise, just call me Hope."

"Is that your name?" Reese raised an eyebrow, pulled out the chair by the desk for her and returned to the bed. "Perfect for a chaplain!"

"Yes." She pulled the chair close to the bed and sat, crossing her legs. "My full name is Hope Springs."

"Wow, Hope Springs eternal! Your parents must have adored you—and expected great things of you!"

Hope shook her head and spread her hands. "Well, Springs is my married name—separated now—but yes. Your parents must have loved you, too, with a name like Cherise."

"Well, they named me for a cordial anyway. I prefer Reese." She twisted her long hair into a knot on top of her head. "They loved their partying—more than me sometimes, I think."

"Yes, I've seen a lot of that in my time here. Champagne, Martini, Brandy, Mary Jane, Crystal, Snow—you are not alone. Reese. May I?" She plucked a stray hair from Reese's pant leg.

"Thanks." Reese smiled. Perhaps she could open up to Hope. "I hated my parents' drinking and drugging. While they slept in on Sunday, I sneaked to church—just to sit on the steps and hear the singing at Trinity United Methodist Church.

"Finally, Miss Leigh invited me to her Sunday school class and helped me believe that Jesus really did love me. I even got my parents to sign me up for Daily Vacation Bible School. But here I am today, worse than they were. They never went to prison."

"So many people never get caught, Reese. But you don't have to go any lower. This can be your bottom."

"But what about consequences? The girl I killed—and the prison hooch gang. I broke with them soon after I joined, but they turned me in anyway. That's why I'm in here."

Chaplain Springs frowned and took a small notebook and pen from her pocket. "Are you saying you're not making hooch anymore?" She searched Reese's face.

"Yes Ma'am, I'm six months sober." She held the Chaplain's gaze. "Tubs, my service dog, has been my higher power."

"Surely, a gift from your higher power."

"Yes, Chaplain. He's been helping me stay sober. I would love to get back to him and hope I haven't lost ground with him. Will you help me, Chaplain?"

"Sure Reese, I can put in a word for you. As for consequences of homicide, the law will punish us."

Reese bowed her head. "I don't think I'll ever get over it."

"Reese, prisons were designed by Quakers to be places of repentance, and I like to hold out redemption."

Reese nodded.

"I like to create a place where people are not held hostage to the past. God says that if we confess our sins, he is just and will forgive us. In his economy, forgiveness is justice."

"Amazing." Reese leaned her fevered cheek against her cool hand.

"Yes, so even in here, you can be free from condemnation—freer than most people are on the outside. Would you like to receive that now?"

"Yes, please, Chaplain. Can I—I mean will it be real if I do it in prison?"

"Nothing's more real, Reese! Believe me, I've seen lives changed. What's more, four letters in the New Testament were written from prison—from prison to prisoners."

Reese laid the open Bible on the cot between them.

"Paul was sick and beaten in prison, yet he found joy and purpose in suffering. He wrote, 'I can do all things through Christ who strengthens me.'" The Chaplain offered her garden-hardened hands. Reese took them and bowed her head.

"Just tell Jesus how you feel about your past."

"I'm so sorry, Jesus, for all I've done." Reese's nose dripped and tears flowed, turning her scrubs dark blue.

The Chaplain handed her a tissue from her pocket. "Tell him how you feel about dying for you."

"Thank you for dying for me."

"Are you willing to give him your life?"

"Oh yes, Jesus, I want to give you the rest of my life."

The cell glowed with a warm light. Reese felt carefree for the first time in her life. "What now?" she asked.

"Now you want to tell the next person you see what happened to you in here today. And live in that joy forever." Hope beamed and glanced at the Bible. "Oh, I see you've started in Genesis. Every page tells how God loves his people—us."

An officer knocked, and Chaplain Springs looked surprised. "Do you have a watch?"

"No, but I have lots of time."

24
Valley of Trouble

The door clanged shut behind Hope, and echoed in the narrow cell. Reese picked up the Bible again and read about Adam and Eve getting kicked out of the garden, into a hard life. Painful childbirth. Then how God called Abraham to a new land, how Abraham went, and that was counted to him as righteousness. She wanted that, too. That call and reward.

When dinner came, it was her favorite, chicken and rice. She took her tray to the bed and kept reading. Was this new landscape her new land? Words had power, and these were giving her new vision for life.

But then the story turned horrible. Abraham pimped his wife to Pharaoh—what was that doing in the Bible? And yet, Pharaoh gave her back without sleeping with her, plus lots of sheep and cows. That seemed unbelievable—as though God were the hero—not Abraham. Because he sure wasn't perfect.

Reese returned the tray to the door and read about Sara being promised a child and not getting pregnant. But then Sara, disbelieving, gave her servant to Abraham as a mistress. That seemed utterly foolish. The servant had Ishmael, who became Abraham's firstborn, and later, Sarah's son Isaac's enemy for all time.

Talk about consequences; that seemed almost too harsh for a loving God. And yet, what could he do? His people were always losing faith and messing up.

Just as crazy was Abraham tying up Isaac as a sacrifice, putting him on an altar, and preparing to kill him.

She could feel those jute ropes slicing through wrists, cutting to bone; the terror of helplessness, the necessity of escape.

She'd struggled but Tyrone had cut her cheek, breast and thigh and threatened more.

If it hadn't been for his Spanish girl, Maria, screaming, *Police!* Reese might have been killed. Instead, there was pounding at the door and shouts. "Police. Open up." Tyrone cut her ropes and shoved her out the window, jumping and running after her. He didn't dare let her go. She was still his Capitol Hill hooker.

Later, she wondered if Maria and the girls had called the police raid to save her, risking their lives for hers. Like God did for Abraham and Isaac, proving he could save them—if they believed. The ram in the bushes.

It was nearly lights out by the time Isaac's son Joseph was thrown into a pit and sold to slavers from Egypt—by his brothers. That was human trafficking thousands of years ago. What a sinking feeling for Joseph to go from favorite son dreaming of ruling the others, to slavery. But he behaved so well that he was put in charge of a rich man's house, only to be thrown into prison for a crime he didn't commit.

Typical.

Reese's first sentence she served for Tyrone. He convinced her that she'd walk if she claimed the drugs were hers—though it was his third rap. Besides, she didn't want to find out what he'd do to her if she didn't. Well, she didn't get off, but at least in prison she got free of him.

The overhead lights blinked and went out, but a yard light sent a shaft into her room. Reese snuggled up to the window and read how Joseph went from prison to serving as Pharaoh's second in command. Wow what a bottom—and what a top! She could only wish—or could she hope —for a climb like that?

She didn't stop reading until she'd reached the end of Genesis where Joseph's brothers were on their faces, begging him not to kill them. By then Joseph had forgiven them for selling him out. "What you intended for evil, God intended for good to save many."

Reese lay down weary and hopeful. "That's what I want, Lord," she said. "That, and Tubs, and let me sleep again."

She woke to keys in the door and metal sliding on metal. An officer announced, "Chaplain Springs."

"Good morning, Reese!" The chaplain appeared in a gold and white dress. "I looked into the matter and it seems Greta has been suspended, pending an investigation. You're free to go."

Reese jumped up and took the chaplain's steady arm as they descended the stairs.

"Does that mean I can have Tubs back?"

"I would go straight to the director—"

"And jump into the program where I left off?"

A guard buzzed them through into warm spring air, blinding morning light. Reese toed the yellow line, and Hope walked beside her, past the snapdragon beds and lettuce garden.

"And Reese, there's something else. May I ask if you were ever held by anyone against your will or forced to have sex?"

They turned towards the breezeway. "Yes, Ma'am, all the time. But I blame myself."

Hope raised an eyebrow. "Why?"

"Because I had to survive; that's how I made my living." They paused before entering the echoing breezeway and passing the security offices.

"Reese, if someone is forcing you to sell your body, that's not surviving. That's a death sentence. So, tell me again, were you ever kept behind locked doors or forced to have sex against your will?"

They waved a few women past. "Yes, Ma'am."

"Did you know Florida just passed a human trafficking law that creates a process for expunging crimes committed while under threat or force?"

Chills ran down Reese's spine. "You mean—I could be pardoned?"

"Possibly. Write your story and take it to the paralegal at the library."

"Yes, Ma'am."

"Here daughter, I want to give you this blessing." She slipped a folded paper into Reese's hand, and hurried to the chapel.

Reese headed straight to the dog dorm, and spied Cinny, Mindy and Lexis approaching in the chow line.

Remembering the Chaplain's words, Reese shouted. "Guess what? I have a new man in my life!"

"Who?"

"Jesus!"

"Woohoo!" Cinny high-fived the air between them. And so did Mindy and Lexis behind her.

Reese had never felt so naturally high.

At the dog dorm, she waited to be buzzed in and went straight to the director. The spike-haired woman in garnet track suit poured herself some coffee and emptied the pot into a paper cup for Reese.

"Reese, you just caught me before brunch!"

Their instructor started her day before dawn and kept the dog dorm filled with the earthy scent of coffee. She called breakfast *brunch*, then worked through until four, spending the most time possible with dogs and students. Would she take Reese back?

"Boy am I ever glad to see you again! Tubs has been moping for days, not eating, looking for you whenever we go outside."

"Really? Can I come back and pick up where I left off?" Reese glanced down the line of bunks to her bed and to Tubs, ears pricked.

"Well, if you're ready, we're counting on it. Look, he heard you."

Reese ran to the crate, to Tubs yipping, jumping and squeaking inside. He wagged his whole butt and tail.

Her fingers shook on the latch so that she could hardly work it. Finally, she flung the door open and Tubs leaped into her arms. She laid her head against his soft, squirming self and received his kisses. Then she leashed him and took him outside to the play yard.

She led Tubs over and under the play structure, commanding his movements and rewarding his obedience with praises and treats. Tubs frisked in the early morning chill, blue skies, perfect day. Reese picked up a stick and tossed it, playing along with him.

In the free play minutes before service-training class, Tubs dropped into the shade under the ramp and Reese scratched behind his ears and stroked his back. This was just like her happiest mornings at home when she gathered her strays from under the porch and day-dreamed her animal shelter.

At last she opened Hope's note and read her bold handwriting aloud. Tubs cocked his head.

But then I will win her back once again. I will lead her out into the desert and speak tenderly to her there.

She drank in the mockingbird song, the deep green grass and crystal sky. This fenced compound was her remote wilderness, the wind his tender whisper. His was a care deeper than any man had ever shown. She scratched Tubs's scruff and he crept closer.

I will return her vineyards to her. All that cheap wine gone; she would start with fresh, new grapes. *And transform the Valley of Trouble into a Gateway of Hope.*

Chaplain Hope had told her how that gate might swing open if she would only push on it.

She will give herself to me there, as she did long ago when she was young, when I freed her from captivity in Egypt.

Reese slid the paper back inside her pocket and shook her shoes at Tubs. He nipped her laces just like old times before she went to lock.

"Go ahead. Take off my shoes."

Tubs pulled and yanked at the laces until they came undone.

"That's right! Good puppy!"

Tubs pulled on the shoe heel and toes, gently, then more insistently until her foot slid out. She gathered him into her arms.

"Good, good puppy!"

The instructor returned from brunch for class and she leashed Tubs and led him back to the dorm. One day, there'd be a dozen Tubsies at her heels.

25

Human Traffick

In the drug therapy dorm, Reese zapped a paper cup of instant coffee and stirred in some powdered creamer. She breathed in the earthy aroma of dog dorm and Tubs. Tubs was off serving his boy, untying his' shoes, fetching his pajamas, pulling back the covers and nosing the boy into bed.

Reese was getting on with her court-ordered drug rehab program. She carried the cup carefully down rows of bunks and set it on the desk beside Cinny.

Cinny put down her parenting class notes and picked up the brew, grinning. "You know what I like, don't you?"

"Yeah! Wanna read something with a plot?"

"Depends…"

"It's my human-trafficking story. You can read it before I turn it in to the paralegal."

"Can I mark it up?" Cinny looked a little too eager, adjusting her new, prison-issue dark frame reading glasses and waving a red pen. "Please, please?"

"Oh alright. But I have to write it first."

"Oh, ho ho." Cinny laughed and took a sip. "Okay, it's worth it."

Reese hopped up on the top bunk, headboard against the wall, and pulled out her pen and paper from under the pillow. A gold bordered certificate hung on the wall, featuring her in white scrubs kneeling beside the Comfort Retriever® Tubs, their smiling faces lit by the morning sun.

She tried to remember what the paralegal had said about writing her story like a timeline; describing how she was coerced and trafficked. She had already started it once, telling it to Cinny in county jail.

I first met Tyrone when I was 14, a freshman in high school, the start of spring break, 2008. Reese printed, neatly, slowly.

He roared through campus on his Harley with some other bikers. One picked up my friend and I screamed, "Bring her back." Writing this was easier since she'd already told it to Cinny before.

Tyrone circled back and convinced me I had to go along and look after her. They took us to a party at a big old house in an empty field. There was hip hop blasting from the bike stereos, booze, weed and crack. My first puff hooked me. I was on top of the world and felt I could do anything. I just wanted more. I was not in control; crack was.

The police chased us, but we hid at Tyrone's place, and after that, he sold me to hundreds of men over two years. He kept the crack pipe ready, and I stayed hooked.

It was an ugly story, hard to push through, and Reese paused. Was it even worth it? She caught Tubs's smiling face over her shoulder. Maybe, maybe if it could free her to start her animal shelter, and help other girls too. She could hire ex-prisoners. The love of animals was so open, total and healing.

"Are you done yet?" Cinny growled. "Because I need more coffee."

"Fat chance, Sasha."

Cinny laughed. "Just call me first princess." She rose to get her own coffee.

Reese kept writing. *Tyrone paraded me in Frenchtown. If the police came, he'd duck me into an alley. If I got angry, he'd pet me like a puppy. Grr.* Reese didn't realize she'd growled aloud.

"Getting into your story there, werewolf?" Cinny ran her cup under Reese's nose.

"Shush, Miss Priss." Reese faked a kick to her head and Cinny ducked.

I tried to escape but he tied me up, broke my nose and cut me. I felt so trapped, I didn't know how to get away.

I was still tall and curvy then—but dropping weight and getting more scarred and jittery every day. Men in suits and hot cars stopped and Tyrone took their cash. He'd show the gun in his waistband and point two fingers to his eyes and mine. He was watching me.

Then I found out he kept other girls high at Bud's house. They were Mexican, and hardly spoke English. They were working off $15,000 Tyrone said they owed him for room and board.

He marked me inside and out, calling me slut *and* whore, *no good for anything but turning tricks. The police busted him for drugs but he ratted me out instead.*

At first, I was pissed. Reese crossed that out and wrote angry. *But then I realized prison might be a way out.*

From prison, I called my mom and she came to visit, saying Dad had left, maybe for the best. I thought I'd get my life back on track, and we'd be a family again. But during one of her benders Mom had a stroke and was put into nursing care.

I was released on probation and stayed far away from Tyrone, but could not even get cleaning jobs because of my felony. I answered an ad for dancers, and was hired. We were put up in our manager's house, locked in 'for our safety.' He kept us drunk and high so we'd keep turning tricks.

Reese's fingers shook, her paper a mess of cross-outs and blotched ink. She pushed on.

In that poisoned house, I was hardly ever sober. One night I was coming off shift, blitzed behind the wheel, when I hit a runner and killed her.

I was going to prison again.

And it all started the day I met Tyrone, on spring break, 2008.

She handed it down to Cinny, waving it under her nose.

In a few minutes, Cinny had made some edits, crossed out the *grrr* and the part about "poison house" and "hardly ever being sober." She ended by writing encouragements. *I am so glad you told this story to me first, and then wrote it down here, even if it was hard. I want you to get out fast so you can help other girls, and strays, by telling it.*

She drew a flying armadillo, ropes flying off her, and handed it back. "You're ready, Reese."

"For what?"

Cinny threw back her head and laughed. "For re-writing that."

Reese laughed too, her sharp, two-toned, "Ha-ha."

"You're ready for seeing the paralegal in the morning, making case history and releasing other trafficked women. You're ready for your new identity as a human traffic rescuer, dog whisperer and inspirational speaker."

"All that, huh?" Reese grinned and climbed down.

The pixie-haired group therapist arrived and their dormmates unstacked plastic chairs at one end of the dorm, circling up for their group time. It was Reese's turn in the "hot seat" and that meant she'd have to listen to put-ups from the other girls. For an hour.

This was designed to undo years of negative self-talk and failure mindset.

She took her chair and squirmed in anticipation, gazing at the women in blue around her—all ages, shades and sizes—gentle faces scarred from accidents or trauma. They were more sinned against than sinning.

"I'll start." It was Cinny, grinning crookedly.

"Oh please, don't say I snore." Reese could shake the rafters, trying to breathe through her broken nose, and she had told her bunkies to roll her on her side if she did.

"Oh, I won't. Reese, you don't snore. You roar—like a lion!"

Several women snickered and snorted.

"Besides that, you talk with a country twang—like Carrie Underwood." Cinny paused. "You are a star and a sparkling gem. I had no hope until you became my bunky, first in county jail, and then in here. You were so kind, sharing your instant, microwave coffee and powdered creamers. For once, I wasn't transparent. You didn't look right through me."

Reese was surprised by joy. It had been years since she'd felt so happy. Was it possible she was healing from deep inside? Her drug-addled brain seemed swept of cobwebs and her anxiety and panic had subsided. She felt content, like the day she got Tubs.

"You are beautiful in your own way, Reese." Pepper, her bunk neighbor, flipped back red curls, a smile crinkling her freckled face. "There is no one in here as tall and elegant as you. You're head and shoulders above us all. The way you handled your dog was amazing—so amazing that he sailed to top of class."

Reese nodded. She'd seen the video of him placed with a loving cerebral palsy child, fetching the boy's brush, toys, clothes and even untying his shoes.

"I know you miss him, but you have us, and you care for us—just like puppies." Several women chuckled. "I'm so glad I got to know you. I will never forget you."

Others spoke, cheeks glowing, as they practiced a new language and opened new brain pathways. These were visions she couldn't imagine about herself and had never seen before.

"When you sing, I hear the nasal twang of a country singer and it just fills me with joy. I love being your friend and having you listen whenever I feel down."

"You encourage me every morning with your *good morning!*"

Another dorm mate shone as she spoke. "When you came to our dorm, the mood improved ten notches. Especially the way you started leading us in stretches and mindless twirling 'til we were dizzy. At first, I couldn't even touch my toes but now I can touch my forehead to my knees! I have become so flexible. You are such a great influence on me. I love you, Reese."

"Thank you all! You've changed my life, too." Reese could not contain her radiance. "Your open praise reveals to me how much negative self-talk I've done all my life. Plus, stretching is a positive part of my life as a dancer. I'm convinced we need it, just like we need each other to feel treasured—and I just enjoy being around positive people like you."

The group closed and stacked their plastic chairs. They stood in a circle for Reese to lead them in stretching. She started with swaying palm trees, flowing arms like rivers, and, finally, twirling like leaves in the wind, wild and free.

"Let go, just feel helpless!"

They laughed and fell in heaps, letting go, releasing control. Wooed in the desert, they had found a sweet oasis.

Breakfast the next morning was gray oatmeal, toast and jam. But Reese was hungry, eating every meager calorie for strength, and even grateful for the weak coffee with sugar and powdered creamer. Between bites, she reread her human trafficking narrative, written and rewritten until it was perfect.

She returned her tray to the conveyor belt and strode to the library. Opening the door to the quiet, air-conditioned room, she crossed to where the paralegal, Ms. Lawson, sat at a table near a narrow window.

"Oh, hello Reese, I've been reviewing your case." Ms. Lawson held a file gingerly with nails freshly blue-sequined.

Reese eased into the chair across from her, folding her long legs under the table. "Do you think I have a good case?"

Ms. Lawson adjusted glittery glasses and patted her curls. "Well, what else do you have for me?"

"Here's my story." Reese pushed it across the table.

The woman read. "Ah.... Hmmm." Finally, she looked up. "Did you ever turn tricks voluntarily?"

Reese frowned. She wanted to ask, "Did you?" but bit her tongue. "Ma'am I was lured into the sex trade by a pimp. It's all there. When I finally escaped, I was again lured into a job and locked in with other women. Wait a minute, are you saying I can't use that defense?"

"I'm just asking, anticipating what the defense might say."

"Why didn't you answer my question? Can I use the human trafficking defense or not?"

"Well..."

Reese stood and reached for her papers but Ms. Lawson pulled them away.

"Ah, you do want the case then." Reese felt color rising in her neck and cheeks. "It's probably a good enough case to put you in the reference books."

Ms. Lawson scrabbled with the files and made a little squeaking noise.

"Well, call me when you have it worked out." Reese headed for the door. She knew when to leave—when her anger had reached the boiling point.

Reese stepped into the midday sun, pursued by little heels clicking behind her.

"I'm ready." The little paralegal struggled to hold the heavy door open.

Reese reached up and held it for her, trying to calm herself on their way back to the table. Evenly, steadily she spoke, defending her younger self like she had never done before.

"You need to focus on how my pimp hooked me on drugs and brainwashed me, teaching me everything I know. You need to tell the judge—just like I said there—" Reese pointed to her story. "Tyrone beat me and convinced me I was good for nothing else." She couldn't believe the power and strength of her conviction.

"Got it," the woman said.

"So, you'll file it then?"

"Yes. Thank you."

"Today?"

She nodded.

Once more Reese strode for the door. Where had the power and strength come from to defend herself that way? *Thank you, Jesus*, she breathed.

Chaplain Springs met her on the sidewalk, and Reese waved. "The paralegal is filing my human trafficking plea today."

"Good for you, Reese! May God bless your resolve."

Jesus take the wheel, Reese hummed, and headed for recreation.

Part III

Double Vision

Tornado (Daphne Zaras, NOAA photo, via Wikipedia, unchanged)

26
Hope's Call

Hope crossed the compound under fluffy grey clouds, turning pink in the sunrise. One was a perfect heart, a love note perched over the chapel. She turned around, but no one else was in the yard. It was meant just for her.

She turned the key in the chapel door, and headed toward her office in the back. She straightened the rows of plastic chairs on her way—not with a yardstick, as she'd once done—just opening the aisles a bit.

Perfect was often enemy of good, remnants of the "perfect" family she'd been raised in. Compelled by many things—adventure, vision, others' expectations—they'd signed up for risky missions on hardship posts in Congo.

Her radio crackled, and she turned it up. "Senior staff to the warden's office."

The call was unusual, and Hope turned and relocked the chapel door, heading for Guard Station One. She hurried to catch up with the school principal and librarian already buzzing through the sally port. There, the guards buzzed her in, locking the door to the compound before opening the door to the outside and permitting her to *sally* out.

The spring sunrise blazed golden through her dark glasses and she had to enter Administration, and pause to remove them before adjusting to the cool darkness of the orderly offices.

This space outside the prison compound seemed quiet and insulated from the clamor inside. Maybe that's why the warden knocked off at four each day to join the women in a lap around the track. Or to walk through education, asking students about their studies, and teachers about supplies. Often, he joined the women for lunch, and sampled what the kitchen served.

Warden Torres sat at his desk in the corner office, shirt sleeves rolled up, tie loose, brow drawn, a storm gathering in his brown eyes. He smelled of oranges, his hair combed back, emphasizing a tanned face and receding hairline.

The beefy Security Chief Ramsey brought in chairs, long hair pulled into a ponytail, beige uniform neatly pressed. He dipped his head when Hope greeted him and kept ushering people in until the large office strained. Hope perched like a bird on a twig. Was this about a prison break, inmate overdose, untimely death?

"Colleagues." Torres waited for everyone to hush. "Sixteen of our last forty random drug tests came back dirty. That means there's a new access point. Or points.

"We are facing a spike in prisoners' deaths in 2012 and contraband drugs are to blame in many cases. We will do all we can to resolve this. So I need your full cooperation. Please be alert and act quickly if you suspect something—anything. We will respond to any report you bring us.

"Remember, we do these women no favor by ignoring this. Any questions?"

"Should we ask the inmates?" Ms. Lawson pushed back black curls, her turquoise nails, matching her shoes. To Hope's mind, she was drawing attention to herself. Perhaps she'd been neglected as a child. Did she have a parent in prison?

"No, Ma'am." The warden paused.

"They sometimes confide in us." The paralegal pushed on.

"No, Ms. Lawson, please. Let's not leak anything that would chase the suspects underground. Do listen closely, but there'll be no loose talk in the yard. Remember, once it's out there, you can't take it back."

Hope followed his gaze around the room as he searched each face. Was he looking for access points in this group? Almost everyone had the opportunity. The chef who brought in saucing liquids, the master gardener with his seeds and seedlings, the librarian who received donated books, the maintenance man with his paint thinners. And on and on.

"Well then, back to your posts. Work smart."

The day seemed ten degrees warmer when Hope returned to the yard and hurried to the chapel. Women in white scrubs were walking dogs around a large wooden ramp and barrel structure, training them to crawl through or run over obstacles. Each woman focused on her greyhound, whippet, yellow or black lab as though schooling a child.

If only women were permitted to raise their own children in this sheltered place.

The dog program was doing a great service for the inmates and the community, and had received plenty of praise and press. Why not bring in a nursery with cribs at the foot of mother's beds, just like the crates in the dog dorms? Why not a preschool and playground with slides, swings and climbing structures for new mothers? Would it not help heal emotional rifts if women were allowed to mind their own preschool children inside?

Hope entered the cool chapel and was met by her chirpy assistant chaplain, Emily.

"You have a visitor, Hope. It's Cinny, said she had an appointment?"

"Really? I don't recall—."

"Well, she's a great leader in Lamp Steps, so I let her in. She said you gave her permission to paint butterflies on your wall."

"Oh yes, I recall something about that."

"Good. Because I got out the poster paints and let her work while she was waiting."

"Ok, but listen, Emily, I need to let you know. We just met with the warden about dirty drug tests again." Hope took a tissue from her pocket and wiped sweat from her brow. A photo of two dark-eyed teens, fell to the floor.

Emily picked it up. "Who are these long-haired beauties?"

"Yes, aren't they? My daughters." Light sparkled in their eyes and their white teeth shone.

"They look so happy!" Emily held the photo up to the light.

"You really think so?"

"Oh, yes, and bright-eyed! They could be ambassadors or world leaders".

"My twins—Brook and Rain—mean the world to me."

"I can tell! You've given them such poetic names! Yet, you'd never confuse them. They're not even the same height."

"I know, right? They're fraternal, not identical."

Emily handed the picture back. "Sorry, what were you saying?"

"We're to be on the lookout for suspicious behavior and access points. I'll be checking DRs."

"DRs?" Emily asked.

"Disciplinary Reports." With Emily two weeks new, Hope still had to spell out acronyms—EOS, End of Sentence, VOP, Violation of Parole.

"To see whose UAs came back dirty," Hope added.

"UAs?"

"UrinAlysis."

"Oh!" Emily laughed. "What we need is an AFA."

"AFA?" It was Hope's turn to puzzle.

"Acronym Free Agency."

"LOL." Hope followed Emily through the chapel, toward their offices in the back, past rows of bright blue chairs and walls painted with Bible scenes and verses. "I'll check the DR list. Then we can divvy it up and visit the women in lockup."

She hurried to her office, sorting keys.

But wait.

Her office door was open and a girl was painting wild, psychedelic colors and shapes on her clean, white wall.

Hope slowed, heart pounding.

Luna moths live only one week, just long enough to reproduce. (Faith Eidse photo)

27
Butterfly Wings

The petite woman in blue scrubs, hair corn-rowed and banded into a round pouf focused on painting in a purple butterfly above orange flowers.

Still, Hope's heart pounded at this invasion of her immaculate office. What was this woman cartooning on her walls like the first lady of graffiti?

Hope leaned against the doorjamb transfixed, thrown back to her pot-smoking, fantasy-art days in overseas high schools. There murals unfolded with vines dripping over jungle waterfalls, leopards prowling dense forests and pygmies sitting on hydrilla rafts, stroking lions' teeth breastplates and smoking pipes; puffing rainbow smoke rings over glistening mountains. Had she turned her back on art and cut herself off from dreams and visions and endless possibilities?

She entered quietly, not wanting to startle, yet feeling dazed. She thought she recognized Cinnamon Rose's familiar profile, her full lips drawn in concentration.

"Hello, Rose?" She was so slim after having her baby. And she must have melted someone's heart, because here she was, outside of her normal schedule and movement.

Plus, someone in cosmetology had done an amazing up-do. Some of the women did signature work in here. Hope's own copper-highlighted hair, and all the staff's and prisoners' were offered free of charge. She tried to tip well since they were only paid $50 a month.

"Yes Chaplain, 'member me?" Cinnamon turned and held out a purple-spotted fingers. Hope shook the paint-slicked hand

and wiped the glistening color on a tissue from the box on her desk.

"Remember, we talked about my painting, and refreshing the chapel walls? This here's a thank you card."

"Thank you." *I think.* Hope dipped her head, still disoriented by the trippy art. "How did you get permission to come here?"

"Oh Chaplain, we have our ways." Cinny smiled, coyly, it seemed.

"I'm afraid that's not good enough." Hope went to her desk and checked the petty cash drawer and toilet paper cabinet. Still locked. She had been conned too many times to be easily amused. She looked hard at Cinny. "Yes?"

"An officer escorted me from drug therapy." Cinny had returned to her work, kneeling and dipping her brush in purple poster paint, brushing in an elegant, foreshortened wing. "I thought you liked my butterflies." Her eyes glittered in the morning light.

Hope had hung Cinny's wild butterfly coloring on her office bulletin board. In fact, there it was. Still, she had to be careful. "Oh, I do, I do. But I need to know who brought you here."

Cinny ducked her head and dipped her brush. She had a cute pout to go along with her large, pleading eyes.

"Don't dodge me, Rose," Hope said firmly. "Cinnamon," she added, softening her tone.

Cinny paused and faced her. "Chaplain, for me, painting has always been better than any drug. Miss Hope, my son is one-month old today, and I miss him.

"Oh Cinny, that is so hard." Hope sagged into her chair. Babies torn from their parents' arms were the worst consequence of mass incarceration, especially for women prisoners who had increased eight-fold since the 1970s. "And that's all it took, Cinny?"

"I was having a hard time in group therapy today and told the counselor it would help to start my painting project here today. She called a guard; I showed him the pattern you approved, and he brought me here."

"Did he ask you for favors?" Hope pressed the power button on her computer and waited while the screen turned blue.

"Well..." Cinny painted, cocking her head. "Just this." She said it lightly, touching her empty earlobe piercing, shifting on her knees. The other ear held a tiny gold cross.

"Cinny, that's an elevator going down. You can get off now or you can ride it to the bottom."

Cinny's lower lip quivered. "I miss Tony, Ma'am."

Hope walked around her desk and knelt on the cool linoleum, laying a hand on Cinny's frail shoulders. "That has got to be the hardest thing."

Cinny leaned her fuzzy poof on Hope's arm for a moment as if soaking up creature comfort. Then she sat up, stirred a pot of red paint and added circles to the purple wings. "Wing eyes."

"Pretty, Missy." Hope returned to her desk and typed in her password, 1Corinthians13, a reminder to do all in love.

Cinny added yellow quarter moons, green diamonds and pink hearts and Hope wondered what drug she was on. Her email loaded and she scanned the DR list. Cinnamon's name was not on it.

"I am concerned, though, Rose. You know, before I came here, there was an inmate who had a baby by one of the guards."

Cinny stopped mid-stroke. "Chaplain, that girl was me."

Hope started. "And you're back here?"

"Yes Ma'am, it was hard to steer clear. I had my baby girl, sued the prison and they let me go and locked him up. When he got out, he came after us—killed my daddy and my boyfriend. Tony, father of my baby boy."

"Cinny, that's awful!" Hope rose again and came around the desk, kneeling despite her screaming knee. Every addict she knew was dealing with some intense pain. Her choice had been endorphins juiced by long distance running. It helped ease the pain of losing her father in a rebel shoot down.

"Yes Chaplain, I didn't handle it well—I went back to my drug dealer and he shot me up."

"Against your will, Cinny?"

"Yes, but I didn't resist until it was too late. Then I died and went to hell."

"Hell, huh? And here you are." Hope grimaced.

Cinny smirked back, her dimples deepening. Then she turned out her arm and Hope reared back. Three raised, purple scars mottled it.

"Demon prints. They tried to pull me in." Cinny shook and dripped yellow paint on her scrubs. She set her brush down on paper towels. "I was dumped at ER and they gave me antibiotics. My sister said I should make it my last fall, my healing fall."

Hope nodded. "And did you?"

"Yes, yes, Miss Hope."

So much trauma in one young life. Hope pulled over a chair and sat down. "You are blessed to have a such a wise sister."

"Yes, Ma'am, but I find it hard to forgive myself."

"Of course you do, Cinny. You're not God." She held out an open palm. "But Jesus is offering you forgiveness. Just take it."

Cinny placed her small hand in Hope's large one, as if seeing it that way for the first time.

"Do you know why it's so hard to accept?"

"Why?" Cinny's forehead wrinkled.

"Because it requires agreeing that He's right—even with the consequences."

"Hmm." Cinny tipped yellow centers on her flowers. "You're right."

"I wish we could change our prisons, though, and not release people worse than when they came in."

"Chaplain!" Cinny protested. "You do everything you can to care for us and help us change for the better."

Cinny shaped and filled a pointed leaf. "I like coming to the chapel when I'm down. It turns my day around. But I'd probably still be using if I weren't sitting in here trying to stay clean. Pray for me, Chaplain. Please."

Hope bowed right there and prayed. "Dear heavenly Father, we thank you that you are not mad at us, though you could be. We confess that we have done wrong and deserve our troubles. But we accept the new life you offer us from now on."

"Amen," Cinny said.

Hope glanced at the drawing Cinny was working from. "May I?"

Cinny nodded.

Above the bright butterflies, Isaiah's words that Jesus had read, commissioning himself. *"To provide for them that mourn in Zion, to give them beauty for ashes, the oil of joy for mourning, the garment of praise for the spirit of heaviness."*

Cinny smiled. "I spent yesterday drawing my baby. His springy curls and chubby cheeks, his soft eyes, adorable face, cute little nose and sucking, rosebud lips. Oh, Miss Hope, I miss my baby." Cinny laid down her brush. "I just want to hold him close, nurse him and read his wide, searching eyes. I want to lock onto them and say, *Yes, yes I love you, yes I will love you always.*"

Hope dabbed her nose with a tissue. "Doesn't your sister bring him on Sundays?"

"Yes, when she can, and it's the best, Chaplain."

Hope leaned down and hugged Cinny's hunched shoulders

"Thank you." Cinny sniffled leaving Hope's silk blouse wet with her tears.

Cinny sighed and picked up her brush again.

Hope went back to her desk and printed out the list of women in lockup. As a DOC chaplain, she would support them in whatever they believed. She had just helped a Jewish prisoner paint a star of David and menorah on the chapel wall and helped provision Muslims through Ramadan with their sundown feast. Belief was better than doubt.

As though she were still in Africa, and had no scissor, Hope folded the lockup list in half and tore the paper down the middle.

Cinny hummed softly, *Someone's cryin' Lord, Kumbayah.* The sun warmed the room and wrapped them in a golden glow. Hope would not write her a DR for coming here to express her sorrow in this creative way. Yet was living by faith ignoring reality? Especially the harsh reality of living behind razor wire?

Her husband had stood on the doorstep in shadow, suggesting she give up chaplaincy and needy people. She agreed that the women inside were often poor. And needy. To her husband, lingering in gray dawn, she added that she would train successors. Yet she knew he could not feel her joy each time a woman stopped fighting, let go and surrendered her struggle to God. No one could take that away.

Painting way outside the purple lines, Cinny swooshed huge yellow swallow tails on the butterflies. She shifted and looked up. "Miss Hope, it hurts so much with daddy and my boyfriend gone. And my big brother. Shot himself after Iraq. Why can't I take care of my baby in here?"

Hope looked up sharply. Had Cinny read her mind?

"Oh Cinny! I had the same thought today. Women's prisons could only benefit from nurseries."

"Right? Miss Hope, that would be perfect!" Cinny's voice shook.

"I had something in my email this morning. Let me see." Hope went back to her desk and typed in her password. She scrolled down to the email from the National Chaplains Association.

"The trend for prison nurseries is growing." Hope read aloud.

Cinny squealed. "Yes!"

"Oh hey, I know some chaplains serving in those prisons! They're in Indiana and New York and a community-based program in Alabama.

Hope read further and clicked a few links. "It says here that babies born in prison can spend a year to 18 months with their moms while the mothers deal with the issues that brought them to prison."

"Oh, Miss Hope, can we try to do that here?" Cinny dipped her paintbrush in the red and added hearts for eyes on her other-worldly butterflies.

Hope did a double-take, but read on. "Yes, and they're better prisoners for the experience. They have built solid relationships with their children so when they get out, they don't come back."

"Miss Hope, do you remember the officer in here who tried make me sell my baby?"

"Yes, you mentioned that. But how can she do that?"

"I was thinking she might work for some church or adoption agency."

"That would be a conflict of interest. That is, if she gets any sort of benefit for it."

"Well that's what Mindy was saying. I'm so glad you helped Mindy sue to keep her baby."

"Hmm." Hope knew more, but couldn't discuss what she had learned, so she and Cinny kept working in silence. She had called the chaplain at the reception center who discovered HeavenSent had recruited correctional staff to inform them of available babies. For this, recruits were offered 10 percent of adoption proceeds.

Cinny straightened on her knees and, with a fine brush, neatly painted, *"the oil of joy for mourning."* Hope marveled at her free-hand control, like a surgeon's. That must have taken hours of practice.

"Miss Hope?"

"Yes Cinny."

"Some women who give up their babies are the saddest, angriest women I know. The law is far too hard on us in here."

"Yes, Cinny, I know. Have you heard the expression 'butterfly on a wheel'?"

"No Ma'am." Cinny turned, brows raised.

Hope moved her monitor to better see the budding artist. "A butterfly or Catherine wheel was a torture device used in the Holy Inquisition to break victims who would not recant various beliefs. They were fragile and harmless as butterflies. The term 'butterfly on a wheel' can refer to abuse victims, like slaves or blacks in the Jim Crow South. Or like drug users locked up longer than their kingpin dealers, or longer than assault weapon murderers. That system is like a torture wheel rolling over butterfly wings."

"I believe it, Miss Hope. I would be so happy—and I'd be the best mom ever if I could just care for my baby. You always tell us that prison is an opportunity to build character, so why can't we be moms raising babies?"

"Well, for one, so many moms and dads have had that chance and failed. People are afraid to give them a second or third chance, or maybe a second third chance"

"Yes, I know, but I want a second third chance—" Cinny's voice wavered and broke. "What can we do, Miss Hope?"

"Let me think." Hope opened an email to Emily and began typing a list. Request nursery proposals from other prisons, ask for budget sheets, annual reports, draw up a proposal for the warden.

Of course, he'd want statistical evidence that nursery moms were not returning to prison after release, and that their families were thriving. The legislature was a tough-on-crime bunch, though they were also pro-birth, despite cutting programs poor moms and kids needed to survive. Still, they should have a heart for prison moms wanting to raise their own babies.

If they shot this down, they'd look like prison baby robbers.

Swiftly, Hope searched her inbox for a prison chaplain she'd met in Alabama.

Prison nurseries, she typed in the subject line.

Dear Teresa,

Please put me in touch with the director of your nursery.

Also, have them send any data, reports or stories about how well those mothers do when released.

Love & prayers,

Hope.

She looked up to see Cinny adding a hummingbird with blurred wings. The effect looked surreal. "That bird looks like it's flying right out of the wall!"

"Right? That's what I want too. I want to fly right outta here to Tony, Jr.—and Annie."

Cinny would be marvelous in a nursery full of children. "Maybe you could paint a mural of moms pushing kids on swings—blurred like that—their feet coming right out of the wall."

Cinny lit up. "Can I do that, Miss Hope? On the outside wall, facing the dog dorm—and highway? "Sure, you could do several scenes—"

"Hey, how about some with kids and service dogs?"

"My thoughts exactly!" Hope's inbox dinged a new message, the Alabama Chaplain responding with success rates. Hope opened the email and read aloud. "In a Nebraska study where women kept their children for up to three years, only 9 percent returned to crime compared to 33 percent of the women who gave up their children." She forwarded it to the warden with an FYI, then hit print and took it to Cinny.

"I think we've got evidence!"

Cinny's joy was contagious. It felt like ages since Hope had imagined something so big. It was as though Cinny was led to her on a pink valentine cloud day. She had been staring up at the treads of a rolling tractor wheel, and had seen Cinny's delicate butterfly wings freed.

Cinny was mesmerized by the photo of mothers in prison scrubs building block towers, coloring and reading to their babies.

"This is the picture I have to paint." Cinny said. "Pictures are so powerful—sixty thousand times more powerful than words."

"Exactly." Hope savored the moment. "I'm sure it's exactly 60,000 times more, not 58,000 or 59,000. Habakkuk said, 'Draw your vision, make it plain.' In fact, now that you have your mural in hand, I want you to draw me a plan of that nursery. Maybe measure your dorm layout and add private rooms and a common area."

Cinny clapped her hands over her head. "I am in Computer Aided Design now. That could be our class project."

28
Laying Out Fleece

Chaplain Hope printed another copy of the news story. It was weeks until the legislative session ended and she would need time to discuss the idea with the warden. Together, they'd have to think of the barriers people would raise like the jersey barriers lining the field across the highway.

"Cinny?" Hope wanted to make sure the tender-hearted girl understood.

"Yes, Chaplain?"

"We've had a vision here today but we need to guard it. I want us to enter a time of spreading our plans before the Lord, of consulting him about every aspect before we speak to anyone else. Let's wait for clarity and complete understanding."

Cinnamon cocked her head and glanced sideways at Hope. "I understand...." She painted a few strokes of lavender grass. "But don't you think that's a bit like spreading a fleece?"

Hope looked up with new understanding. Was laying out plans like spreading a fleece? Perhaps Gideon spreading a fleece had merit. Maybe there was virtue in not rushing into battle, but spreading sheepskin to test God's call to lead Israel against the Midianites.

Perhaps it was strategic to evaluate risk before rushing headlong into battle. First, he had asked God to keep it dry while all the ground around was wet with dew. When he still lacked certainty, he asked for the fleece to be wet when all around the ground was dry. The next day, he rang a bowl full of water from it. And yet, was Cinnamon suggesting that was disbelieving? Resisting God's clear direction? Cinny had caught her out with a single word. "Fleece?"

"Yes, Ma'am, isn't that what we're doing?"

Gideon was so insecure, his faith so small, that he hadn't trusted at all. If this was saving God's daughters and sons, why would she hesitate?

"Thank you, Cinnamon. Often, I find that prisoners are more willing to trust God for every little thing than I am. Why is that, do you think?"

Cinnamon put down her brush, rose and came around the desk. "It's easy Miss Hope. We are not in control. We have far less control over our lives than you do. We don't know the next rule we'll break, while you probably break the speed limit every day."

Hope nodded. The prisoners had seen her pulled over for speeding—to get *inside*.

Cinny nodded back. "I'm a widow, Miss Hope. All I have is my widow's mite—and this is it." She gestured at her wall flowers, butterflies and whirring hummingbird.

"Yes, and may this wall be the beginning of great things—breakthroughs, transformations, solutions and mites multiplied."

Hope knew in her own arms, Cinny's longing to hold and nurture her baby. That was another benefit of keeping mothers and babies together. The deep bonding, the immunity benefits, the confidence that came from watching babies grow and gain weight on her milk. Her resolve and drive, and theirs. Few things were as healing for mothers or babies.

Cinny went back to her painting. "It's just that we have no choice but to trust God."

Hope jotted a reply to the Alabama chaplain asking about breast-feeding classes or support. Did they focus on lifelong health benefits of mother-child bonding?

"You're right, Cinny. We have no choice but to trust God."

A heavy tread echoed across the chapel floor, and Program Warden Kerry filled the door. A former basketball player, Kerry was tall and muscular with short gelled hair and a decided frown.

"Chaplain, may I talk to you a moment?"

Cinny put her brush in the water jar and rose to leave.

"Rose?" Kerry folded her arms, blocking the door. "Aren't you supposed to be in group therapy this morning?"

"Yes Ma'am, but I got excused." Cinny looked down and tried to brush paint splatter from her shirt.

Hope was on her feet in an instant. "Please Warden, she's had a rough day. Imagine if you'd lost your brother, an Iraq veteran, four years ago today. Then imagine your father murdered eight months ago, and being separated from your baby boy, born a month ago."

"And my boyfriend." Cinny absently wiped paint on her face.

"Oh yes, also her boyfriend was murdered eight months ago."

Program Warden Kerry frowned and crossed her arms. "That's rough."

"I had to paint, Miss Kerry." Cinny said.

"I did let her stay." Hope gestured to the brightly colored wall.

"Yes, well. What is that?" Warden Kerry cocked her head. "Butterflies from mars?"

Cinny sniffed and laughed. Hope smiled slightly, crossed her arms and tapped her toes.

"Ok stay, Cinny." Warden Kerry said. "What I have to say is for you, too."

Cinny sat on the floor, legs crossed and Kim pulled a chair in from the activity room.

"Chaplain, Rose, we are planning to bring in a new program from Children's Network specially designed to reunite families. It's a one-year pilot, formatted for children whose parents are incarcerated. There's a video and book I'll send you, a touching look into the lives of children who have a parent in prison." She looked hard at Rose.

"We want inmates willing to help run the program for six hours on Sundays. The children can come and play with their mothers in here. All the books, games and activities will be supplied by the broadcast network. I'm looking for volunteers to help lead and coordinate those games. Rose?"

"Me?" Cinny leaned back, knocking over her brushes and rinse water.

Hope grabbed some paper towels and helped Cinny soak up the gray water.

"Why not?" Warden Kerry said.

"But Miss Kerry, that's when my children come to visit."

"Yes, and this will be even more fun for them."

"No, please, Miss Kerry. It's my special time with my kids." Cinny grabbed Hope's arm. "Chaplain, what about our nursery idea?"

Warden Kerry frowned again, her tan brow furrowed. "What nursery idea?"

"It's in research." Hope gathered the sodden mass of paper towels and faced the program warden.

"Without consulting me?" Warden Kerry's fists clenched, her biceps tightened.

"Don't worry, Ms. Kerry." Hope threw the towels in the waste can. "I'll be happy to gather a few of my chapel volunteers to help with your program. This has been a difficult day for Miss Rose. I'm sure you understand."

Ms. Kerry stood, towering over them. "Okay, please get back to me with a list, and we'll begin working out details. I'll send you that link."

Hope turned to see Cinny, head down, mixing an angry reddish-gray color.

"I thought we had a vision!" Cinny drew a dark V on the paper towels.

"Oh Cinny, I know it's not what you wanted right now. But what about practicing? We could help host a Sunday play school where kids can play with moms all afternoon in the Visitors' Park. Prison moms who are far away from their kids could help plan activities, take pictures and play with their friends' kids. What do you think?"

"Not the same as a prison nursery." She drew a butterfly sliced by the V.

Hope was puzzled. "Cinny, what are you doing?"

"Crows. Crows eat butterflies."

Hope had once chased a plane down a runway in Congo. Had run 'til her legs gave out, trying to catch her parents who'd dropped her off for school. She didn't want any dorm parent substitutes, any rules that got her whipped for wearing shorts instead of dresses. She wanted her own mom and dad and their loose, easy-flowing love.

"Crows are going to eat our nursery idea. I want to hold my Tony and play with him every day. And my Annie. I miss her so much. Do you know that whenever I call, she asks, 'Mama when are you going to come get me?' And I want to, Miss Hope. I want to bring her to live with me. If only we could have a dorm just for Moms and kids. It breaks my heart."

Hope could see the longing in Cinny's eyes, how the need to mute it was shredding her heart, stunting her growth, leaving her grieving. Her children, loved and raised by others, still felt a piece of themselves lost and missing.

"Cinny, I've written away for more information, but you'll have to bear with me. A lot of people will have to change how they think of prisons. They will have to become more compassionate toward prisoners and see them as redeemed and redeemable."

Cinny looked up, a golden light in her face.

"In fact, seeing babies in prison presents a problem for many people. Babies are innocent. In their minds, prisoners are not. They'll have to face their desire to hold people hostage to their past, and hold babies harmless."

Cinny was concentrating, biting her lip.

Outside, women in scrubs passed on their way to rec. At the back, a small woman and her two towering daughters hung back. "When I see moms with grown daughters in prison together, I wish we could stop that cycle before it started."

"Yes Ma'am, and make the tractor wheels realize the damage they're doing to butterfly wings."

Hope turned. Such a sharp image, revisited. "Oh Sweetie, you get it! But please don't let prison sap your joy. Isaiah said, 'With joy you will draw water from the springs of salvation.'"

"Springs?" Cinny asked. She pointed to the white cabinet doors beside Hope's desk, aqua dripping from her brush.

"Oh, I think not, Cinny." Hope laughed. She had to visit the girls in lockup sometime today. "Not today anyway. Don't you have class?"

Cinny rinsed her brush, but turned abruptly when a shadow darkened the door.

29
Busted

Hope straightened at the sight of unlaced jack boots, just outside her office door. Officer Damon? How long had he been standing there, watching and listening, and why was he hiding? What did he have to hide? Designs on Cinny? He should know there could be no consent in prison. She rose slowly and the boots slipped away. In three steps Hope was at the door, watching Mario disappear out the side chapel door, unlaced boots flapping.

Hope turned slowly back to Cinny. Was this the man who'd received her golden cross earring token, the guard she'd persuaded to escort her here? Cinny shifted on her knees, head down. Then went back to painting—a wobbly W.

"Cinny, what was Officer Damon doing here?"

"What?" Cinny seemed shaken. "Pardon, Ma'am?"

"Remember your gain time, Cinny."

"Pl-please don't do that Miss Hope." Cinny flailed. "He was just checking on me. It's time for count and movement soon."

"Why? Why is he checking on you? Does he think I can't call any other officer to come escort you?"

Cinny clamped her mouth shut.

"Do you want me to ask him?"

Cinny jumped. "No please."

Hope picked up her radio, Cinny's vulnerability and the warden's drug alert raised her hackles. "Officer Damon to the chapel."

"No, please." Cinny dropped her paint brush on the floor.

"What are you two up to?"

"It's not me—"

"Yes? Continue. Cinny, we've had dirty drug tests inside. Is Damon involved?"

"It's not what you think."

"What is it then?"

"Someone found a way to get cigarettes into the compound—it's not illegal in the real world."

"It is in here—" Hope felt she was trampling daisies and softened her tone. "How? How are they doing that, Cinny? Think of your sentence." Worse, Cinny would be in trouble for colluding if this was a drug access point. And she'd risk beatings, or worse, from the inmates for telling. She would have to go to lock or be moved to another facility, further from family.

Cinny nodded. "Cheese Puff bags in the canteen—"

In a moment, Hope understood. The first time Cinny had mentioned snacks being tampered with was before Christmas and since then she'd noticed women leaving the canteen with red-orange snack bags. Oddly, they would hide them behind their backs when she came along. And weirdly, they almost never bought anything else. But the dirty drug tests—was it just cigarettes, or was there more?

The outside chapel door banged and Officer Damon's flapping boots echoed across the floor. He arrived at Hope's door, lithe and tense, one dark brow raised.

"You called?"

Cinny seemed stuck to the floor, trembling. Hope helped her to her feet and laced arms with her. "Escort us to the canteen please, officer."

Officer Damon scowled as he fell in behind them. It was perfectly correct to request an escort, Hope reasoned. It was almost time for count, and Cinny was not in her designated place. Prisoners weren't free to roam the yard; they had to have callouts, destinations and guards. But Damon seemed to feel caught out. His hand flew momentarily to the gold cross in his ear. He had lost his swagger and good humor.

"Emily," Hope called into the next office. "We're going to the canteen; here's the DR list." In a moment Emily was at the door and Hope scrawled on the page: *Urgent! Call Warden to canteen—then join us.*

Hope prayed for calm and order as she again laced arms with Cinny, Damon following. The asphalt radiated midday heat and a dark tar smell as they crossed between the dorms. They passed through the shaded security breezeway and reached the canteen. Emily trotted after them and Warden Roman Torres appeared in a striped orange and blue shirt.

"Warden." Hope tried to control the tremor in her voice, to speak evenly with confidence and authority. Things could still go wildly wrong. "Officer Damon and Cinny would like to cooperate with your investigation."

"Okay." The warden planted his feet and tensed his muscles, blocking them in and looking like a tiger set to pounce. Dark shadows cut his tanned, sinewed arms. He met Hope's eyes and she felt a jolt as though he'd connected a live circuit. He seemed to transmit that he got the message, would follow her lead and could handle any sudden movement by the suspects.

Officer Damon glared at Cinny, whose eyes grew wide and terrified.

"Spare us, Officer." Torres's voice could freeze boiling asphalt. "The Chaplain knows something, and cooperating right now would be a good idea."

Officer Damon shifted in his open boots, Cinny's gold cross glinting in his ear. "Sir, the canteen had to stop selling cigarettes but the prisoners demanded it, so the clerks sold cigarettes—in snack bags."

The warden glared at him. "How did you bring in contraband?"

Damon scowled, tightened his lips and looked down.

Hope lacing her arm tighter in Cinny's "Someone had to open the Cheese Puff bags, put in the cigarettes, and glued the bags shut again."

But Damon just shook his head.

"Chief Ramsey!" The warden barked into his radio. "Come to the canteen—at once, with backup."

"On my way." It was more like rumbling than speech.

Damon tensed, eyes wild, as though gaging distances, places to hide. Hope stepped on his laces—a pouncing panther — in the lightening moment he lunged for an opening. Torres tackled and pinned him down, twisting his arms behind him.

The canteen clerk ducked when Chief Ramsey arrived with two lieutenants. "Cuff these two." The warden motioned to Damon and Cinny. "Hope, let go of Rose and check the snack bags."

Before unclasping Cinny's arm, Hope said, "I want you to know she cooperated."

Tears rolled down Cinny's cheeks as a lieutenant pulled her hands back and cuffed them. Chaplain Emily arrived, out of breath, to stand beside her.

Hope opened the door to the concession stand, and the round-faced clerk cowered behind the counter.

"Leylani." Hope had often greeted her in broken Spanish. "Leylani, I need to examine your snacks."

"Ma'am?" The clerk hesitated.

"Your snack bags." Warden Torres growled. "*Bueno*. This is a good time to cooperate."

Hope noticed that the floor was stacked with bins of Cheese Puffs, one with $10 scrawled on bags in black marker, another with $20 and another with $30.

Hope tore open a $10 bag and dumped cheese puffs, a wooden match and cigarette on the counter.

"$10 for a smoke?" Her eyes drilled Leylani's. "*¡Es un robo!*"

Anything could be hidden in these cigarettes. A bag marked $20 yielded cheese puffs, match and a brown, hand-rolled cigarette. Marijuana soaked in hashish?

She opened a $30 bag. Cheese puffs, match, cigarette. *Why $30?* Hope opened the cigarette and a small rock crystal rolled out. "Warden, we have funny cigarettes."

"I've seen enough. Cuff the clerk." Into his radio, Torres said, "Call the Sheriff. We have civilian arrests on campus."

To Chief Ramsey he said, "Take them to lock for now. Emily, back to the chapel, the women will need you. Hope, I want to debrief you."

"Warden?" Hope caught his eye as the others left.

"Yes, Hope?" He took her elbow and turned her into the walkway.

"I want you to know that Cinny was our source."

"And you acted decisively, Chaplain. You helped me bag Damon and earned a commendation. In fact, is there anything at all you need?"

"Yes, sir! There is. If you have a moment?"

The warden steered Hope toward the breezeway, hand on her spine as though leading in a waltz. Hope stiffened and he laughed.

"Dance much?"

"Not nearly enough." Hope's spine blazed under his touch.

Several inmates approached the canteen. "Closed! Back to your dorms." He barked into his radio. "We're on lock down. There's been a security incident. Stop all yard movement."

To Hope he said, "What do you suppose those women are after? Do you know them?"

"Sure, Rave and Crystal."

"¡Ay Chihuahua! Given or chosen?" His angular face contracted.

"Their names? Oh no, their parents gave them those names."

"Keep an eye on them, will you?" He raised one arched eyebrow, and swept his dark hair off his forehead.

"I will, Warden."

Women were hurrying through the breezeway, back to their dorms, and Hope hesitated. But Torres steered her by the elbow through the maze of prisoners and officers. This time, Hope stilled an anxious tingle up her arm. Lives were on the line, Leylani's, Damon's, Cinny's, and many more.

In the distance, sirens wailed.

A line of women hurried to their dorms, clutching book bags, eyebrows raised at the approaching sirens. "What's happening?"

"We're in lockdown. Hurry back to your dorms." Torres waved them on. "Security issue. We have it in hand."

Hope nodded, acknowledging each woman as she passed. "It'll be okay." The sirens screamed down Greensboro Highway toward the prison, and she hoped it would be. *Keep Cinny safe and calm*, she breathed.

They reached the visitor's pavilion and Torres paused, hand on the door. "You bring a powerful spirit of calm to this place."

Hope's cheeks burned and she shook her head. "Warden, it's not me."

"Well, today you helped. Anything you want, up to half my kingdom." He swept his hand at the barbed wire enclosure.

Hope half-grinned.

"I'm serious, Chaplain. We were about to get some bad press and DOC was not happy. They insisted I get these dirty drug tests under control. You, Senorita, saved my neck."

Officer Greta emerged from VP and Torres held the heavy metal door.

She glanced up, then looked down again, head bowed. "Sir."

Torres nodded, and Hope thought Greta seemed muted. She had told the warden about her confronting pregnant women. Had the warden warned her about prison baby adoptions?

Torres strong-armed the next door, alert to police cruisers sweeping toward the prison.

30
Chief Ramsey's Rule

In the prison yard, Chief Ramsey had a solid hold on Officer Damon, marching him stiff-legged toward solitary confinement. He ordered a guard to unlock the nearest holding cell and uncuffed Damon inside. "Just until the police arrive," he said.

Cinny and Leylani, escorted by younger, wirier lieutenants, wavered when they entered the lock building, blinded by the sudden darkness. Shrill cries rent the air; banging metal echoed down the hallways. "Help me, please." "Get out of here." "Damn you all to hell!"

Leylani trembled and whirled on Chief Ramsey. "We shouldn't be in here. I want to call a lawyer."

"I'll get to you in a minute," Chief Ramsey said to Cinny, who waited quietly with one of his lieutenants. He locked Leylani in a cell opposite Officer Damon's. "Try quiet meditation. This can be a noisy place. Don't let it scare you."

He dismissed his lieutenants and walked Cinny past the picnic tables in the common area, up some metal stairs to the mezzanine. He opened another metal door, and stepped into the cell with Cinny. He removed her cuffs, and said, "I am Native American. My people believe in the strength of silence. You are strong enough to remain calm in here."

Cinny breathed deeply again. "Yes," she said, "I'm part Seminole, too. And I want you to know, I'm not part of the Cheese Puff gang."

"The who?"

"It's the name I gave them." It was the first time she'd said it aloud.

"Oh good, your lawyers will be happy to hear that." Chief Ramsey bowed slightly at the door, his slick dark hair reflecting the fluorescent light. "Meanwhile, a quiet talk with Creator can make this hell a paradise."

He closed the door and turned the key in the lock.

31
Warden's Hope

Hello, my name is Roman, and I don't know how to introduce myself. Co-dependent, I guess.

Three police cruisers swept into the parking lot, lights flashing. Chief Ramsey thundered toward them in his huge jack boots, passing the warden and chaplain. "I got this, Warden."

"I know you do, Chief. I'll contact the DOC."

Roman Torres slowed to the meet six police officers in blue. "Leave your weapons at the security office." He gestured toward the sally port.

"I'll get them," Chief Ramsey said. "These are my old colleagues. We'll get right to work on the canteen. My lieutenants have it taped off."

"I know you will, Chief. Keep me informed."

Torres and Hope entered Administration, passed the intake desk, and were buzzed through a heavy metal door to the warden's airy, sunlit offices. It felt spare without the senior staff gathered in, furnished only with a desk, bookshelf and a few chairs. Windows overlooked the entrance walkway, parking lot and highway with a clear view of visitors and staff coming and going. Across the road, heavy cranes loaded concrete barriers onto semi-trailers with that piercing *beep, beep, beep*.

Torres pulled a chair near the desk. "Sit please while I email the secretary."

Hope sat, while Roman typed a brief email of record, no doubt marked urgent and covering *drugs impounded, three arrested, investigation continuing.*

She smoothed her tie-dyed skirt over calloused knees, all that gardening, weeding, praying. On his desk was a stack of hardback books, *Les Miserables* on top.

Roman hit the last key and looked up. "So how did you uncover the Cheese Puff affair?"

"Cinny spilled it. As you know, she's a mother—had a baby by one of our upstanding officers three-four years ago. The officer got out in July and killed her father and boyfriend. He was the father of her second, born exactly a month ago. She came to my office today, distraught at being separated from the baby, and I let her paint butterflies on my wall. That's when she revealed that the snack bags contained cigarettes."

"Yes, go on."

"I was on alert today, Warden, because of your staff meeting this morning. But I realize now that she had already tipped me off even before she had her baby."

"How so?"

"I was coming from the canteen eating Cheese Puffs and she asked, *Whatcha got there*? I felt she was trying to alert me to something. Then she said, outright, *You've got to watch out, Chaplain. Some of those bags have been tampered with*."

"And you said what, exactly?"

Hope shook her head. "I didn't snap to it at the time because her friend Mindy was with her and wanted to see me urgently."

Outside, several police officers passed with plastic bins full of orange snack bags.

"After that, I noticed girls leaving the canteen, hiding those cheese puff bags behind their backs when I came along."

In the parking lot, the men in uniform battled wind gusts, heaving open cruiser trunks, setting bins inside and slamming trunks shut. They grabbed their hats and jackets and ducked into the cruisers.

Hope frowned. "Crazy weather out there."

"Yeah, we're supposed to have thundershowers." The warden peered a moment at his computer screen. "Oh, a tropical storm. Good thing we're on lockdown."

Then he turned back. "Go on."

"So, when Cinny showed up in my office, I pressed her about the officer who'd let her into the chapel. After he checked back on her, she came out with the cheese puff story. I called Officer Damon right away for an escort to the canteen and told Emily to call you. Thankfully, you responded."

"Yes, she said it was urgent. You are to be commended, Hope."

He had used her first name. Perhaps they were forging a friendship through all this turmoil?

"Now tell me what I can do for you, Miss Springs. Maybe you have a solution for all this law-breaking inside?"

"Warden, I would like to start a prison nursery."

Torres reared as though hit by a tidal wave. "You want to put babies in prison?"

Hope sat forward. "I know it sounds barbaric, like Javert in *Les Miserables*."

Torres laid a large, tanned hand on his stack of books. "I've just started re-reading that novel. Javert is the policeman, right?"

"Yes, he's the former prison guard who recognizes that the town mayor is Jean Valjean—the escaped convict."

"Ah yes, when Valjean lifts the cart off a crushed man!"

"Yes, you do know the story! Well, Javert was born and raised in prison—the worst in France."

Torres blinked. "So how does that recommend babies in prison?"

"Exactly, it doesn't. Not that kind of prison anyway. Not that kind of nursery. We would need a much nicer dorm; a safe, well-staffed nursery. And mothers would have to qualify. They would have to be serving short sentences for non-violent crimes and planning to continue primary care of their babies on release."

"I would say so." He moved some papers from his blotter and leaned forward.

Hope pushed on. "Do you remember how the novel opens, Warden?"

"Something about the degradation of men by poverty, ruin of women by starvation and dwarfing of children by spiritual and physical night."

"Exactly, Warden! You do know Victor Hugo."

"Yes, I wrote my criminal justice thesis on him. I called it *Hell on Earth Versus Hugo's Redemptive Justice*."

"And you ended up here?" Hope raised her eyebrows. "In our hell-on-earth?"

"As you can see, I'm trying to change the system from within."

Hope nodded and pointed outside. Torres followed her gesture.

In the parking lot, Damon and Leylani bent against the wind, along with two police officers escorting them in handcuffs to the cruisers.

Hope wanted to reach out to them, to follow them to their jail cells and hear their hearts' cries. She wanted to assure them that there was renewal and hope.

The police ducked their prisoners' heads into the cruisers and closed the doors, backing out and heading onto the highway.

Torres raised an eyebrow. "I know you want to crawl into that cruiser and go to jail with them."

Hope nodded, clasping her hands.

"Sometimes you have to let people feel their failure, Chaplain."

"That's where I end up too." Hope unfolded and spread her hands.

"As long as laws create social blame, we'll produce hells on earth." Torres turned back toward his desk, picking up *Les Miserables* while cruiser sirens faded toward Quincy, drowned by the wind.

Hope breathed a wordless prayer before speaking again. "My goal, though, is to make it a little more like heaven down here."

Torres opened the novel at his bookmark, and showed Hope a woodcut print of a ragged, barefoot girl in a puddle. She was pushing a large straw broom, tendrils escaping her hat. She looked deserted. "Cosette, the way she looked when Valjean freed her."

"Thank you, Roman. This is a priceless reminder." Too late, Hope realized she had lapsed into the familiar, too, using his first name.

"After all, we are in the business of rescuing Cosettes."

Outside the wind gusted, and Chief Ramsey struggled toward administration, hair whipped and tossed under darkening skies.

"Gettin' bad out there." Hope frowned and sat forward, wondering if she should sprint to the chapel before the rain hit.

Roman turned toward the window, and back to her. "Tell me again, how does this make your case for babies in prison?"

"Exactly, we don't want baby enslavement. We want family freedom. But Roman.... May I?" Again, she had used his first name, closing a gap between the professional and personal, forging a friendship.

He nodded, signaling her to go on.

"We offer a hollow recovery unless residential rehab includes real responsibility, like raising and bonding with babies."

Roman gestured her to continue.

Hope pushed on. "Think about it, Roman. Raising prisoners' children is yet another expense prisons force on poor families who are already reeling from paying their toiletries, phone calls, and scraping for gas to come visit."

Torres stood and paced to the window, frowning. "Not raining yet." He picked up the next book in his pile, *The Rich Get Richer, the Poor Get Prison*.

Hope grinned. "More subversive reading, Sir?"

Torres laughed. "How can we deny that social class defines what we call crime? Bank-robber- murderer Patty Hearst gets a commuted sentence and clemency. The banks rob us; no one goes to jail. But steal a loaf of bread—" He shook his head. "Do you know that in Florida, no white man has ever been executed for killing a black man?"

"And I imagine the opposite is not true?"

Roman's inbox dinged and he jiggled the mouse. "The DOC chief inviting me to a meeting on drugs in prison."

"Warden, here's your opportunity. I sent you several news stories; life-altering prison reforms to take with you."

"Yes, I noticed. Catch me up, in your own words."

"A prison in Alabama is allowing women to serve time in community-residential programs with their newborns. They've found that women who bond with their babies are three times less likely to violate parole and come back to prison."

"Interesting," Torres paced again. "How do you propose we do that?"

"I suggest we free up some dorm space. I propose granting more clemency requests for non-violent drug offenses and doubling gain time for good behavior. We could release model prisoners after serving sixty-five percent instead of eighty-five percent of their sentences."

"Well, the governor is politically ambitious." Torres rubbed his stubbled jaw.

"Oh yes, at the national level, the U.S. Board of Prisons is recommending reduced sentences for long drug sentences. Also, surprisingly, prison nurseries are one way to stop this family cycle of addiction and incarceration. A good way to lower taxpayer costs."

The warden turned from the window. "I have your email about prison nurseries. I will take that to the meeting."

"Sure, Roman. Also, did you know that DOC has filed a lawsuit against at least one adoption agency for coercing prison baby sales?"

"Yes, that did come to my attention, and I am acting on it."

"Ah," was all Hope said. That could explain Greta's contrite attitude. Cinnamon had more influence in this prison with her outside-the-lines thinking than she knew.

"Chaplain, how much are we talking for a nursery?"

"It's $24,000 per baby per year and we want 8-to-10 cribs to start."

Torres whistled softly. "A quarter of a million dollars? That will take an act of God."

Hope rose and leaned over his desk, her heart beating in her throat. "But Roman, every $24,000 we invest, we save in productive community members and reduced prisoner costs."

Torres nodded. "Okay, Hope, convince me in writing as though I'm the governor. Write me a bill." He paused and jangled the keys in his pocket. Dark clouds scudded low over the parking lot, throwing the yard into shadow.

"Sir, we put the mothers in here, and we're already paying for it with more social ills, more prisoners, more dwarfed children. A prison nursery can save us millions in jailing fees down the road. After that, who knows?"

"Well for one—" The warden paused, glancing out the window at cascading clouds. "The public will react. They'll demand that we release the babies. We need buy-in. Can you do that, Hope?"

"Certainly, Roman, I will draw up a media plan—." Lightening flashed, filling the room like a spotlight. Hope counted the seconds to thunderclap. Four miles.

The warden frowned at his computer screen and jiggled his mouse. "We have some heavy rain headed this way." He straightened. "With red cones—tornadoes. We need to send non-essential staff home and alert emergency staff—that's you, right?"

Hope nodded, assured Roman would manage and safeguard their compound.

The warden handed Hope an umbrella. "Hope, the prison is built pretty solid, but do your best to hunker down away from doors and windows, will you?"

As Hope reached the door, Chief Ramsey entered, report in hand.

"Hope, wait a minute," Roman said. "You should know what came of your rapid response. Chief, what do you have?"

"Yes sir. We removed snack bins containing contraband to be analyzed in the crime lab. We believe there may be hundreds of bags filled with street drugs. That means the net may spread very wide."

"Thank you, my man." Roman shook his hand. "Also, we've got a storm coming."

"Yes sir, I'll alert emergency staff, send the others home; check the generators and prepare for blackouts."

Hope pushed out the door against howling wind, struggling to keep Roman's umbrella right side out. The wind whipped her dress and hair, rain pricked her face. She waited for guards to buzz her through security and pushed on. In the eves, pigeons huddled, clucked and puffed their chests. Oh, for moms sheltering their babes in storm.

It seemed a mile to the chapel between the dorms where women gathered at narrow windows.

Chaplain Emily met her at the chapel door, concern clouding her eyes. Hope lowered her umbrella and shook it outside.

"Thank you so much for your help." Hope shook out the warden's umbrella and set it by the door. "It's a doozy. Maybe even tornadoes. Let's hunker down—under my desk."

She steered Emily toward her own office at the back.

"Was Cinny in on the drug fiasco?" Emily wrung her hands.

"Well, she knew about it—and many women are serving time for not telling what they knew. She did drop hints, and finally, exposed it."

The lights went out and Hope got down on her hands and knees, leading Emily under her desk.

32
Cinnamon Alone

Alone in my cell in solitary, the room chilled and darkened. Storm clouds rolled in. I shivered in my sweatshirt and scrubs and curled up in the white linen blanket, trying to shut out the voices echoing from the cells downstairs.

If only I'd spoken up louder, sooner. When Mario dropped his bag in my garden plot, or when I noticed digging in my flower bed. I had played along, hardly looking for a way out. This was it—through lockup after finally ratting out the Cheese Puff Gang. What would they do to me? Officer Damon was sitting in jail and the cheese puffers would be getting sick, perhaps sweating and shaking through withdrawals now.

Then too, I felt miserable for letting Hope down; Hope who'd declared me forgiven and assured me I was never alone. I tossed under the pilled blanket, turning over and over on my mat. If only I hadn't told; if only Hope hadn't turned us in. If only...I had called my sponsor.

"Jesus, my true sponsor, I pray for favor and blessing in this matter.... And, as always, hold my babies for me."

Lulled by the wind and rain, I drifted to sleep. In my dream, I was walking down the metal staircase in solitary when hands reached through the grating and grabbed my ankles. I fell headlong to the concrete floor and woke crumpled beside the bed ledge.

I groped in darkness for my mat and heard boots at the door. An officer called and let herself in. I hardly recognized her. It was Greta, but different. Her grown-out hair was pulled back in a neat pony tail and her expression was soft and gentle. "Is everything alright? I heard you fall."

"Bad dream." My voice shook, and I shivered.

Greta helped me up and pulled the cover to my chin. "It's okay. I'm right here if you need me. There's a bad storm, and they've shut down the yard."

I leaned up on my elbow, rubbing my eyes. It looked like midnight outside. "What time is it?"

"It's four in the afternoon. But we're preparing for blackouts. You're the only one left up here on the second floor. Cinny, I want to apologize to you." She sat cross-legged on the floor as though she intended to stay.

"Pardon?" Since when did a guard apologize to a prisoner? Especially Greta. To me. Still, I wasn't going to kick her out in the storm.

"Warden Torres had a long talk with me.... I was hard on you when you were pregnant, and in the hospital having the baby. I was so bent on you adopting out your baby. I knew Willie Hutchinson in here."

"Oh, Doobie?" It still hurt to speak the name of Daddy's killer; the name Daddy had given him.

"Yeah, I was pissed when you filed that suit. But then the paternity test came back positive, I realized you were justified."

I hesitated. "Okay, but then why were you so angry about me not giving up my baby?"

"I was raised by a young aunt and never found out why until I was six years old. That's when she beat me one day for taking a truck from her son. She told me I was just like my grandpa I had never seen—didn't even know I had one. That's when she told me my grandpa had murdered my mother and father, then shot himself."

I gasped, dismayed for that little girl. "That's horrible, Greta!"

"Life was never the same after that. I felt so bad, as though I were the murderer. I didn't know how I would ever live with myself or my aunt who had accused me of being like my grandpa." Greta's face was lined and drawn. "I felt like my whole family was defective, like gross mutants."

"That's awful, Greta." I saw her pain, but couldn't see her logic. "And that's why you wanted all of us to give up our babies?"

"No, there's more. I began to realize that when I grew up, I wanted to be a police officer to make everyone behave, including my aunt. You see, another part of me understood she was wrong in accusing me. But I took responsibility after that to keep everyone in line, alive and make sure no one else was murdered." Her voice broke.

I handed her a corner of my blanket and she comically pretended to blow her nose in it, shifting to her knees, leaning on the bed.

"I was the first woman in our local police academy." Greta sat beside me, folding her arms around herself, shivering.

"Come under the snot blanket." I grinned and held out my blanket, knowing it was a long shot, such closeness between a guard and a prisoner. But she rose and sat huddled under my blanket, her muscled arm warm against my shoulder.

Outside, the wind howled and she raised her voice above it. "As the only female police officer, I was assigned to investigate child abuse. I teamed up with social workers, trying to find safe homes."

Greta paused, brow furrowed. "One was a tiny baby found in the prison dumpster, thrown out with the trash last January. It was a miracle he survived or even that we found him. He was light chocolate with loose dark curls and a sweet, rosebud mouth. Nearly died of starvation and hypothermia. I named him Nate after Nathaniel in the Bible, because he was completely innocent, no guilt in him. Also, a gift of God.

"DNA tests found the mother, a mentally ill prisoner who should never have been locked up. She was released to a group home, and her baby placed in state guardianship. I applied to adopt him, and arrange visits with her."

I shivered and pulled at a blanket corner, wanting to hold Tony and Annie. Rain whipped the window and the damp cold penetrated our shared blanket.

"Last year Nate was diagnosed with autism. He will need me the rest of his life." Greta straightened. The wind had picked up and was roaring toward us like a freight train.

"Quick! Downstairs." She opened my cell door and we raced down the metal steps. I slipped on the last steps, but Greta grabbed me before I could split my head open. She dragged me around a picnic table to the cells under the stairs, wrestling with her keys. "Dang! I can't find the key. Down on the floor, hands over your head!"

"What about the others?"

"They're three, all on the ground floor." She threw herself over me, crushing me to the floor.

Every hair stood on end, my ears pricked to every sound. The wind slammed into the double entry doors and threw them off their hinges. Glass shattered, shards flew, sand scoured us. That wind sucked all the air out of the room. It rose like an atomic bomb, pulling us off the floor, exploding the skylights, and slamming us down on rubbled concrete.

I died in an instant and woke alive the next. The doors, door jambs and picnic table severed their bolts, twisted through the room and crashed down, shattering like giant toys.

Greta screamed, and I found her in the darkness.

She moaned. "Something hit my back—"

I found her outstretched arm, her shoulder, a jagged piece of metal sticking out. "We need to take you to medical."

"If there is a medical."

Through empty window slats, I saw the twister cloud howling through the compound and out to Rocky Comfort Creek, stripping and uprooting trees. Balls of razor wire rolled around the compound and several voices called from their downstairs cells.

"Are you okay—" Greta couldn't raise her voice or get the words out. So, I tried.

"Are you okay?"

"Yes."

"Just scared."

I crawled under Greta's good shoulder and lifted her to her knees, then to her wobbly feet. She leaned heavily on my shoulder so I called out brokenly. "We'll be back. Greta's hurt. I have to get her to medical."

"Okay, I can wait."

"Come back when you can."

Greta sagged over me and I wavered, planting my feet and strapping my arm around her waist. Gradually she moved in step with me, the metal shard still stuck in her shoulder. We picked our way over piles of dirt, leaves, branches and shattered glass. The metal doors flung around like Frisbees at a barbecue.

The clinic was still there, missing its foyer roof, a tree driven into its front window, roots pointing to the sky. A nurse stood at the door, dazed.

"We need help." My shoulder screamed from Greta's weight. The nurse ran toward us, slow motion. Greta had stopped moving and I lowered her to the ground, on her side, turning her shoulder to keep the jagged metal from driving in further. Finally, the nurse reached us and knelt, her hand on Greta's pulse.

"Stay with us, Greta." She examined the metal wound and squinted up at me. "Moving it could do more damage. We'll have to wait for help. Cinny, can you get a blanket from the infirmary?"

I ran to the building, searching blindly in the dark. Wood surfaces soaked, cupboards locked, closets full of brooms and mops. An examining room helter-skelter—no beds or blankets. I stumbled back down the hall, feeling my way in pitch blackness to a sick room. There at the back, a bed with a dry linen blanket. I grabbed it, wrapping it in a ball, and dragged my hand along the hall wall, feeling my way to the yard.

Sirens approached from Greensboro Highway, and I inhaled deeply, gratefully. I raced back to Greta, laid the blanket over her and tucked it around her. Her eyelids flickered.

"Nate—" Her words stuck, her breath rattled.

"Don't talk," the nurse directed, fingers against Greta's pulse at her neck.

"Yes, we'll take care of your baby." I laid my warm arm across her cold one. She wheezed and lay still. I looked at the nurse.

The nurse bent low, hair loose and flying around her face, fingers flailing. "I can't find a pulse."

Police cars rushed to the southeast fences hanging in tatters. The forest beyond lay in ruins, like pickup sticks. Ambulances roared into the yard and emergency technicians raced toward us with collapsible stretchers.

They slid the pieces under Greta, secured them, lifted and carried her away, passing the warden and Chief Ramsey on the way. Voices reached us from lockup and I raced with the warden, chief and several emergency technicians to the shattered building. We picked our way over crumbled cinderblock and around scattered doors, past crumpled picnic tables, glass shards and mud.

I led the team to the ground floor cells where women were calling behind locked doors. The first door revealed a white-haired woman spattered in glass, bleeding. The second, a large brown woman lying on her back, her leg at a crazy angle. The third, a wild-haired teenager, huddled on her bed mat, wrapped in a blanket. The medical technicians placed each on a stretcher and rolled her to a waiting ambulance.

"That's it, I think. Greta said three women on first floor."

The warden and Chief Ramsey checked a few more cells to be sure, then turned to me.

"Thank you, Cinny." The warden gripped my cold, shaking hand in his solid, warm one. "We'll walk you to the other side where the cells are intact. We'll have to keep you in lockup for your own safety."

"Yes, I understand. Thanks." We headed past dozens of shattered cells until we reached the far end. Chief Ramsey opened a separate section of segregation cells, kicking on backup lights and heat. The cell windows were intact and Warden Torres checked to make sure the locks worked.

I checked the blanket, dry but thin. I needed more. "May I please have another blanket—and send the chaplain—?" A fiery sunset glowed through the west window and I drank it in, knowing it would soon turn dark and cool.

"Check next door for a blanket, Chief." Warden Torres gazed at the sunset too. "And yes, Cinny, I was just going to check on the chaplain. We have to get going."

Chief Ramsey returned with two extra blankets and pillows and stood with us, watching the dramatic light display. "All the dust in the air is making it extra red."

"Beauty from ashes," I whispered.

Warden Torres helped me spread out the blankets. "Cinny, we're keeping you as safe as possible, but please stay alert."

"Yes," Chief Ramsey said. "We don't know how many of my security staff were in on the drug-smuggling. Or who will see you as a threat. I will send my most trusted staff to guard you."

"Thank you, Chief. I'll be careful not to mess with the cheese puffers."

"You know who they are, then?" Chief Ramsey's brow wrinkled and the crease above his nose deepened.

"Oh no, just hunches. And a few who smoked them." I didn't want to be pushed into a witch hunt, accusing people on a whim for seeing them with Cheese Puffs bags. But I also wanted to cooperate, reduce my sentence, and get back to Annie and Tony.

Chief Ramsey nodded, a man of few words. "We have some dirty UA evidence of our own."

It was clear what the chief expected of me. Pretend to be a prime suspect to keep me safe, then turn state's evidence. I just wanted to get back to my children—alive.

"Fair enough." The chief followed the warden out the door.

I started after them. "I want you both to know that Greta saved my life today."

The chief nodded. "As harsh as she seemed sometimes, she was one I could trust to keep her nose clean."

"Greta?" The warden grinned. "Your arch enemy?"

"Yes, Warden. Greta wanted to take my baby away for adoption. But today, before she died, she asked my forgiveness."

"Wait, are you sure she's dead?" Chief Ramsey swept his lank black hair off his forehead.

I bit my lip. "It seemed that way. In fact, she may have given her life for mine today. She threw herself on top of me before that door jamb tore loose."

"I don't know, Cinny. She was critically injured, and rushed to surgery." The warden's voice was soft and low.

Chief Ramsey cleared his throat but his voice still rumbled a little. "So, all's forgiven?"

"Yes, and Warden, Chief, she asked me to look out for her baby."

"How are you going to do that in here?" The warden raised an eyebrow, his hand on the door.

"Well, can we at least make sure he's okay?"

They nodded and started closing the door.

"Wait!" I would soon be alone with my grief and I wanted distraction. "Do either of you have a pen and paper?"

Ramsey patted his pockets and produced a pen. The warden took out a pocket-sized notebook. He tore out the first few scribbled-on pages and handed me the whole notebook.

"Warden!"

"If you don't fill that with drawings, I'll feel gypped."

I laughed and the men let themselves out, closing the door behind them. The lock clicked and echoed in the empty building. I opened the notebook and sketched the shattered tree line in sunset. A finger of light burst through the broken limbs. "He touched me," I wrote, "and made me whole."

I woke in darkness with aching arms wrapped around my pillow. Tony, Annie, Greta. *Save them, spare them, bless them and give them joy and peace.* Dex, Daddy, Tony. *Just hold them for me, Lord. You loaned them to me for a moment and now I give them back. I'm not in control; you are.*

33
Greta in the Balance

Greta hurtled through the storm on her back, headfirst and backwards. Lights flashed, sirens blared and she tried to get her breath, plunging 100 miles per hour under black, boiling clouds and dark pine trees.

She took another shock from the defibrillator, stirred on her stretcher, hanging between pain and death, wheezing, coughing, moaning. As the ambulance pelted through the storm, Greta's pain cycled out of control.

A balding man leaned toward her. "I'm your EMT, Jim Hertz. But I don't want to hurt you."

Greta tried to smile but pain racked her chest.

"Yes, that's his real name, and I'm Brook." The other EMT had boyish, spiked hair. "We just need to loosen your clothes and insert a needle."

Expert hands opened Greta's shirt and inserted a needle beneath her ribs. There was a sharp pinch and then huge relief as the EMTs drew off the air that had leaked into her perforated, collapsed lung.

"Emergency unit to Surgery...we're ten minutes out ..." Mr. Hertz radioed. "Prepare to remove a projectile lodged in patient's thoracic cavity."

The ambulance driver weaved around brake-lit cars on I-10, veered into Tallahassee on Thomasville Road, carefully running lights, aiming for the nearest hospital emergency room.

A trauma team was already masked and gloved when the EMTs lifted out her stretcher and rolled her to the surgical theater. Greta watched x-rays on a TV screen showing where the metal had lodged, until the anesthesia pulled her under.

Greta woke in a feather white bed, with a nurse checking her stent and wound dressing. Rosy light filtered through coral window blinds.

"Good morning, Ms. Green. You are a lucky lady."

Greta touched the bandages wrapping her tender, inflamed rib cage.

"How are you feeling here, and here?" The nurse touched just the raw tips of her rib cage and seemed to know just where the pain was.

"Ouch."

"Yes, exactly. Let me get you some heat." The nurse returned with a heating pad and Greta wanted to sleep under it forever.

"What about my mom and baby?"

"Oh yes, they'll be back today. They were here before dinner, when you were still under. We assured them you'd make a full recovery."

Greta wavered between consciousness and sleep. When she woke, Nate's chubby arms reached for her, but her mother held him back in solid arms.

Greta could not yet sit up, but she did receive Nate's slobbery kisses and her mother's whispered praises as she bowed her gray head over her, kissing Greta's forehead.

34
Roman in Charge

Roman Torres hurried through moist air, past an open breezeway, its roof hurled into the yard, shattered. Chief Ramsey had peeled off to the wrecked security area, rounded up his staff, and was reassigning them to broken perimeters and limited yard movement.

Broken kiosk bulletin boards strewed the walkway. Flower beds were ripped up and light poles toppled—thousands of dollars in damages.

He dodged around them between the dorms, where dim generator lights glowed and prisoners watched at long, narrow windows. He flashed a sign language "o" for okay, and they flashed "o" back.

He hurried on, focused on the tornado path leading straight to the chapel. Had Hope and Emily survived?

The doors were gone, plastic chairs thrown into jagged piles, lights still off in the sanctuary. He picked his way to the back through dirt, leaves, scattered shelves and books.

"Hope?"

"We're in here." Hope and Emily sat by her office door in rescued chairs, hair tousled, limbs trembling. Hope rose on wobbly legs, shoving curly hair out of her face.

"Are you okay?" He couldn't help but embrace her, relieved. She trembled and sagged against his beating heart.

"Just a little rattled." Hope found her feet again and paced around Emily who sat rigid and speechless.

"It's Emily's first tornado. She's still in shock. We heard the wind roar through the door, lift all the chairs and even hover my desk for a moment, suck all the air out of the chapel. Then it blew out the windows and the chairs and desk came crashing down again. It all happened in 30 seconds."

"Yes, it was a bomb blasting through here." Roman reached for her again, but this time she lingered only a moment, then found her feet.

"And we survived." Hope stepped back, hand on hip, trying to look stern. "Warden, we're going to need new furniture."

"That's my chaplain, always demanding something." Roman laughed at the comic relief.

"Well at least I'm not demanding a stretcher—for Emily." Hope shook her head at her own gallows humor.

"I'm okay, just processing." Emily stood unsteadily, then sat again.

"We heard the ambulance. Are the others okay?" Hope rubbed her bruised forehead.

Roman squinted at the bump rising there. "You need ice, Hope. You'll prob'ly get a black eye."

"Naw, I'm okay. What about the others?"

"Greta was taken to emergency with a piece of metal in her back. We're hoping she'll pull through." He looked hard at Hope through dim light. "She took the hit for Cinny, throwing herself on top of her before the tornado rushed through solitary."

He led the women outside where the sunset still glowed a deep purple, and clouds lifted and scattered.

Chapel chairs were flung in all directions, some hung up on the basketball court fence. Roman checked his radio, depressing the call key. "Chief Ramsey, any word yet from the hospital?"

A voice crackled, then came in low and clear. "Greta's out of surgery, resting fine. The three inmates from lock are resting too, one with a reset leg, one with first-aid wounds."

"Thank you, Chief. The chapel was hit, but our chaplains are okay, just shaken up a bit. How's security?"

"We're fine, getting emergency backup in place. Over and out."

"Emily?" Roman leaned down, checking her full face for any sign of lingering distress. "You live in Blountstown, right?"

Emily nodded and stood, opening her purse and fetching her keys. "I'll be okay."

"Great!" Roman breathed deeply. He had never seen staff in such shell shock. "I want to make sure you can make it home alright."

Hope lifted her face and stepped forward.

"Hope, would you get some ice on that goose egg—try station one refrigerator. And see Emily to her car? Also, will you look in on Greta when you get to Tallahassee?"

"That's my warden, always demanding something." Hope took the warden's outstretched hand.

"Thank God, and thank you." He pulled her long, lithe body into a solid bear hug and thought he could dance that way forever.

35
Cinnamon Awakens

I woke to dim light, soft shapes, swinging children in their arms. Sweet-faced prisoners danced all around my bed with babies cooing. Mindy was holding her Jason, and Reese holding Greta's baby, Nate.

I fell asleep again and woke to broad daylight, the shapes clearer in my mind than ever. Smiling moms in prison scrubs, down on the floor, playing with their babies.

My pencil lay beside my bed on my notebook, right where I had left it the night before. And my face and hands, braised from the wind, couldn't prevent my holding it, even if stiffly. I drew bright-eyed moms and babies, crawling around on a clean rug, sitting at tables coloring, and cuddled in a big nest, reading. Kita had said she wanted to include all my drawings in the sketch book, even if it had to wait. She had a local publisher ready to print it, too.

In my parenting class, we had learned the importance for academic success of babies hearing 30,000 words a day from birth to age 3. And words are free; it had little to do with economic status. I drew a finger painting table and toddlers drawing letters in chocolate pudding. Touch and action were important too.

A guard knocked, announcing Chaplain Hope, and opened for her. She entered, with a black eye, half-swollen shut and frizzy hair. She had dressed down, too, in a sage work shirt, khaki pants and tennis shoes.

"Geez, Chaplain! What happened to you?"

"I got a goose egg where the desk crashed down on us." She rubbed it comically and sat down on the only chair. "I should be in bed, but it's too critical to be here today. I heard you and Greta were right in the tornado."

"Yes, and she was hit, protecting me. I pray she lives."

"Oh, I saw her in the hospital yesterday. She is resting and stable after her surgery. She gave me this for you." Hope held out a metal-worked, enamel butterfly clip, bright pink, yellow and blue.

I smoothed my hair into its clasp, and turned for Miss Hope's approval.

"Nice!" Hope helped me straighten it on my braided poof. "And guess who else was recovering after surgery, in the very next room?"

I tried to think. "Chaplain Emily?"

"No, she's fine—despite surviving her first tornado. It was your mother. She had knee replacement surgery and was doing well. She should be going home this week."

"What happened?"

"She fell on her steps and banged her bad knee, she said. That right knee had been giving her problems anyway, and now it's repaired and healing. She sent this big hug for you." Hope rose and wrapped me in a long, tight embrace, her soft curls smelling of raspberry shampoo.

Until that moment, I didn't realize how my face stung. "Ouch."

Hope stopped and examined my scratched-up cheek and nose. "Oh, it's red and swollen. We'll have to get some triple antibiotic ointment on that."

"Just whenever. Thanks, Chaplain."

"And this hug's from Greta." She hugged me again, more gently. "Greta is still tender and could not even hug you that tight. But she wanted me to. Her lung collapsed when that metal struck her. I am so glad you got her medical help—dragging her all that way, must have taken all your strength. And I'm glad that the metal didn't hit you. She is a bigger, stronger woman and they said her dense muscle slowed the projectile."

"Oh Chaplain, I've lost so many people in my life. I thought she was dead when they put her on the stretcher. I prayed and dreamed about her, begging her not to go."

"Well, it helped. Greta was in shock, but the EMTs responded quickly, applying AED shocks to restart her heart, and treating her collapsed lung. The surgeons removed the metal, expertly, without doing further damage, and stitch her up. She'll probably be back at work before too long."

I felt a deep joy for myself and Nate. The dark struggle of the night before was giving way to peace. Outside, a mockingbird trilled. She, too, had survived. "Whenever I hear the mockingbird, I think of that song, 'I dance for my father; my father sings over me.'"

"Yes, exactly, he lives in our praises."

Hope picked up a few drawings from my desk. "Amazing, Cinny! You seem possessed with a creative spirit. Is this what the storm crisis dredged out of you?"

"Yes, Chaplain, the vision is coming true! See, I'm drawing it real. Look, each bedroom has a theme!" I showed her a round manatee rolling with her baby underwater, surrounded by angel fish. "This is the underwater room.

"Oh Cinny, these are awesome!" Hope examined each sketch carefully.

"This is the tree house room. See you're standing on a tree house balcony, overlooking a crashing falls, right at bird's eye level."

"And there's the eagle soaring! What you need is a sketchbook and pastels or paints. May I take these to the warden and get his permission?"

My eyes bulged. "Really? You can help me do that?"

"Oh, I think art can be as powerful as stories to persuade people to act."

She rose and hugged me again, then knocked on the door to be let out. Her warmth lingered as though I'd been visited by a companion spirit. I went straight back to work, humming as I sketched. *What if your blessings come through raindrops? What if your healing comes through tears? What if a thousand sleepless nights are what it takes to know you're near? What if trials of this life are your mercies in disguise?*

Gone was the scouring wind, the dark clouds, the roaring train and any regret for anything I'd ever done. Lemon fresh light filled the room and I filled one page after another with detailed arms and hands reaching around toddlers, heads bent, building a block tower, or pulling a dump truck full of sand. Strong arms pushed gleeful curly-headed tots in safety swings and chubby feet splashed in a wading pool. Razor wire blurred in the background.

Part IV

Hope Persists

Camellia (greennurseries.com)

36
Nikita's Moon Shadow

Nikita tuned into her driveway while the children chattered about catching Pokémon. But wait, what had happened to her neat lawn? As if struck by a tornado, it was strewn with clothes, toys, shoes, bedding, dishes. How had her trailer vomited its contents like this? Burglars? The hair on her neck bristled.

"Stay here," she commanded. She threw the shifter into park, stepped into the brisk March wind, beneath whipping Spanish moss. She crept up the steps and peered in the windows. All was dark and empty inside.

A chain and padlock secured her door and barred her entry. She slumped against the bannister, rubbing something from her eye. Yes, she was late with the rent and van payment again. Mama's knee replacement had required follow-up surgery and costed more than expected. She had given up shifts and hired a church woman to help Mama with rehab. But Kita had begged her landlord to let her pay the penalty and catch up next month.

All she wanted tonight was to gather the children around a warm pot of chili and focus them on homework, baths, story time and bed.

A clang of wood hitting metal spun her head. Behind the trailer, a plump pink man and woman in red sweat suits were loading her recliner, kitchen table and chairs onto their truck. They glanced her way and raced to the cab, climbing in and slamming doors.

The van doors opened and Kita put up her hand. "Kids, stay in the van!"

She ran toward the truck but the driver squinted straight ahead. "Hey, you're stealing my stuff!" The truck raced onto

Marvin Street, squeeling tires. A lamp fell off the bed and smashed in the street.

"Bring back my stuff," Nikita yelled. But the truck was gone in a puff of sulfur.

Nikita kicked through the heap at her feet, turning up Cinny's sketches. They were wet and dirt-smeared. Could she still salvage and publish them?

She was late paying the utilities, too, and had been threatened with a cut-off notice. In fact, Saturday morning, she had just soaped her hair, when the water stopped. She opened the bathroom window, sticking her head into the raw cold and begging the city utility man to please let her rinse off. He had opened the valve briefly, laughing, straightening, hands on his hips, swaying a little. She had stoppered the tub to save what little soapy water she could for cleaning and washing floors. She would have to scrape $600 to reconnect.

It was a double-whammy for people already behind in bills. Could she raise that with Cinny's books? Maybe if she sold boxes of them to charities transitioning prisoners.

Perhaps she'd made the wrong choices, emptying her bank account to pay the medical bills and church lady sitting with Mama instead of the utilities and rent. Her twelve-year-old, Ruby, might have babysat ten-year-old Dex, but how could Ruby handle wild Annie and baby Tony?

Besides, Ruby was captaining the traveling soccer team and that had also taken a toll her savings. Ruby had worked so hard for it, and it might open doors to athletic scholarships.

Kita had taken her last $10 to buy bread, milk, eggs, and now they were smashed in the yard. She righted the toy bin and threw in trucks, dolls, balls, building blocks and stuffed toys. She piled up Annie's bright pink tutus, the boys' orange Rattler t-shirts, blue jeans and running shoes. She started a fresh stack of quilts, pillows, towels, soaps, lotions and toothpaste; nested pots, pans and dishes, cereal, milk jugs, eggs and flour. She set aside the potted plants.

A van door creaked open. "Auntie Ma, Auntie Ma," Annie called. "I have to pee!"

Nikita grabbed a paper towel and led Annie behind the Moonshadow camellias she'd cultivated. It always amazed her that the rose-edged winter roses had no scent.

Annie giggled as Nikita helped her crouch out of sight.

"Life's a big adventure, isn't it?"

Ruby and Denny clattered out of the van. "Mama, can we come out, too?"

"Sure, come on, kids; the thieves are gone. Ruby and Denny, take turns behind the bushes, then help me sort this out."

Annie came running, gathering up stuffies and dolls from the toy chest.

"No Annie, leave those."

When Annie couldn't hold anymore in her little brown arms, she sat down on a pillow and rocked as though her heart would break, "Mama, Mama." There was something so sorrowful at her core. The school therapist called it separation anxiety and a heightened fear response.

Ruby and Denny sat with her.

Nikita gathered them all in strong arms and rocked them. "We're going to have to load the van and find someplace else to stay tonight. Maybe Nana Mama's?"

Tony hollered from his car seat. "You all sit here and hug each other. I gotta get Tony."

Nikita unbuckled and lifted out darling, cuddly Tony. His diapers were soaked through. She laid him on the front seat and dug into the diaper bag. He crooned and giggled, and she rubbed his cute button nose with hers. Tony was clean and dry again and she pulled his hoodie up over his ears against the brisk March wind.

The other children huddled, arms around each other, heads bowed, singing something. She joined them, hugging Tony and joining in the chorus. "He's a good, good father, that's who he is—"

Ruby led them all, voice raised. "—and I'm loved by him, it's what I am."

Nikita would not trade a moment of mothering these children. Prison may not be the best rehab, and poor families bore the costs, but she was going to try to be the best mama these children knew.

The kids handed her piles of clothing, pots and dishes, and she placed them in the back seat. Yes, she knew city law was harsh about not paying utilities and risking mold in landlord properties. Or at least that was a policy concession the landlords had won.

The children handed her books, shoes and crayons, and she didn't try to organize them anymore. In Tallahassee, at least, the sheriffs could throw your stuff on the lawn and lock you out. Still, she was sure her landlord had violated some law in throwing her out with the kids.

But when she turned back toward the children, they were beaming at her.

Annie's tears had turned to joy. "Auntie Ma, can we have a sleepover in the van?"

Ruby paused, a pillow and blanket in hand.

"Sure." Nikita helped Ruby spread them on the middle seat and floor. Denny opened the van's back gate where she was going to put the toy chest, and shoved in his FAMU bean bag chair. It filled the entire cargo hold. "This is my side. The girls can have that side."

Nikita couldn't help herself. She laughed. Helplessly. "Let's see if the neighbors will keep that 'til we can pick it up again."

She did have some options. "Let's finish up and go to Nana Mama's for night."

The children squeezed in their last toys, clothes and shoes, just as a black Escalade drove up and the landlord stuck out his large, waxed head, not bothering to heave his bulk out of his leather bucket seat. "Exactly when were you going to pay me your back rent?"

Nikita wanted to hurl the eggs she was carrying.

Instead, she plucked and handed him a rose-edged Moonshadow camellia from the bush she'd cultivated. "We were blessed to live here—and now that we're leaving so are you—with these moonshadow camellias I cultivated."

He sniffed it, cluelessly, and Kita laughed. Something good would come of this, sneaking up like moon shadow.

37
Cinnamon Zest

Silver light penetrated my corner cell again the next morning, and I felt a familiar presence—Jesus beside me, his white-robed arms around me. "Fear not, for I am with you." Peace covered me like a blanket. I stirred, feeling rested and ready for more dream vision and drawing.

The door slot opened and a guard called, "Good morning, Cinny! Shower?"

"Yes, please."

I stood in the warm waterfall feeling pure adrenalin on my spinal cord. We'd have a waterfall room for bright-eyed babies, a fountain filling a splashing pool. The possibilities were endless.

When I returned, the guard had placed oatmeal, canned peaches and cooling coffee on my door tray. Once I would have laughed that, so close to Georgia, the kitchen could only serve canned peaches. Instead, I savored the fragrant fruit and nutty grain.

I returned the tray to the door and sat on my bed mat drawing light bursting through leaves; an orchard of fruited peach trees, pecan trees and the pokeweed Nana Mama used to fry up with bacon grease. That was the savory part of a haunting summer that had steeled my resilient mother in jail, and nearly broken me. We were all more cautious after that. Like pebbles along the railroad tracks, we faced tumult and, at times, disarray.

I had run out of paper and was drawing on my knuckles when Chief Ramsey knocked and unlocked the door. He stepped inside, surveying the drawings scattered everywhere.

"I give you my pen, and this is how you thank me? A blizzard of scribbles?" He smoothed escaped hair into his ponytail, and picked up a sketch of a jungle pond with monkeys swinging over it. "Where are the bananas?"

"Oh, good idea, Chief!" I gathered up a stack to show him. "Will you help me with these?"

He looked long and hard at the first two—the waterfall tree house and underwater manatee caves. "What are they for? I'm afraid to ask."

"Room themes. Each nursery room will have its own adventure setting, and I'm sketching them as fast as they come to me."

"Well, do you have my Apalachicola River with a dugout canoe and Indian princess? You know, I've been carving that 40-foot canoe with an axe, the way my ancestors did it." He showed me his banged up hands.

"Brilliant! Yes, the Big River. I can do that if I have more paper." I flipped through my pages looking for a blank side. But I had filled every inch, both sides.

The chief's interest in my art was almost as good as Daddy's in his good seasons. Chief Ramsey was adding a new perspective. I was a pebble jettisoned from the railroad track, and skipping over shining water.

"Cinny," the chief said, "we have only just completed the damage assessment. I don't know where we are with getting reconstruction funds."

I sat down. "What are you saying? That I'm coloring way outside the lines? What if our construction plans were to build a nursery?"

Chief Ramsey grinned. "In place of solitary confinement?"

"Woohoo!" I hooted.

He looked at me from under heavy brows. "Meanwhile, today we're taking you to give a deposition. We'll have to cuff you, but it's just a formality."

He pulled my hands back gently in his large, rough ones and read aloud the words I'd written on my knuckles. "*Poke? Salad?* Cinny, are you Poke Salad Annie?"

"In a way, Sir. My mama was lynched by her co-workers, falsely accused and jailed when I was four. I missed her terribly, cried every night; Daddy took us home to his nana mama, a

Seminole, and we ate poke salad. And now, look at me, I'm in the poky and my kids are falling asleep every night without me."

Chief Ramsey cleared his throat. "Cinny." He bent to look into my face. "Just remember this, you are stronger for all you've been through. You can endure more, expect less and make more of the little you have. That poke salad you ate while your mama was in jail will nurture you the rest of your life."

He turned me around and clicked the cuffs closed. We stepped into a naked world, trees ripped up by the roots, the forest a pile of raw timber. Our gardens and flowerbeds were bare, snapdragons and pansies gone. I gasped. "Chief!"

"I know it's a moonscape." He pressed his calloused hands gently on my bound ones, and steered me the back way to avoid the women staring out dorm windows. A work crew and truck cleared rolled razor wire at the perimeter fence; police officers paced around the yard.

Crisp air hit my lungs, a chill wind blew through my thin prison sweatshirt. But the sky was crystal blue, not a cloud in sight, as though it had sucked the dark, roiling clouds into outer space.

We cut through Education and the Visitors Park to Administration. Chief Ramsey hummed soft and low. "Poke Salad Annie... makes the alligators look tame." His voice was deeper, more monotone than Daddy's.

We were buzzed through security and, for the first time in months, I was outside the razor wire. I turned and saw Hope crossing the shattered compound in cargo pants, green shirt, work boots, with a backpack slung across her shoulder. Her sleeves were rolled up and she looked ready to work.

Chief Ramsey noticed too. "Well, she's not slacking today. Worried 'bout you too, she said. Thinking of you in deposition."

A burden lifted and I walked lighter and breathed easier. We reached Administration, amid beeping from cranes lifting broken concrete barriers into dump trucks.

"The tornado smashed those barriers, too?" What was it Hope said about people throwing up barriers to our nursery vision?

"Yes, Ma'am, we're lucky to be alive." The chief escorted me past reception and down the hall.

Two young lawyers sat in the conference room, pink-cheeked and serious-toned in dark suits. One wore a University of Florida gator lanyard, and the other an ice-blue tie. They were both smooth-toned and pink-faced.

38
Hope Delivers

Hope crossed the yard, shifting her backpack in the crisp, clear air. Her boot heels echoed along the empty walk and she waved at the women standing at the dorm windows. It had to be tough for them stuck inside all day while crews repaired fences and security systems. How hard would it be to give them furloughs to see their families?

And yet, she knew the cost in security to escort them all home and back.

The women pointed at her work boots and mimicked her rolled sleeves. She had deliberately avoided blue shirts after being mistaken for an inmate and throwing off prisoner counts. She waved, hoping to lift their spirits. Chaplain Emily had helped assemble her nursery proposal, and had offered to visit dorms today so Hope could meet with the warden. She felt a chill and tried to calm her nerves. So many of her dreams were rising from this vision.

Hope again shifted her backpack full of binders. It, too, differed from the prison-issue blue mesh bags. As she rounded the corner, women at the window would see its giant print of Vincent van Gogh's "Starry Night." The backpack had appealed to her during a gloomy low after her husband left.

Hope hummed Don McLean's *Vincent* as she opened the heavy metal door and crossed VP. Van Gogh had freed himself through insanity to paint bright ochre-yellows against dark nights. In the asylum, he was free of behaving well, free of rigid expectations. Just like she was, free to recommend a prison nursery.

Hope greeted security in the sally port and picked up the soaring, anguished tune as she hurried to meet the warden. *This world was never meant for one as beautiful as you.*

Why did sad songs speak so deeply to her and lift her mood? Did they underscore how sweet life was in its simplicity? The morning sun glinted on her upturned face, the brisk breeze filled each breath. It was a privilege to make a difference because of her own suffering.

She had struggled with her sanity for years in her marriage, and separation seemed freeing at times. Yet she missed her man and wept with the women inside who were separated from families in crisis, aching for reunion.

She had, one Thanksgiving, wanted to stick the carving knife in her own heart, to end the pain. Marriage had set up such impossible expectations. And she was so hurt by the way she had been raped on a research trip, and how that had consumed her and her husband for years.

But even that wound was healing with time, distance, acceptance. Her husband had texted her after the tornado, invited her for coffee, and Hope had searched his warm expression for a promise of reunions to come. Perhaps. One day.

Reassured, Hope had worked through the weekend after the tornado. The adrenaline of surviving, the miracle of life—Greta's, Cinny's, hers and Emily's—had permitted her to draw up the nursery budget, prepare policy, articulate mission and vision and even work up returns on investment.

This morning before seven, the warden had forwarded the facility repair blueprints, and she had worked with those too. She was ready for detailed meetings with him, and his superiors, to review and plan next steps.

One thing she knew, separating mothers and babies topped the list of ways to deepen pain, aggravate mental illness and derail restoration and healing. She had read Claudia J. Ford, a social worker who'd adopted a prostitute's baby. The edgy memoir title had caught Hope's eye in the prison library. *Why do I scream at God for the Rape of Babies?*

Hope found the answer deep inside. Ford was called to the hospital and asked if she would care for a prostitute's raped baby.

Only with her consent, would the surgical team attempt repair and reconstruction. Ford had struggled with slim odds of the child's full restoration, but finally agreed. The baby grew into a joyful, dancing child, and the author realized the answer. It was because God was saying, *Do something about it.*

Like Ford, Hope wanted to give her life to restoring hope in traumatized, hurting women and children. It was a pursuit she couldn't put off, a path she trod every day, a door she must keep pushing open. She entered Administration and was buzzed into the inner offices.

Warden Torres opened to her knock, and flung out his arms, a huge grin spreading across his tanned, lined face.

Hope stepped inside, warmth rising in her cheeks. "It's lousy to see you, too, Warden." In another time and place she might have walked into his embrace, secure despite storm and tornado.

Instead, she walked to his desk. "Roman, look at these." She laid out her line item budget, covering three nursery staff, furnishings and supplies.

The warden put on half-moon reading glasses and studied it carefully.

"And look at this comparison." Hope flipped to a second page, holding her breath, hoping she wasn't pushing too hard. It compared costs of repairing the lockup facility to converting it to a nursery. "If prisoners paint their own nursery rooms, and we convert the shattered building to a one-story nursery with play yard, the conversion would cost the DOC only $250,000, compared to restoring it to confinement unit requirements, costing $500,000."

She opened her binder to a business proposal that showed the state saving money due to moms improved behavior and their qualifying for early release.

She turned the page toward Roman while he read the mission statement she had crafted. It was clear, she believed, if not simple. "To rehabilitate women prisoners by strengthening mother-child bonds and restoring primary attachments in a safe, secure environment for mother and child."

The return on investment was next. Her heart beat in her ribcage and she stilled it with a hand to her chest. "It's good, right?" she asked. It belonged on his bookshelf next to the black, red-titled tome, *ROI.*"

He looked up and smiled. "Yes, you've been thorough. I like how you include reduced costs when women don't return to prison. And you add that women who increase family bonding time, decrease their chaos. Clever, Hope."

He studied it further, his dimples deepening. "You're pulling the rug out from under private prison's profits from numbers of prisoners. You focus on more global, community economics."

Hope nodded, stilling her thoughts and damming the rush of words.

"Yes, I see it. This value extended to prisoners' families who experience reduced costs, burdens and traumas of having family in prison. You've even drawn a process map of how nurseries enrich impoverished communities."

"Chaplain Emily did that." Hope sat and folded her jumpy hands in her lap, the caffeine and lack of sleep didn't help.

Roman examined it carefully. "Hold on. This depicts prison nurseries helping to reduce the odds of one in three black boys, and one in six Hispanic boys, going to prison?"

Hope rose on shaky legs, cautious in her conclusions. "It's quite a claim, I know, but it's borne out by research."

"I would do anything to change those odds." Roman turned, full-faced, stance opened.

Hope read his consent, and rushed in. "And yet, in my experience, many people inside are repentant, redeemed and ready to give back to their community. We need to create a place where they are no longer held hostage to the worst thing they've ever done."

"Hope, Hope." Roman took off his glasses and studied her. "That's your spirit, infusing this place."

"Not mine, Warden. It's the Lord's, especially in visionaries like Cinny."

"You are so idealistic. After all this time, you should be properly jaded."

"Sure, but let me finish." She shifted in her boots, wanting to run a marathon, but knowing she should walk.

"No, Hope, let me finish. Congratulations! You've done a marvelous job."

Hope felt a spark as he gripped her hand. "Would you meet me at my papa's Mexican restaurant in Quincy tonight, six?"

Hope swallowed hard. "Is that permitted?"

"*Si.* I'm permitting it, to celebrate your genius, and review your proposal more thoroughly."

Hope hesitated.

"I assure you, you will make an old man very happy."

Hope stepped back. "But, sir, you're not an old man."

"Not me, Sister." The warden teased her like she was some cloistered nun.

She ducked her head.

"My papa has ordered me to bring in my colleagues. He's trying to build his business."

"Well... I-I have more to show you." Hope flipped to the next section. Listed were certificate programs in *Meeting your Baby's Needs, Finding Community Support, Self-care, Stimulating your Child's Development* and *Producing Happy, Confident Children.* "Each of these programs is accompanied by online videos."

Hope looked up. "In fact, without early cuddling and nurturing—"

"Well, are you going to say yes?"

"—you can't produce secure children. Warden, are you listening?"

"Yes, are you?"

"Okay, Roman, tonight at six. Your papa's restaurant."

"Thank you. Now, how did you cover this so thoroughly?"

"I consulted with the prison nurseries in Illinois and New York, and the residential community program in Alabama. They not only sent me their documents, but reviewed and edited our adaptations. Emily helped with the policy and process map."

Next, Hope laid out Cinny's sketches of mothers and babies stacking blocks, reading picture books and playing on toddlers' swings. "Sir, may we get Cinnamon Rose to paint these to accompany the proposal?"

"Hey, that's my grubby notebook paper! I had no idea she was going to turn it into art."

"Yes, Roman, she could make a killing off your notebook paper." Hope pushed up her sleeves. "Do you see how all our resources are being stretched and multiplied?"

"I'm just following your lead." Roman opened a drawer and handed Hope a jumbo sketchbook and box of acrylic paint tubes. "I had my secretary order these, like you asked."

Hope was amazed at the generous size of the sketchbook and acrylic paint tubes. He had spared no expense. Was this from his own pocket? She accepted the gift, permitting his hand to linger on hers.

"Thank you." She breathed. She had to think clearly. "But wait, Cinny's here, giving her deposition in the conference room. You can give it to her yourself."

Roman followed her to the door. "I am so indebted to you, Hope."

"Your reward will be Cinny's paintings capturing the press and legislators at the Capitol when we present this next month."

"I still have to face the Corrections committee under threat of firing for dirty UAs."

Hope nodded and murmured, "Yes, and may God save you." Hope permitted Roman to open the door and guide her through, hand on her spine. A solemn waltz.

The phone rang as they passed his assistant's office, and the woman signaled Roman to stop. Placing her hand over the receiver, she held up her hand. "Warden, it's for you. Cinny's sister, Nikita Rose."

39
Cinnamon Answers

Security Chief Ramsey released my handcuffs at the door to his private conference room, his dark ponytail, high Seminole cheekbones glowed. "Just do your best, okay?" His broad shoulders filled the doorway, and his voice boomed. "Cinnamon Rose," he announced.

To me, he added, "You're allowed to take a break; I'll be at my desk. Just knock if you need out, okay?" He closed the door, his footfalls thudding to his desk. He was like the protective father I had longed for all my life. Chief Ramsey was genuine.

I faced two young men in dark suits with legal pads and laptops. One was tall and lean with cool, blue eyes and tie. The other was compact and muscled, with dark frame glasses, thoughtful brown eyes and green tie.

The one with a Gator-lanyard smiled, raising one eyebrow comically, as though he didn't care that his green tie clashed with his blue-checked shirt and blue-orange lanyard. He reached a warm hand. "Hello Cinnamon. This is Leonard and I'm Andrew. Call me Drew."

"Call me Len." The tall one straightened and leaned back, stiffer, more reserved.

Drew looked familiar, as though I had seen him before. But where? "Call me Cinny."

I shivered a little as I took the office chair opposite them. What did these school boys know about me? Technically, I was an accessory since I knew about the Cheese Puffs gang, had known for months, and hadn't told. Women here were serving years for what they knew and didn't tell. Would these attorneys be willing, or able, to separate me from the charges they were pursuing for others? I was dependent on them for leniency.

A drip coffee maker burbled on the credenza behind them and filled the room with a dark roast aroma. It was like Nana Mama's cozy kitchen on chilly winter mornings.

I breathed it in, unable to resist. "Mmm, that smells good."

Drew rose and poured me a Styrofoam cupful. "Cream and sugar?" His bent, over-sized head; that sweet, serving presence. Who was he and where had I seen him before?

"Just cream, please." He brought several creamers and a stir stick to the table.

For a moment, my jitters subsided as I breathed in the warm steam. "You can't believe how I've missed brewed coffee." I poured in the creamers and took one small sip and then another, savoring the dark creamy taste. "Mm, especially isolated in lockup, and especially after the horrid tornado."

"Yes, I heard it was bad here." Caring, friendly Drew was striking a cord with me. Where had I heard his voice before? "How did everyone do?"

"Oh dear, it nearly killed Officer Greta. She threw herself over me and was struck by flying metal that would have sliced me in two. They operated, and she's recovering now."

"That is fortunate," Drew said.

"Yes, it is. She gave me this butterfly clip." I touched the ornate clip in my hair, and took another sip, and another, savoring every drop. "And so is this, thank you."

"Oh, you're making it look so good, I almost forgot to pour us some. Len, are you having some?"

Len nodded, staring at the screen and keyboard. "Thanks, Drew."

Drew rose, took off his jacket, hung it over his chair, and poured two more. He offered Len some creamers, sugar packets and a stir stick.

I shifted in my worn blue scrubs, pulling down my sweatshirt sleeves. I'd have hell to pay from the women inside if I ratted on them and they found out. Would the lawyers understand if I hesitated? I tried to read them through the fluorescent glare in their glasses.

I sipped more creamy coffee and glanced out across the parking lot full of red, gold and silver cars, into a spreading bay in the meadow. Tangy bay leaves spiced Nana Mama's savory chicken soup in those uncertain days when Mama faced life in prison. Before we ate, Nana Mama folded her calloused hands. *Help us to sit quietly before you like King David, to play our flutes even when the king is trying to spear us to the wall. Help us to trust you completely.*

The attorneys stirred and sipped their coffees. Drew loosened his tie and sat forward. So down-home. "Cinny, we represent the Department of Corrections against the drug dealers inside Rocky Comfort Correctional Facility. Our goal is to end drug trafficking inside this facility. To achieve that, we're prepared to offer you immunity and commute your sentence if you tell us all you know about the cheese puff drugs."

"May we record you?" Len stared at his computer screen.

"Wait, I need to consider this carefully." I folded my arms, trying to stop my shivering and still my beating heart. These men were offering me what I needed and wanted. Yet they looked so relaxed in their dress shirts. Did they know I could be sock-locked, stabbed or smothered in my sleep by any number of angry women? "How will you grant me immunity from the cheese puff gang?"

"The cheese puff gang?" Drew's eyes reflected a kaleidoscope of emerald, blue and orange. "That's what they call themselves?"

"Oh, no." I paused, choosing my words carefully. "I'm sure they don't call themselves anything. They barely admit what they're doing. No, that's my name for them."

Len had started typing something, but paused, his eyebrow raised in question.

I nodded at him. "Okay, go ahead." I wanted him to take down every word I was about to say. "Cigarettes are still legal on the outside, and Florida's mayors sell roxies while legislators snort coke. We never see them inside. What do you wanna bet they get their records wiped?"

Drew breathed deeply, nodding. "Yes, yes, good point." His willingness to listen reminded me of someone else I couldn't quite name.

"What's the difference between us and them?"

"What do you think?" Drew's tone was soft, gentle.

I inhaled. "No difference, except class. Poor people are punished; rich people are rewarded."

"Agreed, I grant you that." He reached his smooth hand, palm up. "I think we should change that, and I'd like to start with you. I want to offer you all I can, immunity and protection, as much as you need."

I took his hand, feeling a surprising warmth and strength. He seemed concerned about me and my safety, just like—like…. "That's fine, but first I want to know how."

"Cinny, we can't realistically follow you everywhere. But we can move anyone you implicate—anyone you fear—out of your way, into a more secure facility."

"Do you realize, Mr. Drew, that my ex-boyfriend threatened me from prison, and the moment he got out, killed my father and boyfriend? Your world is safe as Finland; mine is deadly as Rwanda."

"Mine was deadly too," Drew unbuttoned his cuffs, and rolled up his sleeves, revealing webbed scars on both forearms. "This is from a meth explosion my Mum sparked. I was lucky to escape."

Len stopped typing and gaped at Drew's arms.

I gasped. "I know your mom! She's my good friend in here!"

Drew pulled his shirt sleeves down and buttoned them. "Lexis? How is she?"

"She's great. Prays for you all the time. You'd be so proud of her."

Drew nodded. "I believe it. I've felt her prayers all my life. She's a good woman who just got involved with the wrong people."

"Mr. Drew, she is hoping to see you again! You should try to visit her while you're here."

Len cleared his throat and tapped a few keys.

Drew glanced at him, then back at me. "Maybe so, but this is about you, and how we're trying to get at the truth and protect you."

"Yes, I'll be a marked woman when I walk out of here. How will you protect me then? You know there's a woman in here with a scar face?"

"Meaning?" Drew trained his focus on me.

"The guy she ratted on tied her down and cut her from eye to chin." I dragged my finger down my cheek. "Lucky he didn't blind her."

"I'll say." Drew glanced at Len who raised an eyebrow, and paused in his typing again.

"You're right, Cinny." Drew's brow furrowed. "We can't completely protect you but we'll do our best to move people out of your way. Right, Len?"

"Right." Len resumed typing.

Compared to Len, Drew was more open, more understanding of me as a person with feelings, experiences and fears. He helped me feel I could trust in him. It seemed he might be able to help me out.

"For you, then, I'll talk." I searched Drew's brown eyes. "But may God help me if no one else can."

"Thank you, Cinny. I know this must be hard for you. May I record you?"

I nodded.

Drew pressed a button on his iPhone and started writing on his legal pad. Len continued typing.

"Officer Mario Damon is my dead boyfriend's cousin; we used to play hide-n-seek and cops-n-robbers. So, one day, after I came back to prison, he needed to ditch a Cheese Puffs bag fast. I was digging a hole in a flower bed and he threw it in. I teased him about trying to grow Cheese Puffs. He said there were smokes inside and to mind the g-code. That pissed me off. Just by telling me, he had made me an accessory."

Drew nodded gravely. "Yes, I can see how that compromised you."

"Hold on, let me get that down." Len typed rapidly, then paused. "The g-code?"

"Yeah, you know, gangsta-code. Don't rat out your buds to the po-po. I didn't know how or when the Cheese Puffs gig started, but when the governor banned cigarettes in state prisons, the racket was on. Prisoners got antsy and demanding, and would pay $10 for a smuggled smoke. Damon and the canteen workers somehow, somewhere opened the Cheese Puffs, added cigarettes and glued the bags shut again."

"Can you give us names?" Drew flipped to a clean page, pen poised.

I stalled. How could I mention Reese ducking behind the greenhouse or lighting up on the track? I wanted immunity, but why would I turn in my friends for smoking? "You have the dirty drug tests, right?"

Drew looked up.

Len frowned and cleared his throat.

"Most of us inside are trying to go straight—"

A rumbling engine and backing beep pierced the room and I dove away from the window.

Part V

Healing Rises

Behind the waterfall (Source unknown)

40
Andrew Wakes

Hello, my name is Andrew. I'm a recovering co-dependent. I miss my birth mum, but I was given a new life outside while she lives hers inside.

Cinny lunged from the window, and I glanced at the truck backing right toward us. It was a trash truck filled with tornado debris. Len and I dove for the opposite wall. The truck swerved last minute, but hooked the corner and shook the walls.

"Whew, close call." Len said

"Yeah, cutting corners with tornado repair?" My hands shook and I waited for the engine racket to fade.

Cinny and Len laughed nervously.

I laid down my pen and picked up the coffee pot. "Well, does anyone want some calming caffeine?" I poured while Len and Cinny held out their cups, all of us still shaking a little. Caramel liquid filled the Styrofoam and bubbles rose and clung to the edges.

I watched the bubbles burst as I stirred in creamer. I knew enough, had known before I was adopted at age six, about rolling your own weed or tobacco. You cooked the hash and soaked the toke in it. But my birth mum's friends had drugs of choice.

To Cinny I said, "So what if I paid $30 and got one hash toke when I wanted ice?" I was always careful to use "I" not "you" or "they" when interviewing a witness. Making the statements about myself, avoided accusing anyone else.

Cinny squirmed and scratched her inked hand. "Poke," it said.

"Remember your commutation," I prompted. "I know this is hard."

Cinny laid her other hand on top. "Salad." Poke Salad Annie? Had her mother served time too? I knew the guilt she must have felt, the shame or responsibility for her mom's choices, or her own. And there were consequences. Sad as it was, the addictive flash of a meth high could cause brain changes, sheering off dopamine receptors, and leaving users without natural highs.

"I don't know." Cinny shrugged. "Other than Hope finding ice in one of the bags."

Len still shaking, pushed his chair back. "I need a break."

Cinny rose too, and knocked on the door. Chief Ramsey led her across the hall to the women's room.

I stretched and gazed across the meadow surrounding the prison. My reflection in the window showed olive skin tones, dark curly hair, broad smile, like my birth mum's. She was just yards away somewhere on this broken compound. Dare I see her or not? Oh, to clear my confusion by galloping my chestnut mare Chance across that inviting expanse, her mane flying.

I strode down the corridor, nodded to the receptionist and stepped into the bright cold. A guard was walking the perimeter, hunched against the wind. The clearing assured direct sight of the fence breaches. A constant watch was set to stop anyone trying throw in drugs or cell phones.

I paced the parking lot, annoyed by a constant beeping from across the highway. The wind rippled the water in the storm pond, whipped through my hair and up my shirt sleeves. My scars burned in the cold and I headed for my Prius to get a hiking jacket.

When Mum went to prison, her friends came to see me in the hospital, calling me "Poke Salad Andy...." I had smiled but missed her terribly, crying hot tears into my ears when they left. My burning arms cradled carefully at my side, kept me facing the ceiling, an ache like a peach pit stuck in my throat. My big sister, Pixie—named for her cute, pointed chin and dark-haired widow's peak—found me that way. She sat beside my bed, smoothing my hair with trembling fingers smelling of tobacco.

"You know our mum wants the best for you," she said. "She wants you to live with a nice married lady who can give you more than she can."

I wanted my own mum, like she used to be, dark eyes laughing, brown hair flying as we drove to the corner store for Slurpees. "Drew." That was her special name for me. "Drew an ace," was her special phrase. "Means you're too blessed to be stressed."

"Mum" was my special name for her, from the public TV Britcoms that streamed on our no cable TV. They kept me laughing at screwball families, like the Buckets in "Keeping Up Appearances." The Buckets were so stiff and fake, compared to ours. But mum's friends ended up partying all night, lying around the sofa or floor like zombies.

They started cooking meth and turned into the insomniac, agitated, living dead. The house stank like cat pee, and stayed messy and dirty. Mum got worried and panicky, too afraid to take me to my school play, a friend's birthday, or even trick-or-treating. She had stopped functioning as a mum.

In the prison parking lot, I closed the Prius door, put on my jacket, stuck my chilled hands in my pockets and headed back to Administration.

In the hospital, my arms healed from the meth burns, but I hugged my pillow to fill the giant hole at my core. If only…. If only Mum had gotten better. If only I'd been able to stop her. If only she hadn't left me and gone to prison.

At first when Mom Joy Weaver came to sit with me in the hospital, I froze. She was a school teacher with gray hair, wire rim glasses and long dresses. But when she spoke, her voice was like a lark and her songs were haunting with strange words like "abide" and "eventide." Her husband Day—lanky, bald, plaid-shirt— joined her with his melodic tenor, and the words seemed written for me. "…help of the helpless, oh, abide with me."

Day teased me about "shirking" work. He promised to make me feed horses and run the dogs when we got home. A week later, Joy and Day took me home to a bright yellow house in south Tallahassee with acres of meadows and woods. They made me pancakes and hot chocolate on cold school mornings and helped me with homework. At their Old Mennonite church, a rock band struck up dance praises, and I found myself moving along. *I'm trading my sorrows*.... Women in net bonnets that Mom Joy called *sin-sifters*, swayed and clapped, their apron dresses flying.

"We're old, but not stuffy," the Weavers said. In fact, they had a fun streak. They took me to barn dances and taught me the fiddle. They read from the Bible at breakfast and Harry Potter at bedtime.

I dreamt of being the despised wizard who had to hide his scars and real identity among muggles. I galloped across the meadow on Chance with a quidditch bat Day made. I even had a best friend named Ron. Well, Rhonda, but everyone called her Ron. She'd ride over on her bay named Crookshank and we'd pretend to hit bludgers and grab the snitch. Mom Joy sewed me a hooded red cape that covered my scars—around muggles.

Don't focus on your scars. Day's voice was deep and gentle. *Your problem is only as big as you make it*.

I gripped the cold metal handle of the heavy door to Administration and pulled against the wind. My cold fingers trembled a little when I showed my visitor's badge to the braided receptionist and was buzzed into the corridor. I had tried to live up to my name when the Weavers told me that Andrew was the trusting disciple. He had trusted God with a little boys' lunch, and Jesus multiplied it to feed 5,000 people—with twelve baskets left over. I would try to trust God about seeing my mother again, too.

I heard Chief Ramsey's voice in the conference room and knew the others were waiting. I rushed to the men's room to comb my wavy, windblown hair, peering at my serious, boyish face; angular yet large—like my mom's. Why hadn't I written her more than a few Christmas and birthday cards?

No use envying others their height, Dad Day had said, stooping a little. *You want that, you'll have to take the whole package. And you're ten times smarter than most kids your age*. He had given me confidence and encouraged me to study hard and use my gifts.

I took off my glasses, rinsed and rubbed them on my soft jacket lining, then put them on again, bringing the world into sharp focus. I stepped into the hallway, caught a whiff of lemon polish, and Len heading from the vending machine. That string bean was always eating, hungry as a wild animal.

When I turned eight, Joy handed me a letter. It was from my birth mum asking me to visit her in prison. I read her scratchy-pen writing. *Please, son, come see me. I'm clean and sober now going on two years. I'm doing all I can to improve myself and make you proud of me. I'm taking my Class C drivers so I can drive trucks, and cosmetology so I can fix trucker's hair—haha. I will be so ready to make it up to you when I get out of here.*

I looked up, and read the doubt in Mom Joy's blue eyes. Those eyes had poured so much love into mine, morning and evening over cereal and soup, walking me to the school bus, taking me to soccer practice and violin lessons. Dad Weaver, too, had sat on the sofa, arm slung over my shoulder, doing math with me. I had handed the letter back, chilled to think my birth mum might take it all away and drag me back to the zombie house.

"Maybe I can just write her a card?" So, we picked out a card that said, *God's doing more than your faith can imagine.* We could hardly send it without promising to see her. The next month, we did.

She had aged, her brown hair turning salt and pepper, her cheeks sunken and her body skeletal. Her beauty was marred by a chipped tooth and pock marks. She had aged so quickly on meth. But she was clean again, and had been for years. In fact, she was a Lamp Steps leader.

She could not stop smiling, laughing and crying all at the same time over seeing me, and hearing that I was riding horses, playing fiddle and acing math. She hung onto me so tight when it came to letting go. "Thank God, I Drew an ace."

We returned to the conference room where Len ripped open a pack of peanuts and offered me some. I waved them away and he poured a handful in his mouth.

"Len, we shouldn't be too discouraged about Cinny's reluctance to turn others in. I think we have enough evidence now to testify in the Corrections committee."

"Okay, I'll answer that email right away. I think it's due today."

We took our places at the table, Len powered on his computer, and I checked the recorded notes on my iPhone. Chief

Ramsey opened the door and let Cinny in, then bowed out and closed the door, thudding back to his desk.

I smiled at Cinny, and she sat forward, clean hands clasped. She had washed off "Poke" and "Salad." I grinned, rubbing my knuckles in a gesture of understanding.

Cinny laughed and sat back. Her colorful butterfly clasp bobbed in her braided poof, and her smooth, full-featured face glowed. How would she fare on the outside? Would she be able to keep her children safe? She certainly seemed capable, secure and relaxed for the moment.

I would have to file her commutation up the chain of command, and wanted to vouch for her in solid terms. The people in my church believed Christ could restore even the brain chemistry of addicts.

And the prisoners certainly carried that message deep inside. But back outside, their lives were often unstable. They had given up years of earnings while sucking scant resources from poor communities. Landlords wouldn't rent to felons, and those who did, took risks. Ex-felons struggled in minimum wage, mind-numbing, body-bruising jobs like housekeeping, dry-cleaning or kitchen work. No longer eligible for welfare, they fell behind in rent and utilities, getting evicted and having to give up their children again. They couldn't vote for better leaders, and often needed the support of entire programs, and church communities. Often they needed years, even decades, to get back on their feet.

Len clicked some keys and waited for his computer to initialize. "Almost there, give me a few minutes."

I had visited my birth mum Lexis a few times when she got out, too, but she was struggling to find stable work and couldn't afford to do things with me. It was the Weavers who found her a job cleaning an old estate. All might have gone well if my sister hadn't relapsed and her dealer hadn't threatened to kill her if she didn't pay up. The Weavers tried to understand why mum stole from the estate to save my sister, and land in jail again. Her life was still too filled with crisis, Joy said.

Cinny was sketching something on the table with her finger and I tore a few pages from my legal pad and found an extra pen for her. She grinned and clicked it, sketching with quick confidence.

I navigated on my iPhone to the DOC website. A click on my mum's name would bring up her mug shot, history and charges. I hesitated a moment, wondering if I'd see the vacant eyes of the living dead or the sparkling ones I'd first loved. The image populated and her brown eyes were clear yet somber after years inside, her hair still long and wavy, was turning white. Yet I recognized her humble heart in the grainy photo and knew I would always soften to the first face I'd ever loved.

I gazed at Cinny's drawing, a room full of children and mothers in prison scrubs. "May I see that?"

"Yes, I'm drawing the vision of a prison nursery—making it real!"

I gasped. "That is an amazing idea and stunning vision. Also, you have real talent! How old are these children in your vision?"

"Oh, they have to be birth to 18 months, born to moms with shorter sentences, so they can transition together. That's the idea for now, anyway."

Chief Ramsey's thudding step and knock at the door interrupted us. He opened and brought us each a glass of ice water.

"Thank you!" I said.

"Okay, ready." Len looked up.

I turned on my recorder, repeating my last question. "What if I wanted crack or crystals?" My purpose was not just to learn more about selling the hardest drugs inside but whether Cinny knew more. I wanted to be sure she was not personally entangled, because then she wouldn't make a good witness on cross examination.

"I thought about that on break." Cinny looked pensive and seemed genuinely puzzled. "I think you took what you got and traded—or sold it."

I nodded, believing her. She wasn't playing stupid. She really didn't know. She would make a good witness for the state.

She pushed up her sleeve, revealing an arrow-pierced heart, *Love*.

Was it a feeling or a choice? Both my moms had filled me with love, and Mom Joy had showed me how to love anyone, even me, a needy child. I did love my own ex-addict Mum, even to the point of completely forgiving her for the scars she'd left me. That's what she had ensured by giving me up, that I would be loved lavishly, and perhaps be able to love her again.

"Sure," Len said, "But how did they avoid dirty drug tests?"

"Well, a lot of them didn't, which is why the warden and chaplain found out. The dirty drug tests could've got them all fired." Cinny paused, letting Len catch up with his typing.

"The rest probably drank bleach—" Cinny shuddered. "It's a crazy old rumor but some people still do it. Put a few drops diluted in a gallon of water. I don't know. Could be the gallon of water that cleanses you, I suppose."

"Oh boy." Drew winced, his throat burning and his skin tightening from his scalp to his scarred arms. His mum had drunk it in milk, when she was trying to keep her job. He swayed slightly.

Len steadied him. "You okay?"

Drew nodded and turned to Cinny. "Go on."

"That's all I know."

"Why would Officer Damon make you an accessory?" Drew asked, trying to think of every question on cross-examination, if he put her on the stand. "Did you also buy Cheese Puffs?"

"No!" Cinny exclaimed, half-rising. "No, you don't understand. He may have wanted me to. But since Tony's death, I have a new man; Jesus."

Anthony rose too, reaching out, touching her hand. "That's good, Cinny." He now knew exactly how to word her clemency order. He knew the governor, had met him at an adoption event. They had made a fast connection, and the governor had offered to help in any way. This would be the way.

"We are trying to understand, Cinny. Remember? I'm Poke Salad Andy."

"Yes, yes you are." Cinny bowed slightly and sat again. "Look, I've already lost my dad, brother and boyfriend. Officer Damon is his cousin, the uncle of my baby, Tony, Jr."

"Oh dear, Cinny. How do you manage all that? And how do we protect you from your own family?"

Len looked up but kept typing.

"Look." Cinny straightened, pulling herself to her tallest. "My family wants the best for us—and Damon isn't right. But he may want to clear his conscience."

"I guess we all do." Realizing the interview was over, Drew extended his hand.

Cinny gripped it. "Getting his confession is worth a try, and it may protect me in the long run."

"Thank you again, Cinny." Len rose and shook her hand, too.

Cinny knocked to be released.

But it was the warden, not Chief Ramsey who opened the door.

41
Cinnamon Rewarded

Hello, my name is Cinny, still a grateful, recovering addict.

The warden held out a large sketchbook and acrylic paints. My heart leaped as he handed them to me.

"Cinny, I'd like to present these to you to help us present our nursery project."

I understood the investment and burden. Could I do it? Genuine studio art supplies would certainly help.

Chief Ramsey and Chaplain Hope stepped around from behind him and shook my hand. Drew and Len joined them, wishing me well.

The warden pushed his hair back. "Also, not to alarm you, but your sister called. We offered to call her back when you were through in here. We can talk on the phone in my office."

I nodded, trembling, wondering who was in trouble. Tony or Annie, Mama or Kita?

The warden led us to his office, signaling Hope to come along, her *Starry Night* shoulder bag, loaded with binders and notebooks.

"Hey Chaplain." I patted the backpack. "Those yellow stars, Van Gogh invented that pigment!"

She paused, surprised. "I did not know, Cinny. You always amaze me. You should be teaching art in here."

I grinned. "Maybe, one day."

The warden set chairs around his desk and entered Kita's number in his phone. I held my breath and Hope patted my knee, smiling, her cheeks glowed golden in the light like her shirt.

Nikita picked up on the first ring, "Hello, Nikita speaking." Then there was Tony cooing. And in the background, pings and whistles from video games.

"Hello, Nikita?" The warden motioned us closer. "I'll put you on speaker, if that's okay?"

"Yes." Her melodic voice filled the room loud and clear.

"Go ahead." The warden gestured to us. "We're all here, Cinny, Chaplain Hope and myself. Tell us why you called."

"Hey Kit—!" I hardly ever called her that, but my voice cracked. I didn't realize until that moment how the deposition had drained me.

"Well, I hope it's okay to say this. Hang on. I'm going to put Tony down. He's crawling now, Sissy."

"Cool! I want to see that!"

"Go ahead, Kita." Hope's forehead wrinkled. "Tell us why you called."

"Cinny told me about your vision of a prison nursery."

"Yes, we've been working on a proposal." Hope pulled out her binder and opened it to show me, leafing through to my sketches.

"Oh, that's great, Cinny! But I'm calling because we've been evicted."

"Oh Kita." I cut in, gripping Hope's hand.

"Yes, I'm having trouble finding a place for all of us, that we can afford."

I gasped and tears sprang to my eyes. "Where are you staying now?"

"We're at Mama's but she's rehabbing from her knee replacement. It's too much for her. She needs peace and quiet, and I want a safe place for kids—not right on the railroad tracks."

I looked at Chaplain Hope, and whispered, *"Can you help?"*

She nodded. "Nikita, Chaplain Hope speaking. I am going to put out an email requesting help with funding and finding you a place. On a park somewhere, perfect for kids."

"Thanks Chaplain Hope! Cinny, I still have your graphic novel. I was going to publish it and sell the books but it got muddy in the eviction. I took it to the publisher and she's working on restoring it."

"Thank you, Sissy."

"Nikita, Chaplain Hope here. I think we can find a patron to buy several boxes of books for fund-raising purposes."

"That is exactly what we need. Here's Tony again, chewing on the phone." Tony cooed again.

"Nikita, this is Warden Torres speaking. Would you be willing to make a statement during our hearing at the capitol?"

"Sure, Warden. What shall I say?"

Hope took the phone. "You can explain what it's like to double your family overnight, why we need a nursery, to relieve the burden on prison families."

"And bring the kids!" I cut in.

"Exactly, they'll see the need then, not just hear about it."

"Sure, if you can, bring the kids," the warden said. "It's scheduled for Earth Day, 10 a.m. You may have to take them out of school, but most schools will be attending the courtyard exhibits anyway."

"I will do my best, sir. When will the nursery be ready?"

"We'll have to get the budget amendment passed first. Your story will help."

"I'll do my best, Warden."

"Meanwhile, thank you for offering to send that email, Chaplain." Nikita had calmed way down, the video games quieted, and Tony cried into the phone. "Come on, Tony." She heaved a heavy weight with an *ooph*.

I realized how much I wanted to hold him again.

"Well thank you Nikita." The warden smiled.

Hope leaned forward. "Yes, meanwhile, we will find the perfect place for you and the children."

I lifted up my sketchbook and paints. "And Kita, guess what the warden gave me?"

"A reduced sentence?"

The warden nodded. "We're working on it."

"It's a giant sketchbook and paints so I can paint the nursery ideas for our presentation.

"Get out, Cinny!"

"Right, Kita? Please hug my babies special for me." I hugged the sketchbook and paints close to my heart.

"Okay, I'll see you all on Earth Day!"

The warden called Chief Ramsey's extension and the chief entered, holding up the handcuffs.

It would be best if I didn't look like the state's evidence on the way back to confinement. He tucked my sketchbook and paints under his big arm and I turned, hands behind my back, submitting to the cuffs.

It calmed me to have him escort me along the corridor and past the women inside.

"Our priority is your safety, Ma'am." Ramsey's voice was deep and soothing.

Hope caught up as we hit the brisk breeze outside. "Cinny, I want to consult you as soon as you have a few sketches ready for our project." She adjusted her shoulder bag, eyebrows raised.

"I'll do my best, Miss Hope." My voice was pitched and amazed even to my ears.

"We depend so much on your vision, Cinny."

42
Reese Steps Up

Hello, still Reese, grateful, recovering addict.

Reese walked the track, filling her lungs with fresh air, feeling good about her writing. She was pretty sure Ms. Lawson, the paralegal, could use her story to appeal her sentence.

Meanwhile her poetry assignment was due. "Tell a story," the English teacher had said. "Doesn't have to be your story, but should be one you know well. Tell it fresh, make it real—take me there in vivid detail. Surprise me."

I'll surprise you, Reese practically sang as she picked up her pace, breaking into a light jog. He'd be amazed how creative the women in here could be. She could zap a birthday cake in the microwave using peanut butter packets, butter pats, cocoa packets, and instant coffee. It tasted just like rich, gooey brownies. Or how about the ramen noodle-tuna bake Mindy invented?

Reese's long legs carried her easily past white-haired, sparkling Lexis. She'd been beside herself ever since her daughter, Pixie, had joined us at Rocky Comfort. Because even if you never want your child to go to prison, sometimes it's better than dying in the street. Now there was a ballad Reese could write. Lexis had been in the Florida prison system for 17 years. She'd come here to finish out her final years, months and days.

Lexis waved, pock marks dimpling her cheeks. It was hard to believe, she'd never used a cell phone or sent a text message— didn't know a bar phone from a flip phone from a smart phone. Her sentence was so long, she'd had to give away her children. Yet her daughter had reunited with her here—not every mother's dream. But, as Lexis said, there was more freedom, drug-free inside than in a haze outside. Lexis beamed whenever she and Pixie could spend time together.

Reese didn't want to interrupt. Instead, she dropped into the shade of the gray stone gymnasium, pulled a pen and paper from her pocket and jotted some random lines.

A pen is a door.
A pen is a door to half thoughts, shards, bit pieces;
It forms letters, small words, whole pictures.
O pen, open my mind.

She heard a beat and wrote. When she looked up, Pixie had peeled off and Lexis was walking alone. Her tanned skin was a sharp contrast to her white hair, making her look fit, trim and youthful even though she was at least 60.

"Hey, Lexis," Reese called, "May I join you?"

"Sure, chain-mate" Lexis said.

Reese laughed. She had almost forgotten where they first met. The unnatural closeness the first time they came to prison years ago, chained together on the bus, strangers who suddenly occupied the same space. They couldn't move without coordinating each step.

"What's happening?" Reese asked.

"Oh, Pixie was talking about her kids. The baby is starting to walk and the oldest starts preschool soon. And, did you hear? I'm leading her group in Lamp Steps."

"You go, Lexis!" Reese tried to match her shorter stride around the track. "Does that mean you can be my sponsor?"

"Sure, what behaviors are you working on these days?"

"Getting my homework done." Reese knew it would be trouble to list more than one. Sponsors kept you accountable for everything.

"Okay, rec is the perfect time. Right?" Alexis tipped up her radiant face.

"Yes, I've written a poem for my English class. May I read it to you?"

Lexis nodded. "Let's sit a bit." She led Reese back to the shade.

"*True Blue.* That's the title. And it's dedicated to you."
Reese folded her long legs and read, while Lexis listened, nodding.

"No more wearing blue, not even jeans.
Unless they're black—I'm done with that!
No more taking my own t.p. or sitting down
With all the guards around.
I'll close the door when I leave here,
And leave my flip flops on the floor
When I step into my shower—all alone!

Don't get me wrong, I have no shame
After all the strip-search-shake-down games
To keep us humble and to blame.
I'll be so free— when I leave here—
In 20 years.

Got my own bed-bath-beyond;
Bar of soap deodorant,
Butter for my hair condition,
Glitter eye shadow rubbed from greeting cards,
Lipstick smeared from glossy ads,
My fashion sense has never been so lean—or keen.

Why 20 years, you ask, when others got just two?
Grand theft larceny—awful—
Wish I could give it back.
But I work hard, earning nothing;
Costing taxpayers buckets while private prisons
Rake in profits. Does that make cents?"

Lexis shook her head. "No."
"That's rhetorical."
"Whatever that means." Lexis laughed. "Go on."

"I had a crazy lawyer, too,
Didn't take the plea—no—
No, he thought he'd win
But he is gone while I live on with all the pain.

And staying sane while guards rain down,
"Bitches," "hos" and "theivin' liars."
(Who they talkin' to?)
I focus on white clouds, azure skies
Sapphire like forget-me-nots;
My family did—will you?"

Razorwire (thinkstock.prison.barbed.wire)

43
Lexis Weighs In

Hello, my name is Lexis, a grateful, recovering addict and co-dependent. And Jesus Christ is my higher power.

"That gives me chills." Lexis gazed across re-strung barbed wire into crystal sky. "It captures so much—the dark humor and the hurt, especially." So many times, she'd taken her children for granted, thinking they'd always be there to cuddle. The youngest, Drew, she'd surrendered—against her will, after burning his arms—poor thing.

She left court that day in tears, sobs wracking frail ribs. She'd lived ghost-like for years, keeping to herself in prison, her arms heavy, her head thick with regret. At night, she woke clinging to her pillow. Oh, to hug Drew close again. She sobbed for the son she'd loved too little, then too much when there was no way to reach him. There was no punishment so harsh and brutal as giving up her sweet, darling son. And yet the judge had declared it.

"Six times sentenced to community treatment. You cooked that lethal mess in the boy's presence--could have blown up your house and killed him."

Horrible, horrible man. So harsh to someone so fragile. She'd worn that horrible mom badge for years. Who would rescue her? It had taken years before she heard the Prince of Peace assure her he would bring the boy back at a better time and place.

"You don't think the poem's clever?" Reese asked.

"Clever? That's not what came to mind. You know, we've all had to give up a lot in here. More than just vanity."

"Oh, I know, but the giving up started long before the crime that got me here."

"Yes, it did." Lexis couldn't stand being closed-up in small, dark spaces. On the bus ride over, tethered in a cage with Reese, she was back in the closet in her room, her mom crouching beside her, trying to quiet the baby. Her dad punching walls, calling, *Lexis!*

Her mother held her back. But Lexis knew what would quiet him.

She slipped out and walked the floor swinging her hips like a showgirl.

You deserve what you get, he'd said.

44
Andrew's Visit

Hi, I'm still Andrew, recovering co-dependent.

I gathered my phone and brief case and followed Len to the door. We'd been partners long enough; I knew the next stop would be a local Mexican restaurant. In the Quincy area, it would be Torres Tacos with its flamenco music, bright colors and cheery family service.

"Go on to the car." I tossed Len the keys and stopped at reception. "I'll be along shortly."

I smiled at the woman behind the Plexiglas. She looked up, squinting through bifocals and brushing aside her beaded braids. "Nice braids. Bet that took a while."

"Why, yes!" She tossed her head and smiled. "May I help you?"

I knew the art of opening doors and coaxing information. I'd learned it long ago from Mom Joy, the way she focused on me, or on perfect strangers. "Do you have a Lexis Brown in here?"

"Yes, we do. Is she on your deposition list?"

"No, I would like to visit her." There was no need to lie— or to reveal more than necessary. *Undiscovered error*, they called it in court or science.

"You have to be an approved visitor. The inmate has to give you an application or, since you're with DOC, maybe you can email the warden or his secretary." She slid a business card through the window tray. "Visiting hours are Saturday and Sunday, 9 to 3."

"She gets out soon, I think?"

The woman tapped her keyboard and looked up. "Yes, soon. Are you a friend or family?"

"Yes, I'm her son."

"Well then, sir." The woman turned to face me through the glass. "As a family member, you may want to get two passes. Her daughter's here, as well—"

"Pixie?" My heart skipped a beat. It would be great to see her again, especially sober. I had lost touch with her through the years. "Thanks!"

I couldn't believe the lightness I felt, stepping into breezy sunshine, gliding beneath crepe myrtles. What had changed in a few short hours? Was it that I had seen life from Cinny's perspective—how so much was beyond her control? Or was it that I had never wanted to see my mum—or sister—locked up. Afraid I'd be next. And now I had let go of that fear.

On Sunday, I brewed some ginger tea, no need to drink caffeine. My hands shook, their nails chewed to the quick. My childhood had ensured a nervous personality and it required all my emotional intelligence to recognize when I was running from fear and how to quiet down.

I had emailed the warden's secretary, filed my background check and been cleared for two passes in record time. I would see my mum and sister for the first time in 7 years. As my Prius purred down I-10, the news played softly. The legislature would be taking up bills to reinstate felons' voting rights and reduce the use of mandatory minimum drug sentences.

I turned it up, as the announcer summed up. "When you turn someone into a prisoner, you transfer their economic and social power to the people who build and work in prisons. Inmates can no longer vote, take care of their kids, or provide for their families."

They were stripped of caring for families, the one role that might give parents hope, the commentator added.

I knew it was more complex than that. Poor people with fewer resources struggled longer and harder than others. After I was adopted, Pixie had stayed in touch for a while until she, too, disappeared into her addiction.

I pulled into the prison lot, under a dense bay tree, emptied my pocket change into the ashtray, locked the car and strode to the guard house through warm sun and soft breezes. What would my mother be like after all these years? Bitter and wounded, or mellow and content? Had prison made her a better person? Had she been helped in here?

I entered security and knelt to unlace my hiking shoes. The dust of Florida's National Scenic Trail flaked off, leaving a tactile memory of the waterfall I'd discovered on Econfina Creek. A gush of cool fresh water spilled over the steep banks in such fresh, clear flows, I'd ducked under it, washing off the sandhill grime, and gulping its sweetness. That would be a wonderful place to take mum and Pixie when they got out, if they were up to it.

Joy had collected mum's letters and given them to me from time to time. But I had let them pile up, unanswered. This weighed on me as I straightened and removed my keys and glasses. How hard would it have been to send a card or a letter now and then? Would mum understand my torn feelings, or would she hold it against me? I walked in stocking feet through the metal detector and the officer called on his radio. "Lexis Brown, Pixie Brown to the Visitor's Park."

A young African American in a dark suit and yellow tie entered with several little girls in pink dresses and hair ribbons. They were younger by half than when my mom went to prison. Curious as puppies, they turned all around looking at the officers, and tipped their faces up to me. I smiled down and let them slap my hand, then fist-bumped their open palms. "Turkey!" I said, showing how their hands were the feathers and my fist and thumb were body and head.

The oldest, about four, giggled and skipped.

The youngest added her own little jig. She seemed happy in her little preschool body. "Again, again!"

We made a few more turkeys and they pulled their daddy down by his tie. He knelt, and played along, making turkeys, all in.

"Let me guess, we're visiting Santa today?"

"Uh-uh." The youngest shook her pigtails.

"The Easter bunny?"

"Noo." The oldest laughed, nudging her sister along.

"Can you believe, I'm visiting my mama today?"

"Nooo."

"For the first time, here!" I turkey-bumped them again, and winked at their dad. "Woo-hoo."

The man laughed and lifted the youngest to his shoulder, grabbing the other girl's hand.

"Nooo." She leaned toward me, and shrieked when I stole her nose and gave it back between my thumb and forefinger.

I longed for children of my own, though my boyfriend was against it. Would I tell Mum? Probably not today.

Mom Joy had reacted badly to my coming out, and had read me several Bible passages. It had turned me against God for a time. Or at least against the people who used God to beat others down. But God, in the end, had left Mom Joy at Romans 1, and raced after me, sandals and white robe flying.

The Prince of Peace, Mum Lexis called him in one of her letters. He would bring us together again one day, and he was still who I called on when feeling down and desperate. *If you made me this way, how can it be wrong?*

It had taken months of listening to Mom Joy and Dad Day and answering their questions, shepherding their emotions, hoping they'd see how relieved I was to reveal my hidden self. They had finally accepted that I could only be who I was. But that had exhausted me, and I resolved not to go there with Mum Lexis—not today.

We were buzzed through no-man's land—or no-woman's land—between razor wire fences. I held the gate for the girls. They skipped and jigged through like eager pups. Their dad laughed and we entered a large, air-conditioned room, painted with *Jungle Book* scenes. Voices echoed off cinderblock walls and everyone yelled above everyone else. Would I be able to hear my mum?

Family groups met at tables, eating chips and drinking sodas from a busy snack shop. Officers stood guard and roamed among the tables, nodding and smiling.

None of the women in blue looked like my mother and an officer pointed out a chair for me to sit in. Just as I crossed to it, a small woman entered from the prison yard. She was much smaller than I remembered, no longer pale but deeply tanned, with chiseled face and flying white hair. I moved toward her, arms outstretched and she ran into my arms. "Drew!" Mum's tears flowed as I embraced her frail frame. We hugged and rocked each other as though nothing else existed.

Behind her, a dark-haired woman with pixie-pointed chin came rushing toward us. "Andy!" Her special name for me, Poke Salad Andy. She hugged and rocked me too. "It has been so long."

Mom crushed us both, weeping. Then dabbed her eyes and nose with a wad of toilet paper from her pocket.

She and Pixie radiated an inner light. Mom's wavy hair fanned out over her shoulders; Pixie's reached to her chair. They sat, holding my hands across the table, not wanting to let go.

"I never thought I'd see the day... My son, a lawyer! Look at your dimples! You still have dimples, Drew!" Mum reached out and stroked my face.

"Mum!" I leaned forward. "So do you! It's like looking in the mirror at myself. And, you're almost out of here. How does it feel?"

"Good." She was clear-eyed and level-headed as the best days I could remember. "And scary. I'm going to have to find a job out there."

"Sure, but you can drive truck, fix hair—you can fix truck drivers' hair, remember?"

"You did read my letters!" Lexis cried some more. "You always made me laugh."

"Me, too." Pixie pulled a photo from her pocket. "Drew, this is your niece and nephew." In the colored photo, Pixie held on her lap a curly-haired boy, sucking his fist, and a young, doe-eyed girl, standing, leaning on her shoulder.

I could not believe my joy at having a young niece and nephew. "Oh Pixie, you have a little prince and princess! He has curly hair like mine; she has beautiful dark eyes like yours."

"Yes, and I want you to meet them. They're coming next Sunday if you can make it. They'll be happy they have a caring uncle like you."

"I'd love to! You have no idea how I long for children. It's as though I want to grow myself up all over again."

"Me too!" Mum grinned. "May I, please? And start over with you two?"

"Mum, you are! Your hearts' desire is coming true. You've been wonderful!" Pixie gazed at her, then me. "She's been the missing mom to so many women in here."

Mom smiled sweetly. "It's as though God multiplied my children 100 times."

The din crescendoed and I leaned in. "How wonderful for you! I never even imagined that God could fill your loneliness like that."

She paused and gazed at me quietly. "Psalms 68:6 says, 'God places the lonely in families; he sets the prisoners free and gives them joy.' I have claimed that. But how am I so lucky to see my own family—you and Pixie—again?"

"You mean, how am I so lucky to see you again, Mum? I faced myself in the mirror this week, while taking depositions in here. I recognized you in me, and all I wanted was to see you again." I wanted to be direct and honest without betraying Cinny's identity.

"Oh, Drew, really? You're defending women in here?"

"Yes, Mum." I fidgeted and hid my chewed nails in my pockets. "I realized that the system can be heavy-handed."

"Yes, yes it can." She looked up. "And that's another thing, you always called me, *Mum*. Oh, that was so long ago—and yet it feels like yesterday."

"Time is a healer." I took my hands out of my pockets and reached for theirs again. "So, tell me, Mum and Pixie, what happens from here?"

"I'll be released on probation to Fountain, near Panama City, to rejoin my family." Pixie slid the treasured photo back in her pocket.

"Are you single or married?"

"Oh, married, but my husband kinda comes and goes, depending how well I'm doing. We're hoping I'll do better this time."

Mum smiled. "You will, dear. I'm praying circles around you."

She grinned big then and squeezed my hand. "I go to Tallahassee work release and find a job. It's six months until I EOS."

I squeezed her small hand back. "A reward for being everyone's mum."

"Yes, prison can be a maturing process."

"Can I take you out on furlough one day, Mum? I have a special place I want to show you—and Pixie and kids, if they can."

"Well, after I'm there for a few weeks and get a job, I think I can apply for furlough and a family visit."

"Perfect! I have a heaven on earth to show you two."

"The beach?" Pixie's eyes danced, reminding Andrew of their trips to the Gulf of Mexico. She'd probably moved to Fountain to be near those emerald waves.

"Oh no, north of the city. High in the sandhills."

"Oh, I've been there—ages ago." Pixie fixed me with a dreamy look. "Camping and swimming in Econfina Creek."

"That's the place." I inhaled, so full of joy, I did not want to lose it ever again.

45
Hope Yields

Hello, I'm still Hope, still a recovering codependent and addict.

Silverware jingled on ceramic plates as Hope entered Torres Tacos at six. Flamenco music laced the air and doors swung open as a dark-haired woman in white apron carried steaming dishes brimming with rice, beans and tacos. Hope's mouth watered at the savory scent of chili, grilled chicken and ground beef. Bright, yellow walls draped in rainbow ponchos muted murmurs, lending a cozy warmth to the air-conditioned room.

The warden was already there at a corner booth by the window. He looked up, square shoulders, muscled arms, calloused fingers marking his place in Hope's binders. He rose to greet her, tall and supple, moving towards her like a dancer.

"It gets crowded in here; I wanted to save us the best table. I've been reviewing your proposal, Hope. And it is so aggravating."

Hope grinned. "Hello to you, too. Aggravating?"

"Okay, I know, I'm a bit carried away. But I've been sitting here since 5:30, reading. And you know what bites?" His dimples deepened with his broad grin.

"Something bites, about my proposal?" Hope slid into the booth and took the menu a waiter offered.

"Gracias, Miguel. This is Chaplain Hope." Miguel bowed and Roman took his menu. "Un momento."

Miguel nodded and returned with tall glasses of ice water and a bowl of fresh-cut lemons.

"Yes, extremely annoying. The only thing I can find to mess with is your budget."

Hope grinned. "Well, how badly did I screw up?"

Roman turned the binder her way. A few red marks in the margins. Increased construction figures and reduced staff numbers.

"That's it, Roman?"

"Chaplain, I believe that I must try to find something to fix when I review proposals. I also found a mis-numbering. Here, when you went from VI. to VIII., see and this misspelling. My name, Hope. Really?"

"Let me guess, I added 'a,' Roam-an?"

He laughed. "No, you left out an r, it spells 'Tores.'"

Hope clutched her shirt. "That tores my heart."

"It really is thorough. I'd like to send this up if you can manage to get my name right."

She unrolled her silverware. "Are we going to convince them though?

"It's strong, definitely a strong proposal." Roman's irises flashed fire.

"I'm standing on the shoulders of giants. Giants who've known for years that women do better when serving time with their kids."

Hope again broke Roman's gaze, studying the menu. She wasn't free, was she? Even after months of separation, she'd asked her husband if he wanted a divorce but he'd asked to try again. Said they'd go slow. And yet, he'd gone *too* slow.

Roman cleared his throat. "Well, see anything you like?"

Hope was taking too long studying the menu, seeing nothing. At last the first dish came into focus. "How are your Papa's chicken nachos supremo?"

"Supremo! But there's always enough for two."

"Want to share?" Heat rose through her neck and into her cheeks. She hoped it didn't show.

"With you, always."

Hope smiled but broke his intense gaze again, studying the tomato fields stretching for miles behind the restaurant. Large velvety leaves, acres of white blossoms. "Has your family lived here long?"

"Oh yes, Hope. I was born in Quincy when my parents were still teenagers. They picked tomatoes while my abuelo watched me. I was only eight when my parents put a hat on my head, bandana around my neck, and took me out picking with them. They said if I crouched down, no one would know how young I was."

Hope nodded. She had joined children in an African village, carrying gallons of river water uphill, baby sisters or brothers tied to their backs while mamas hoed peanut fields. And yet, in this country, things were different. Farmers were subsidized to grow food and waddled out of air-conditioned tractors, pink and rotund, among their hungry workers. "Doesn't that violate child labor laws?"

"I'm sure. All I knew was terror at being discovered and deported. Torn from my family."

"That doesn't make sense." Hope smiled gently. "You were born here."

"Believe me, I was confused. I didn't understand, except that I was supposed to crouch down and help my family. They could be deported and I would go with them."

"How stressful for a young guy!"

Roman nodded, lips drawn. "One day, a big white car drove up and a large white man in khakis walked toward me. I ducked very low and he walked right past me, straight to my parents. He talked to them, then turned around, came back and stretched out his hand. I was too scared to take it, but my parents nodded, said it was okay. The man was going to take me to school and I should go with him.

"Sitting in that big leather seat, high above the world in his car, I was shaking. The man smiled down at me, handed me a notebook and pencil. When I got to school, the place was huge and confusing. All the kids spoke English and I went completely silent."

Hope nodded. She knew the discomfort and silence of the outsider. When she was the newcomer, the one struggling to understand a new language.

Miguel returned to the booth, accompanied by a stooped man with salt-and-pepper hair.

"Papa!" Roman stood and enfolded the beaming man in his muscled arms. "Gustar tu a conocer mi amiga. Hope meet my Papa."

Roman's papa nodded and held out a gnarled hand.

Hope took it warmly. "Encantado. Your son is a good warden."

Roman translated and added a few more sentences. To Hope it sounded like, "And Hope is a good chaplain. She saved my neck this week." He drew his hand across his throat.

"Si, si, content." The older man's dark craggy face, crinkled. He shook Hope's hand again, then took out a matchbook and lit the candle on their table. He lingered while Miguel took their order, and hurried away.

The dancing flame flickered on Roman's face. "You know he's going to heap that plate!"

Hope nodded. "I bet, knowing how generous you are."

"I helped him set up his restaurant here. After all those years of cooking around campfires, I knew we could make this succeed."

Hope squeezed lemon in her water. "They must have depended on you a great deal after you went to school and learned English." She sipped her water. "That must have been hard for you, a little guy."

"Ai, I was lost that first day, crouching at my desk in my hat and bandana, listening to their harsh language with my head down. It was all I could do to stop shaking."

Hope took another sip, clinking the ice in her glass.

"Then, the teacher called us into circle time and told us a story about three pigs. I found myself looking up, watching the pigs in the big storybook. They wore hats and bandanas, and carried straw and sticks from the field. One even mixed the straw and sticks with mud to make bricks for his house. They were just like us." He watched the orange sun setting into the tomato fields.

"That's it!" Hope tapped the table between them. "The way forward with the prison nursery is through stories. I was like you, sitting in a kindergarten in France, and the way into the new language was through *Le Petit Prince* crash-landing his plane on a little planet. It's perfect—you asking Cinny and her family to tell their story on Capitol Hill."

Roman nodded. "Stories reached me, crouched in a cold, dark field; my abuela telling about Aztec fortresses, how we'd come from greatness. Inside, I was climbing endless steps to a fortress overlooking huge jungles, mighty rivers. In school, I played softball, and practiced that story, too, pitching, batting, running. I made varsity in high school, and a scholarship to FSU."

Roman gripped his water glass with a sinewed hand. "When I read *Les Mis*, I knew we had to use the power of inside stories to fix the system from within." The sunset glowed purple around us.

Papa brought the chicken nachos, heaped up and steaming. Miguel gave them each their own dinner plate to serve into.

"Chaplain, would you care to say a blessing?"

Hope bowed her head and noticed Roman holding out his hand. She took it, feeling a warm jolt. "Lord bless our nursery proposal and this food; the hands that picked it and the hands that prepared it. Amen."

Roman squeezed her hand before releasing it. "You just blessed my entire family."

Hope nodded and lifted some nachos and chicken into her plate. She sampled the juicy, spiced chicken. "Your papa can cook! You must tell him how heavenly this is."

For a while she and Roman savored the crunchy chips, cool lettuce, hot-spiced chicken.

The candle light flickered on the table. "Hope, if this prison nursery proposal goes forward, it could advance our careers significantly. Do you realize that?"

She paused, setting down her fork. "Roman, I'm most excited for the children, women, and families who will benefit."

The sky purpled over the tomato fields as they left the restaurant. Roman walked Hope to her car, carrying the binders. "Hope?"

"Yes." She turned, leaning against her white Honda.

He handed her the binders, his hand lingering on hers. "Hope, do you realize what we've got here?"

"A solid proposal?" She grinned, unlocked her door, and placed the binders on the passenger seat.

When she straightened, he cocked his head. "Bear hug?"

She nodded and let him pull her in.

Hope felt breathless and flustered. "Warden, is this permitted?"

"I just permitted it." He pulled her in again, lifting her in a solid embrace. The restaurant door opened and flamenco music poured out.

"I better go." Hope ducked into her car and waved.

"Don't go too far." Roman turned toward her with a broad, disarming smile.

Hope threw her phone in the back seat, where she'd consigned it ever since her last texting and driving accident, $500 for a new bumper. Never again. She turned the key and backed out, and Roman disappeared into the restaurant.

Heading west toward Tallahassee on Route 90, she crept through Quincy, shivering in the warm spring night. An old grandfather oak spread its eighty-foot boughs over the town square, framing the century-old town hall and stately bronze dome. Redbuds bloomed at the garden club. Colored light poured from the Tiffany stained glass windows. Inside, silhouettes waltzed in glittery gowns and dark tuxedos.

The two-story Victorian had once belonged to the banker who wouldn't lend to farmers unless they invested $1500 of the loan in Coca Cola. Tobacco farmers amassed fortunes in a matter of years. They built majestic two- and three-story homes north of route 90. The little clapboards to the south housed the workers who'd once picked their tobacco, and continued to pick cotton and tomatoes. The workers who cleaned those grand houses.

Hope's heart hurt and soared. Tonight, she'd been embraced by a family that had risen from tomato fields. *Roaman, Roman Tores.* She'd have to fix that.

Had she been praying in the wrong direction? For God to bring back her husband? The prayer had given her joy when roasting turkey, baking sweet potatoes and gathering her husband Kevin and twin girls around for Thanksgiving or Christmas.

But maybe she had been too rigid in drawing boundaries around her heart.

Hope's headlights lit on a dark man in jeans and jacket walking along the shoulder. Just in time she swerved. He stumbled and held up his thumb. Once, she was him, taking her chances on the open road, young pores open for risk and adventure. But rough words and harsh touch had left slivers and scars that she'd tried to forget.

Hope was descending toward the Little River bridge when her phone vibrated in the back seat. She slowed on the highway and gently applied the brakes, her whirring wheels hit warning reflectors on the white line, then gravel. Her lights caught deer eyes shining in the creek. A doe and fawn leapt into the woods.

Was it the girls? An emergency at the prison? Roman using his emergency contact list? Or was it Kevin?

She reached into the back seat, fumbled around, and finally opened it. "Hello?"

"Mom! Dad's been in an accident. He's in emergency at Tallahassee Memorial. He's stable but hurting. Please come quick!"

"On my way, Brook! I'm just leaving Quincy so it'll be about a half hour."

This time Hope stuck the phone in her console cup holder and drove, barely noticing rising and falling speed limits.

Please, please, spare Kevin, Lord. Keep your healing hand on him. Don't let him slip away, not yet, not now. The girls need him; I need him.

Her phone lit up again, and Hope picked up. A text message from Rain. "On my way to Emergency. Dad was in an accident."

Hope stopped at the red light in Midway and hit reply. "On my way. Will be there in 25 min."

If she'd gone straight home today, she'd be there in minutes. She'd been reckless with her heart. If only she'd stopped to consider the risks. Risks of dating a supervisor, speeding through the night, veering off narrow paths.

46
Hope Reconsiders

Tallahassee with its narrow canopy roads and moseying motorists raised Hope's blood pressure. She stood first on her brake, then her accelerator, tearing around a motorist blinking for a right turn and gunning it in front of a honking Escalade. The TMH parking garage was full until she got to the top deck, far from the reception desk and first floor emergency room. She parked, locked up and raced, breathless, to the double glass doors. Inside, she checked left and right for signs to emergency.

The hospital was a maze of mismatched halls, floors and elevators. Finally, she descended to the cement bowels and raced toward the florescent-lit emergency center. Water burbled and a rich, bold coffee aroma filled the floor. Heart monitors beeped and a stretcher whirred past the central desk, bearing a gray-haired woman in some sort of body brace, her jaw set. She was followed by a middle-aged woman, carrying two purses. Hope glanced into several rooms, no Kevin. *Kevin, where's Kevin, Brook, Rain?*

Hope hurried to the desk and excused herself to a woman in periwinkle scrubs tapping a keyboard. "I'm looking for Kevin Springs?"

"Ah yes, let me check. He's in 121." She pointed to the back room.

Hope tried to still her pounding heart as she entered the wide door. The first bay held an ashen, white-bearded man, attached to a beeping heart monitor. A younger, grizzled man, sat holding his hand.

The second bay held Kevin, surrounded by Rain and Brook. They brightened when Hope entered. Rain, the tall, gangly twin, sat on the far side cradling Kevin's hand. It was limp and taped with a plastic port and IV drip. Brook, the petite one, stood and offered Hope her chair. Rain had more of her Swedish grandfather's height while Brook resembled her father's Italian-Japanese compact angularity.

Kevin lifted his stubbled face when Hope bent to hug him. She hugged Brook and then Rain across the bed, sat down, and leaned in toward Kevin again, surprised when he reached up with his good hand and gave her a sloppy, one-sided kiss.

"I'm just running to the bathroom." Brook grabbed her shoulder bag, and Rain followed.

Kevin gripped Hope's hand.

"How're you feeling?"

"Sho-sho-...." His words slurred and his mouth sagged. When he tried to smile, it was crooked and only one eye crinkled. Was he having a stroke? Hope tried not to look alarmed. "Has the doctor seen you?"

He nodded toward the IV in his arm. Meds to break the clot, stop bleeding in the brain, or both? Hope didn't know, but he seemed to be yielding his independent spirit and confident rationality to expert care.

Hope stroked Kevin's upturned face, his rugged, dignified jaw she'd first observed in a college dorm. Kevin, even then, had strummed smoothly, playing U2 to a packed room. "I still haven't found what I'm looking for."

Long-haired students, cross-legged on scattered cushions, swayed and sang along. But he'd gazed around the adoring eyes and found her dark ones. She pushed aside raven curls, poured steaming almond-honey tea, handing out mugs and meeting Kevin's sloe eyes coming 'round to hers again.

Later on the porch, in a cool evening breeze, they'd talked into the night and parted with a soul-bonding kiss. His Asian-Mediterranean gray eyes seared her thoughts as she crept back into the women's dorm, mulling a new name. Not Hope Block, but Hope Springs.

In ER, Hope clutched Kevin's good hand. "Oh dear Lord, may I pray for you?" She almost expected him to say no, and she'd have prayed silently, anyway. But this time, he nodded. He seemed to need her faith, to want to join her at the throne as they once had. Years ago, the girls still in high school, they'd gathered 'round the supper table, read a few verses and prayed together. It had strengthened their purpose as a family.

But after the girls left for FSU dorms, they'd only come home to do their laundry and raid the fridge. That first semester, they often smelled of stale beer and cigarettes, and each flunked a course. Math and science, Kevin's favorites. Hope had counseled them to move home, but instead they promised to study more. Kevin had watched silently as though the ship were wrecked. He had left then, moving into his own place and Hope had given them time and space to heal from her recent rape and years-earlier affair.

Still, Hope felt during the months apart as though she alone were carrying their family—three gilded but broken vessels. She carried them to the throne as she hung the laundry, drove down I-10, raked leaves and pulled weeds—praying hourly, daily. At first, she phoned the girls every evening until they complained about her helicopter parenting. She had lined up gravel pieces for memory stones, on her driveway walls until her girls turned in passing grades.

While the heart monitor beeped in the next bay, Hope bowed over Kevin, petitioning for this man still in crisis, father of her gorgeous children. "Heavenly Father, please lay your healing hand on Kevin. Heal his very cells and tissues. We ask this, believing, in Jesus name, Amen."

Deep down she was praying a different prayer. *If this is it..., if this is my sign to believe and take him back again, move this mountain of doubt. Help me to close the door on Roman and open it to Kevin.*

A shuffle behind the curtain, metal rungs pulled along a steel bar, and a stocky, whiskered man in green scrubs and cap appeared. A surgical mask rested on his neck, and he extended a rough, red hand. "Ms. Springs, I presume?"

She nodded and returned his strong grip, a lump in her throat. *Please, let it be good news.*

"I am Doctor Early. I'm glad you're here while I give Mr. Springs his results. Kevin, it appears you have had a Transient Ischemic Attack, or TIA. That is, a mild stroke. We have stopped the bleeding for now." He nodded toward the IV. "But we'll need to admit you for observation and physiotherapy. Our goal is full recovery of your left side."

Kevin nodded.

Hope gripped his good arm.

"Mrs. Springs, will you be the primary contact?"

"Yes, Sir." Hope answered firmly, knowing the path she'd have to take. And it would not be back to Roman. That clinch was so wildly unplanned; this, so long-awaited.

Kevin's eyelids drooped and he struggled to keep them open.

Dr. Early cleared his throat. "Kevin, we'll admit you, take you up to second floor and let you rest now. Tomorrow we'll run more tests and bring in your physical therapy team. Ms. Springs, you and the girls may want to check back in the afternoon? We will have more results then."

Hope nodded, picked up her purse and leaned in for another kiss, squeezing Kevin's hand. Her phone pinged—an incoming text from Brook. "Are you ready for us?"

"The girls." She explained, then texted back. "Yes come."

Rain and Brook swept around the corner and she held out her arms, taking them in. "We'll let Dad rest for now and see him again tomorrow afternoon." All three hugged Kevin again, murmuring their good nights.

On their way out, the twins clung to Hope like a rock in a gathering storm. She bore them up and breathed deeply. *Let this be their wake-up call, their return to your loving arms.* She called the elevator and accompanied them to the parking garage.

How long Kevin's recovery would take or how much his health would improve, she didn't know. But if he was ready to come home, she was ready to receive him. It was what their family needed; the two of them united and strong, committed again to each other and the twins.

Hope huddled with the girls in the parking garage, breathing in the girls' citrus shampoo, and calming their jitters with a long, solid hug. "Thank you, girls, for being right there for Dad. He's had a stroke, but thank God, he was taken directly to ER. They stopped the bleeding; now let's pray he makes a full recovery."

Someone's phone pinged, and they each dove into their purses, laughing as each pulled out a lighted cell phone.

"Okay, good night." Rain loped to her car in neon green Nikes.

"Yeah, me too. Good night." Brook's heeled boots clicked, echoing through the nearly empty garage.

Hope unlocked her car and slid inside.

She put on her drugstore reading glasses before reading her two texts. Unknown number. *Home yet?* and *Are you safely home?* Oh, yes, Roman. Lovely man. Lovely, off-limits man.

Hope considered her scrambled emotions—fear, love, infatuation. Infatuation was the least important at this critical moment. It would just take a firm resolve, a few cogent sentences, to put things straight again.

Not yet. My husband was in a car accident, now in hospital recovering. Looks like the separation is over. Friends?

She inserted the key and the car rumbled and echoed through the cavernous garage. Still his reply vibrated through. She checked it before shifting to Drive.

Yes, Friend. She liked the capital *F*.

47
Kevin's Hope

Early the next morning, Hope slipped into her gray suit and black boots. Something was different. Her clothes fit the same but the house was smaller. She took the cool patio route to the kitchen pulling weeds out of her daylily border. She no longer doubted the future. She crossed the living room to the kitchen, her footsteps no longer echoing through an empty house. The house felt warm and full again, perhaps overfull. She'd learned to enjoy her own company, though she'd longed for her soulmate.

Hope turned on the radio. The state legislative session was winding down and the headlines crackled. "DOC employees have won their protest to stop further prison privatization. Research shows it won't save taxpayers money…"

Well, at least word was out about for-profit prisons not saving money. Empty promises.

She ran her espresso machine, and steamed milk, spraying the counter. Good thing Kevin's math models weren't lying around—yet.

But wait, what? All these months she'd longed for her companion, and now she worried about fitting him in again?

Kevin would likely be waking up in the hospital at this very hour. She grabbed her shoulder bag and headed for the car, calling Chaplain Emily and leaving a message that she would be a little late. She swung down Capital Circle Northeast and turned onto Magnolia, headed for Tallahassee Memorial. It was a crazy mazy mix of departments, clinics and added wings. The key was to find a parking space near the admissions desk and get directions to halls and elevators to the right floor and room.

Kevin grinned crookedly when she entered and wiped orange juice from his hospital gown. "I'm a little schloppy."

Hope laughed. "I'm the schloppy one, remember?" She stirred his oatmeal and purposely spilled some on his tray until he laughed.

"This hand'sh a little weak." He showed her how he had to move it with the other hand to set it beside the bowl. Then he could dip in and lift the spoon to his mouth.

"You'll build it up again." Hope stirred cream into his coffee and spilled that, too. Kevin laughed out loud.

Hope waited 'til he calmed down and lifted the mug to his lips, again spilling on his gown.

They chuckled some more and Kevin took the mug in his right hand, drinking fine and setting it down, smiling.

"Do you have physio today?

"Umhm." He swallowed his oatmeal and sipped coffee.

"When they release you, would you consider recovering at home?"

Kevin nodded, reaching for her hand, holding it against his warm, thumping chest.

"In fact, would you consider moving home?"

Kevin's lips quivered crookedly. "Yesh."

Hope fairly sang as she cruised west on I-10 to Rocky Comfort. *I'll praise you in the storm....* She crossed the Ochlockonee River, waves rippling and glinting in the spring breeze. She pulled down her visor as the sun crested the stately southern pines—some of God's best creation. Life was so sweet. She and Kevin had survived and they would soon know more of what to expect. She would keep praising those blessings down.

Hope swept off I-10 and waited at the stop sign for a logging truck rumbling past before merging onto Greensboro Highway. She found herself composing a press release.

Rocky Comfort Correctional Facility will consider adding a nursery during a meeting of the Florida Department of Corrections in the Capital this month. The nursery is envisioned to offer new mothers and babies the opportunity to bond in a safe, secure environment. If approved, renovations can begin and inmates serving up to two years for non-violent crimes can apply.

"The object of a prison nursery is to create better transitions to our communities and reduce repeat offenses," said

Warden Roman Torres. "The costs will be offset with reduced inmate numbers when they transition successfully to their communities."

Hope dipped into the ravine at Rocky Comfort Creek, crossed the bridge and swept up the hill into the prison lot. Too late to park in the shade, she crossed the lot and waved as she passed the warden's corner window. Inside he raised his hand, and the plate glass reflected her flying yellow scarf and wind-whipped silver-gray pant suit. She still needed his close support. The press release would be ready as soon as the corrections chief agreed to hear their proposal at the Legislature.

From his desk, the warden knocked on the window and beckoned her in. She nodded and rounded the corner to Administration, pulling slowly on the heavy door, then waiting for her vision to adjust before she was buzzed in and gliding down the hall, calming her nerves.

Roman's office door stood ajar and she entered softly.

"Hello, Hope! Close the door, will you?"

Hope latched it quietly, and stepped into the room.

"Come on in, Hope, please. I don't bite. Here, have a seat." He indicated her usual spot, the chair right in front of his desk.

Hope settled in, smoothing her puffy hair and scarf.

"Chaplain." His tone was formal but pleasant. "First, how's your family?"

"Thank you, Roman. We are well. My girls were at the hospital when I got to emergency, and my husband was being treated to stop the stroke. He has some left side paralysis. But they hope to address it with physiotherapy."

"And how are you doing?" Roman stood and moved around the desk, perching right in front of her.

Hope moved her knees aside to give him room. "I'm happy that it wasn't worse and that my husband has decided to move back home."

"I'm happy for you too." He turned and pulled a paper from his printer tray, handing it to Hope. "This email reinforces all you've done for so many people lately."

It was from the private prison program's corporate headquarters dated the night before with the subject line, Prison

Nursery. *Warden Torres, we want to congratulate you on your foresight in proposing a prison nursery. This is exactly the type of innovation the corporation is looking for to stay significant. Please keep us apprised of the response from FDOC and the Legislature.*

Hope looked up and pointed her gun finger at him. "You are right on target, Roman."

The email continued. *Also, we have advertised the vice president's position and want you to consider applying for it by following this link.*

Sincerely, CEO Bill Wright

Hope looked up in awe, handing the paper back. "Roman, it appears you're in line for a promotion."

"Yes, and it's many thanks to you."

"Oh Roman, how will we do this without you?" Hope wasn't trying to flatter him; she meant it. He was someone who planned and executed. "Will you be requesting a nursery item on the agenda for the corrections meeting at the Legislature?

"Certainly I will. Now that I have the blessing of headquarters."

"Oh good, I came in today, buzzing with ideas for a press release announcing it. I will run it by you as soon as we get the green light. I believe we can be convincing."

Roman offered his hand and pulled her to her feet. "On your way, then."

"And best to you with your application." Hope floated out of the room. Roman had a fire lit under him. It could bode well for the nursery.

Florida's old and new capitols. (Faith Eidse photo)

48
Cinnamon's Call

Hey, still Cinny, still recovering.

I pulled my leather art portfolio, wheels clattering, along the walkway to Florida's old Capitol. I'd been called—with Chaplain Hope and Warden Torres—to show my prison nursery paintings at a special session of the legislature. U.S. and Florida flags fluttered over us, and I could hardly contain myself.

The warden carried several wooden easels in sculpted arms, and Hope hauled thick binders in her shoulder bag. I tried to match their long strides.

Magnolias bloomed around us and I stuck my face in a large, creamy blossom. Its honey-citrus scent just like on Econfina Creek with Dex, exactly this time of year. I had missed so many familiar, sensory pleasures during my ten months behind bars.

Sun warmed the small and large domes of Florida's old Capitol, its gray shingles, ornate columns, sculpted cupola and red-striped awnings. We had been invited, not to the old Capitol, but to the new tower, soaring behind it. Twenty-two stories of smooth concrete with window slats running its length, an observation gallery circling its top floor. From there, you could see forever.

The session was called due to a spike in prisoner deaths—and the tornado-hit Rocky Comfort. Our vision was needed.

The chaplain and I had probably saved lives exposing the Cheeto gang. But would my images of babies in prison offset news of aging prisoners—some sentenced to life without parole—dying inside?

We circled the columned capitol toward the shiny new obelisk, dodging children in bright tee-shirts. Schools from miles around had emptied classrooms, freeing children for Earth Day discoveries. They circled touch tanks, stroking ancient horseshoe crabs, oysters and sea stars from our Gulf Coast. Further along, they studied limestone fossils and pressed clay replicas.

Hope in her sage eyelet shift and jacket, and Warden Torres in his tweeds, walked at my elbows, brows arched like jackal gods guarding the pyramids. I had been furloughed from prison, for our exhibit, on their word and honor.

Miss Hope shifted her stuffed shoulder bag. "The Old Capitol was built in 1845 after Florida finally passed a constitution. Until then, the Pork Chop Gang enforced segregation—Jim Crow laws—like denying ex-felons the vote."

I shuddered, knowing that I—along with a million others, might never vote again. But no one could take my canvases and brushes.

We entered the Capitol's deep shadows, and the warden set down his easels. They were mismatched, lent from the prison's art program, and he rearranged them for a better grip. "There's still, a big wealth gap, north and south of the Capitol."

I pointed downhill to where bulldozers were digging a new stormwater system called Cascades Park. "I was born and raised down there in Smokey Hollow. My sister still lives in that patch on the far side of the tracks."

"Yes, I've been down there." Hope turned to face me. "At least they built memorial—open, metal-frame 'spirit houses'—to recall the old shotgun houses, first cut in half by the railroad, then bull-dozed for state offices."

We passed the old Capitol's back steps, clinging to morning shadow. "Sir, we sang on those steps in middle school— in go-go boots and 'fros."

"What did you sing?" The Warden flicked his dark hair from tiger-gold eyes.

"Oh, ho-ho." I raised a fist and threw back my head. "We Are Family."

"By Sister Sledge?" Hope jigged her head and swayed her hips. "Hmm hmm…"

"That's the one. We got several encores and even senators kickin' it up in the courtyard. That music brought us together. It was my highest day on the hill."

Hope pivoted, the wind lifting her copper curls. "Well, may today beat that."

We reached rows of double brass doors, and I cricked my neck up, up, up at the massive skyscraper receding into a pearly pink sky. I swayed and swerved and nearly tripped over Miss Hope.

"Steady there, Cinny." She had dressed me in her gray silk suit, hemmed up to fit my shorter legs. She was letting me play the professional for a day while she flitted around me in her cotton shift and jacket.

The warden reached a hand to support me. "Careful, that leather case contains the power to sway hearts and minds."

I gulped. "Yes, sir." With bright, colorful strokes, I had painted the adoring faces of babies and toddlers, the intense focus of mothers, all playing and learning together behind razor wire. I had contrasted this with women behind the fence, clutching children's photos, arms empty, full of yearning. Would the images move legislators to approve our nursery?

Hope squinted up, too. "That's as tall as Niagara Falls, twenty-five floors if you count the three underground."

I had never seen Niagara Falls, but I had grown up under the Capitol's torrential runoff, washing down and flooding our homes. Standing right under it, I was a mullet scaling a waterfall.

Miss Hope held the door, and I rolled my portfolio inside. We lifted it like a newborn onto the conveyer belt.

"May I?" A guard waited for my nod and pulled the zipper latch, opening to pure cherub faces gazing up at moms soft cheeks, razor wire reflected in their eyes. He whistled low.

A second guard glanced over. "Look at the color and energy; the contrasts, hard-edged wire and soft baby lips."

I gestured at the chaplain and warden. "They put me up to it."

The warden stepped up and laid his easels on the conveyer belt. "We're trouble." He winked.

The guard gently moved the portfolio and easels down the line. "Your fluid style reminds me of the Florida Highwaymen. We have an exhibit on the top floor this month."

My scalp tingled. How had they gathered the scattered paintings of twenty-six artists who'd sold to tourists from all over the world? No gallery would carry them; they'd sold slapdash out of the trunks of cars for a song, paintings that were worth a small fortune today.

"Oh, please, please? Do we have time?"

Miss Hope, checked her watch. "I've sent press releases, agreed to meet reporters—but we have a few minutes."

Warden Torres groaned. "You women! Always so demanding."

"You better. It's a rare treat." The guard handed me a bin. "Shoes, belt, jacket."

I hurried out of my jacket, new black Mary Janes and belt, setting off alarms anyway and slowing us down. Would we miss the show? A security wand beeped over my head. Oh right, the butterfly clip Greta had given me. I put my clothes back on, and the security officers shooed us upstairs.

We raced up the half-circle stairs to the mezzanine, where the warden deposited his armload and called the elevator. "We'll just leave these—and set up here when we get back."

Chaplain Hope, flitted around us, not permitting me to leave the portfolio behind. Men in pinstripes and women in pale suits and heels, clacked by, nearly tripping over us with their folders and cell phones.

The elevator doors swooshed open and I caught my breath. I had been to the observation deck a few years before in a short sequined dress and thigh high boots. I was not in my right mind that night, nor with the right people, but on the arm of some big shot from South Florida.

The warden held the doors and I ducked my head as a serge-suited man crowded in elevator with us—a young blonde at his heels, scribbling notes as he dictated... *The governor's fish fry, Friday at 7; the crab boil at St. George Island, Sunday at 2.*

I fiddled with my portfolio latch. *Lord, if they know me, help them forget.*

Finally, they got off at the tenth floor.

We stepped off into paintings of vivid landscapes, mysterious green jungles, water reflecting sunset, palms and oaks dripping Spanish moss.

Miss Hope read the description aloud. "Rapid, mass-produced paintings on boards or Masonite, even using house paints. Hundreds of thousands sold from cars on Florida's highways in the 1950s for $20-$35 apiece, now worth tens of thousands, each."

There were some of my favorites. Alfred Hair's red-flowered Poincianas, textured egret swamps, leaning palms and pink clouds; Al Black's muted skies, bold palms and seagulls; and Mary Ann Carroll's rich pastel skies and dense cypress domes.

"Can you imagine if their families had that money today?" The warden strode down one side and up the other, pausing occasionally to take in a royal palm or fiery red river reflecting an autumn sky. At one point, he almost ran into me "Oh, pardon, Cinny. These are stellar."

I nodded. "These are my forerunners. We painted a Highwaymen-style show in high school, and sold out."

"Yes, I can see the influence. For sheer emotional impact these paintings are tops—and so are yours."

"Thanks, but by myself, I'm no Highwayman. They were an entire school of painters mentoring each other. Maybe if we had a stable of painters at Rocky Comfort, we could produce this kind of movement."

He stopped in his tracks. "Why Cinnamon Rose, that's precisely what I want for you. That freeing, creative movement—inside our prisons." He turned back towards the elevator.

"Roman, slow down, not so fast." Hope raised her cell phone and snapped us in front of a turquoise seascape, birds swooping and mullet leaping. "I can see how the painters captured enchanting moments when few people had cameras. They gripped hearts and minds."

A cinnamon cloud outside seemed plucked from the wistful paintings. Below us, church steeples pierced the sky, law court domes shone, high rises and university classrooms circled a shimmering fountain. Why couldn't I just paint that—my bird's eye view reflecting my soaring feelings? What made art good?

There was so much I didn't know or understand. Maybe I could apply for art school and learn all I was missing.

Hope joined me at the window. "What would you say, Cinnamon, if someone loved your paintings so much they offered to buy them?"

"I'd say they were crazy."

Hope checked the time on her phone, and was alerted by a text message. She looked up wide-eyed. "Do you know that we found your sister a house? It's a huge, five-bedroom rental on a neighborhood park. We've spoken for it, and are raising the money to move her in this month."

I stilled my shriek, hand over my mouth. "That would be perfect for us, for me and my kids too."

Warden Torres clapped us on the back, shook our hands and turned to go.

"Wait, Warden, what is that highway to nowhere?"

"Oh, Cinny, you've never been to the airport? Someday, I predict, you will. And beyond that's the Apalachicola National Forest, Florida's largest, full of black bears and fish in the Big River." The scenes burst fully-painted in my head.

Hope led us to the elevator, and I rolled my portfolio case after her.

We descended just in time. The cameras and journalists caught us positioning the artwork. They photographed moms and babies building block towers, finger-painting, and piled in a reading nest, chubby fingers turning bright picture books. Reporters peppered me with questions.

"Yes, I had two babies in prison, two separate sentences, and I had to give them both up within 24 hours. It crushed me. I missed them terribly. I knew I could never replace the bonding hugs and playtime I was missing. And I was only marking time inside." I shifted, trying to read the cameraman's response behind a large video camera whirring in its wheeled dolly. He motioned me to continue.

"These paintings are my vision for a prison nursery, giving moms a second chance to build their strength by raising babies inside." I paused and several reporters moved in. "Instead of robbing women of their most treasured possessions, and sending them back down the rabbit hole."

A tall, soft-faced reporter with long, auburn hair, edged right up to me. "Tell me about that rabbit hole."

"That's where you fall into darkness and chaos in tunnels and mazes. Just when you're feeling strong and hopeful, turning your life around, you lose your heart's beat. The wreckage of it all can keep you in the abyss for years."

"So, are these paintings of your children?"

"Not only mine. Many moms inside have lost children. The chaplain shared our heartaches, and we dreamed up this prison nursery. The warden made sure I got the supplies, time and space to paint our vision. But there's more to the story." I gestured to the warden behind me.

He got right to the point. "Rocky Comfort was hit by tornadoes last month. It destroyed our chapel and solitary block, and we hope to rebuild lockup as a nursery."

The auburn-haired reporter raised her cell phone. "Does that mean prisoners will no longer have to serve time in solitary?"

"Yes, we hope to cut down those numbers with this improved programming."

With that, the reporter stood in front of the big TV camera, and read the headline from Hope's press release. *"Prison nurseries, a critical reform."* She added solemnly. "The idea is ours. It belongs to all of us. What will we do about it?"

The prison nursery images stole the morning headlines, and played in a live loop on the Florida Capitol TV channel. State workers, legislators, teachers and school children crowded the mezzanine, snapped and shared photos on Facebook.

It seemed so long since I'd worried that people would be shocked to see babies in prison. Now, I wanted to hide from the flashing, clicking cameras. But Hope and Warden Torres kept pulling me out from behind pillars and introducing me to state representatives and lobbyists.

"How much?" A gray-haired lady in pearls studied a painting of an adoring child and mother with a razor wire backdrop. I looked at Hope.

"Three—" She hesitated.

"Hundred?" The woman opened her designer clutch.

The serge-suited man from the elevator cut in. "I'll pay three-thousand!" I still couldn't be sure I knew him, but his offer shook me. I glanced at Chaplain Hope.

"Three-thousand-five-hundred." The woman in pearls held up her clutch.

"Four thousand." Drew, Lexis's son, bounded up the stairs behind me and raised his wallet. He shook my hand and handed Hope his legal pad. "Silent auction?"

"We'll have a silent auction." Hope raised the legal pad. "Write your bid, name and email or phone." She placed a bid sheet on the table in front of each painting.

I had forgotten to name my paintings or organize them in any way. And yet people were stepping up and writing their bids. I pulled Hope and Drew aside. "Where does the money go?"

"What do you mean?" She looked down at me her brow creased. "To the artist, of course. The Highwaymen showed us that."

Drew nodded. "Why not? Oh, you think that because you did it for corrections, the earnings go to them?"

"Well, not if you acted independently, voluntarily," Hope said.

I nodded. "Yes, but also, Miss Hope, it was our idea together, and the warden gave me the canvas and paints."

Hope swept the air with long, tapered fingers, dismissing my objections.

"But I want to tithe—at least ten percent to the prison nursery."

Drew nodded at Hope. "She's free to donate."

I bounced on my toes. "Yes, for good paints to paint the nursery rooms—and refresh them all the time. And I want to help."

"Well then, may you be rewarded." Hope turned me back to the rotunda. "We have to get back to your public now."

Drew flashed me a dimpled grin, reinserting himself in the lineup writing bids. "Gotta get back in the queue to get me one— after you used my pen to draw them."

The clean-shaven Governor swept in from outside, and wafted a cool breeze up the stairs. He glided up the stairs, his wife trailing, and stepped in front of the paintings.

Hope steered me over to shake hands. His wife looked up from writing a silent bid, and waved. I didn't understand. After all the opposition we'd expected, why were things going so well?

"Are you going to put babies in prison, Governor?" A white-haired man stuck a CNN microphone in his face. The governor blinked and looked at the warden, who stepped up.

"First, the babies will not be prisoners. If their mothers consent, they can be entrusted to family members and sent home for an agreed-upon time. But we no longer want to send officers to retrieve babies who've been taken from a guardian's care against a prisoner's will."

"That happens?"

"Oh, yes. These women behind bars lose control of their children's safety, and it traumatizes them. With a prison nursery, inmate mothers will no longer be forced to give up custody of their babies, or to yield them to the state, or adoption agencies. That lack of choice will end."

"How do you know this is what's best for babies?" The news anchor pressed on, adjusting his black-rimmed glasses.

"We understand that babies' needs come first. Mothers will have to apply and qualify to raise their babies inside. The ideal candidates will not have violent histories, and will be able to transition with their babies within eighteen months to two years."

"How do you know this will work?"

"The results from prisons in Alabama and New York show many advantages. Mothers will be supported by committed staff who teach parenting classes. And they will be separated from the general prison population. We'll start by running a nursery, not a preschool. Does that answer your questions?"

"For now, yes." The news anchor turned to his crew for a wrap-up.

Warden Torres moved us toward our hearing room.

Hope leaned close and spoke in my ear. "Nikita texted. She and the children are on their way—in the courtyard, petting crabs."

I took a seat in the chamber, but craned my neck, keeping an eye on the door. Legislators and corrections officials presented their reports and bill proposals to board members and lawmakers sitting behind a shining table.

A bipartisan bill would reduce inmate numbers by funding drug courts and community treatment centers, like I'd been in. Another would restore prison staff cuts and benefits.

A public health bill would regulate doctors who'd staffed Florida pill mills along "oxy alley," as inmates called the pain clinics along Florida's interstates. But could it limit doubled oxy production and doctors enriching themselves from it? Or improve mental health services for addicts—women and seniors—the fastest growing numbers.

Chaplain Hope took the podium, and paused when the door opened to Tony cooing. I hurried to meet Nikita and the kids, lifting Tony's cuddly weight from her arms. Annie, in yellow-bobble pigtails and ruffled tee-shirt, grabbed my hand and planted a sloppy kiss on it. I led them through the packed room and Hope motioned us to sit in front.

She threw up slides of brick rubble, rolled razor wire and crumpled tin roofing—hurricane damage to Rocky Comfort's lockup unit. She compared costs of rebuilding it as a nursery, drawn real by my paintings. The kids *oohed* and *ahhed*. She closed with our mission statement. "To restore prisoners, and mother-child bonds, in a safe, secure environment."

Nikita was invited to read her statement next, and I cuddled Tony on my lap, the other kids close beside me.

Tall and regal at the podium, she sparkled in Mom's lilac suit, paired with her sequined headscarf. "Dear Judges." She swept the room with moist, dark eyes as though that were all of us.

"When you sentenced my sister, did you mean to sentence the rest of the family too? Did you intend to punish us all by forcing our hard-working mother, and her innocent grandchildren, into a life of poverty? Did you know you would be burdening us with all the costs of my sister's toiletries, phone calls and clothing? And these at 100 percent markup? A lot of private industries are profiting from inmates, while families and tax-payers pour into a bottomless pit." She turned the page.

"No wonder the US imprisons more per population than any other country." She looked directly at the governor, who lowered his gaze. "Including China."

"And did you know that teenagers are serving time for marijuana cigarettes while *bankstas* walk free after putting our mortgages underwater? Are any of you satisfied that our criminal justice system punishes poverty, and enforces maximum sentencing on minorities at double and triple the rate of whites?"

Committee members and lawmakers nodded, bowed their heads or shuffled papers. "Blacks are twice as likely as whites to be poor, in part, because of this injustice system."

She swept back her scarf fringes, drawing energy from upturned faces.

"Recently, I was thrown out of my trailer for not making rent and utilities. Since our mother's knee surgery, I had to miss nursing shifts to watch her and the children. All while my sister Cinnamon serves time for pain pill possession that would have gotten a *lawyer* a slap on the wrist."

In the chamber, people mumbled and someone nearby whispered, *Who vetted this?*

"When we were evicted, all our belongings were strewn on the curb and white people in a big pickup truck stole my furniture."

Several people gasped.

Kita turned to page three. "'Land order, law and order,' the politicians say to get our vote."

Several people smirked.

"But consider what those words mean in a skewed system where black people do twenty percent more time than whites for the same crimes. Consider what this does to our families." She beckoned us.

"Come on up here, Cinny—and the children."

I rose and straightened my gray suit, setting Tony on my hip, his chubby legs hugging my waist. I grabbed Annie's hand, and Kita's children followed. She gathered us in around the podium.

"My sister, Cinnamon Rose's children miss their mother every day. But they only get to play with her for a few hours on Sundays. The other day, Annie got on the phone and begged her mama to come get her." Annie lifted her face, and I stroked her pointy chin.

"Please consider building a prison nursery where mothers can grow and bond with their babies in a safe environment. And please spare families the heartache of bankruptcy, destitution and disintegration. Please," her voice shook, "give families a jail break!"

Crashing applause echoed around the room and people rose to their feet.

When Kita stepped down, the governor and his wife stepped up to the dais, shook her hand and bent to shake the children's hands. The governor waited for silence, and called for "Chaplain Hope Springs."

Hope swept her copper curls aside and stood on shaky legs. Roman Torres offered his arm and escorted her to the front.

The governor raised a polished wooden plaque. "A commendation for saving lives by exposing a drug ring inside. Please accept this token on behalf of my wife, myself and the people of Florida."

Little Annie shrieked with the approving crowd, then covered her little ears against the din.

"And also, please accept this well-deserved bonus for envisioning and proposing a prison nursery." The governor brought out from behind the podium, a large Styrofoam check for $10,000. The room erupted in cheers. The governor and first lady flanked her for a photo, before continuing.

"Secretary of Corrections, committee members, Warden Torres, Chaplain Springs, ladies, gentlemen—and children—I have another commendation."

He lifted another plaque. "This one is for Cinnamon Rose, our prison nursery artist."

My limbs went numb, and Warden Torres had to pull me to my feet, accepting Tony from my arms.

The governor shook my hand. "For your brilliant vision, I'm naming you Outstanding Social Change Artist of Florida."

I sagged and the warden, jigging Tony in one arm, hung onto my elbow with the other. Had he arranged this—or had someone else?

"Also, I would like to call your advocate, State's Attorney Drew Weaver, to present this certificate."

Drew took the framed certificate, and bowed slightly. "Cinnamon Rose!" He paused amid shouts of, *Bravo, Bring it!*

Drew practically lifted me with his grip, and waited for silence. "First, accept my gratitude for encouraging me to reconnect with my mother—your dorm-mom in prison."

A hush fell on the chamber.

"This certificate grants you clemency from all criminal charges. Please accept it with our humble gratitude."

Though I had been promised clemency, I had not received it until this moment. I was overjoyed to be free at last. I could hardly think to speak, but the words poured out on their own. "Today, I'm the happiest girl alive. And it's thanks to you all—" I gestured to Drew, Hope, Warden Torres, the governor, his wife, corrections officials, lawmakers, my sister and family. "I am finally free!"

People cheered. *Woohoo. You go girl!*

"My dream for moms inside is rising from ashes. And now I can go home to my children, and help extract my family from debt, and set them on their feet again."

Nikita brought my children to me, and put my plaque and certificate in her handbag. The crowd swept us to the rotunda where the corrections secretary had catered a fruit and cheese reception. I ate fresh green grapes and huge red strawberries for the first time in months—and fed them to my children.

Hope grabbed a microphone. "We have our silent auction winners. They are the governor and his wife for the three baby close-ups. Drew Weaver, Representative Windham and Warden Torres each won a nursery playroom painting. And the Honorable Judge Turnbull won the reading nest painting. Thanks to your generosity, we have raised $120,000 here today."

I nearly choked on my strawberry.

"Cinny, your images will forever represent this moment. Not just a moment, but a movement." She held up an envelope. "Please write your checks to Cinnamon Rose and place them in here."

Tony reared up and wailed, then buried his soft, curly head in my neck. Hope stroked his back. "Aw, time for his nap. Do you want us to gather the checks and easels? I believe you have some things to pack at the prison, and paperwork to sign?"

I hesitated. I did not want to go back inside, yet. Not with a target on my back.

Warden Torres spoke up. "We'll take care of packing your things and paperwork. Just come by my office tomorrow. Go home now and enjoy your family!"

When I joined Nikita and the children, Ruby and Denny jumped up and down, and Annie joined in. "Yay, Aunt Cinny!"

I tugged her pigtails. "I'm Mama to you, silly."

We crossed the courtyard, and the kids looked for their classmates. But Kita corralled them. "I got permission to take you home after our event."

Annie shrieked and followed her cousins, running and skipping toward the parking garage, shadows bouncing in the midday sun. It was only noon, and the day was perfect. Just like when Dex took me to Econfina Creek Falls.

"Kita, do you realize what day it is?" I chose my words carefully for the children's sake. "The anniversary of Dex's home-going."

"Yes, it is." Nikita unlocked the van and put Tony in his car seat while I buckled Annie in. I climbed in front, and she turned and backed out.

"How would you like to celebrate?"

I smoothed Miss Hope's gray pantsuit. "May I take you to his special falls? It's a little over an hour away, but it's early and the day is perfect."

"Sure, we can change when we get there. I have some extra scrubs and jeans in the back. You can roll up the legs."

I nudged her. "You giraffe."

Annie and Tony dozed, Ruby and Denny played their handheld games, and Kita described the place Hope had helped find. "It's a large brick house, five-bedrooms, each with its own bathroom and exit to a park with walking trails and playground. I just found out, before the hearing, that the landlord is offering me a rent-to-own deal. Or—" She touched my arm. "If we can create a detailed prison transition program, they will turn over the deed. That will take some time—and paintings by you!"

We high-fived. "I can do that."

I-10 flew by and Denny and Ruby's video games stopped tootling. All four children slept like cherubs, and I had so much to be thankful for. "With the money from the paintings, I can help you with costs and go to Tallahassee Community College, like Hope said, for my Associate in Art degree." It would help me catch up with my education and make up for lost time.

"You don't even have to work." Kita slowed behind a semi and glanced over quietly. "You can study and paint and get to know your children again. You've made such progress since last fall."

"Yes, it's been my healing fall."

"We're ready to release your graphic novel too. I took the perfect picture for the back cover—you with your nursery paintings."

"Well, I really want to give back. When I'm ready and it's safe again, I want to help paint the nursery and teach art inside, too. Create a stable called the Florida High-Road Women."

Kita chuckled. "Perfect."

"And I want to pay you back for all those months of child support."

"You'll do that by spending time with your kids." She passed another semi. "And mine. They've been missing their auntie ma."

We sailed high over the Apalachicola River, a blue heron gliding below us, neck tucked. I straightened a bit, realizing I no longer had to tuck my neck. I would paint and create with my children, making up for lost time.

Ten minutes later, we exited at Marianna and turned south on Highway 276. We passed several trucks pulling into the Family Dollar Distribution Center, and turned south again on 167. Sun filtered through a pecan orchard, reminding me of Daddy and poke salad crackling in bacon grease.

The highway curved west and the afternoon sun glinted off undulating macadam. "It looks like waves rolling in from the sea."

"Really, Sis?" Kita swerved around a gator—tire retread. "You have the eye of a geologist! That's exactly what they say happened here. This used to be the seashore and these sand hills were formed by wave action."

"What Ma?" Ruby craned around my seat.

Annie woke, eyes wide. "What Ma?"

"See how the highway rolls up and down like waves?"

I turned to Annie in the middle seat and tickled her knee.

She shrieked and pulled up her legs. It was so freeing to be sailing out into the world again with my kids. We reached Scott Road before Tony stirred. He woke to us bumping along the dirt road and into the parking lot for the Florida National Scenic Trail.

A kiosk map showed the trail running south along Econfina Creek under hollies, magnolias and oaks. Archaeologists had recently discovered a Native American tool kit for making arrowheads at its headwaters, and pioneers and slaves had settled its cool springs 200 years ago.

Tony called from his car seat, "Ma, Ma." My heart skipped a beat, and I reached for his clutching fingers. That was the first time I'd heard him utter my name.

Nikita spun around, amazed. "Those are his first words! What a day!"

I unbuckled and lifted Tony, hugging him to my once aching chest and letting him squeeze my neck 'til it hurt.

Hope changed from her suit into purple butterfly scrubs, and handed me her extra jeans and tee-shirt. She took Tony while I changed.

He cooed and kicked his round feet in the spring breeze, and I set him in Kita's backpack carrier. She held it high, while I slipped my arms into the straps and buckled it tight. Tony settled in, his weight perfect against my once hollow core. How I had longed to carry this burden, so easy, so light.

49
Andrew Comes Through

Still Andrew, still co-dependent.

I circled the homeless shelter in my Prius, looking for
parking. Men and women lounged among the bushes and trees on
Tennessee and Virginia Avenues, and I finally pulled in between a
a glitter-gold-and-pink, derby-hat car with Louisiana plates, and a
dusty van with a flat screen TV plugged in the dashboard.

The women's work release center was logistically located
near several Tallahassee high rise hotels, and the city's reputed
crack house.

I crossed to the white-columned house and rang the
doorbell. People rustled behind lace curtains, and a diminutive
woman opened and welcomed me inside. "Are you here for
Lexis?"

"Yes! How did you know?"

"That's all she can talk about." She called down the hall.
"Lexie!"

Lexie? She had settled in quickly with this counselor. In an
instant, Mum was racing toward me, crying "Drew!" I braced
myself to receive her impact.

Her hair was neatly combed and swept up in a French knot.
Her jeans were faded—perfect for a walk in the woods—and her
tee-shirt was a lovely emerald green, like her shining eyes.

"You are beautiful, Mum," I said. Time had creased her
face and given her a chipped tooth, but I meant it. My pointed
nose, high cheekbones and broad mouth came from her.

"You like it? Donation closet specials!"

"Ready go?"

The short counselor handed me a binder. "Excuse me, sir, you have to sign in—and out, too. Also, Lexis has to check out." She glanced at the clock. "9:15 a.m."

Mum went to the inmate log book and wrote the time, her first furlough from prison in eight years. She grinned the whole time and nudged me when I blocked the door. "Out of my way."

I chuckled, and followed her across the street.

"Care to pick my car?"

"I pick...the raggedy one!" She pointed to the white Prius, and I opened her door.

"You should've locked it in this neighborhood." She waved at the live-in cars and bushes.

"Oh, I did. But it unlocks automatically when I get near it with this fob." I pulled the remote from my pocket.

"What?" Mum gaped like a schoolgirl. "The car kinda looks like an egg, but I'll take it."

I hooted.

"You still laugh the same, too—like your sister."

"Wow, Mum! Only you would know that." It felt like a homecoming. I pushed the start button and the car glided into the street.

Mum grabbed the door handle. "Hey! How is this thing moving? You didn't even start it!"

"It's a hybrid." I knew the word was nonsense to her, but I tried to demonstrate as we drove. "Look here." The video diagram in the dashboard, flashed a dashed orange line running from a green box. "That's the electric battery working. When we pick up speed, power will transfer to the gas engine."

"I think I'd have an accident watching that." She peered at the street and back again.

"I almost did at first, but you get used to it." I waited at Bronough Street for the light.

"There's oodles more cars than there used to be, too."

What must it be like to wake eight years later and see the outside world so changed—with twice as many cars on the road. "It's like a perpetual rush hour, eh? See, there? Another Prius and a Sonata—hybrids are taking over. They've been around five or six years, but I just got this secondhand. It gets about fifty miles a gallon."

Mom whistled low. "I remember when fifteen miles a gallon was good." She shot me a chipped-toothed grin. "Do you know what I can't believe? *I'm* riding in a car."

"Yes." Too late, I realized how tepid I sounded.

"I'm *riding* in a car. I'm riding in a *car*!"

"Yes, *yes* you are!" I let her enthusiasm infect me. "Oh, I get it. You haven't ridden in a *car* lately?"

"Not in like eight years! *I'm riding in a car.*"

"How did you get your CDL?" We headed up North Monroe.

"Oh, that was on computers and then some parking and shifting practice in the prison lot. It wasn't open-road, free-wheeling like this. It wasn't riding *away* in a *car*."

I pulled into a filling station, took out my credit card and filled up, happy the day was a perfect 74 degrees.

Lexis gasped when I drove away from the pump.

"What?" I asked sweeping around the cloverleaf onto I-10 West.

"You drove-off!"

"What? Pardon, Mum?"

"You just drove off without paying."

"Oh no, Mum, we pay at the pump now. I just swiped my card in the electronic reader."

Mom's forehead wrinkled. "Huh?"

My iPhone lit up and I handed it to her. "You answer. I think it's Len."

She looked puzzled. "How do I do that?"

I showed her how to slide her finger across the screen and talk to it. "Hello Len, I can't work today. Here. Talk to my Mum."

"Len?" Lexis said. "So, you work with my son?" She lowered the phone and peered at the screen, then realized she had to raise it to her ear again. "Yes, Andrew's taking me on a road trip—my first since prison."

I was amazed how open she was about serving time.

"Yes, I'm his birth mum. I'm sure he'll call back when he's not driving." She handed the phone back.

"Push 'End,'" I touched the screen so she could see the button.

"Oh, just touch the screen? How in the…? Neat! Hey, I just talked on a cell phone. For the first time, ever!"

"Yes, you did." I fist-bumped her. "And it'll be old hat soon."

We were sailing along I-10 when the phone dinged again. I handed it to Mum.

"Do you know how to swipe it open?" I asked.

"Sure!" But when Lexis said "Hello?" there was no answer.

"It's not a call; it's a text. Just look at the screen."

"Oh, it's from Len, it says, 'Have a great time with your Mum.'" She hooted. "That's the first time I've read a text on a cell phone."

"That's a lot of firsts for one day, eh?"

"You *do* sound like a Brit."

"Well, Mum, Joy is from Canada. Here, I want to play you a song by one of her friends, perfect for our trip today." I touched a button on my steering wheel and the car filled with stereo guitar cords.

Mum leaned her head back and closed her eyes.

To the river I am going bringing sins I cannot bear;
Come and cleanse me, come forgive me,
Lord I need to meet you there…

She sat up, cheeks wet. "Are you okay then, with my giving you up for adoption?"

"Yes, very. I'm so happy you were able to, Mum. I know it was hard for you, for both of us. I wanted so much to come with you, but it wouldn't have worked, would it?"

"Perhaps not at your age. You were already in school." Mum wiped her scarred cheek. "So many women in prison are moms. I wish corrections departments had more places that let moms care for their children while in rehab. I am just so lucky you came back for me."

I reached for her hand. It was so small and rough in my big soft one. "Have you been working a garden?"

"Not me, son. Cinny did that. My hands are from doing heads. You know, dyes, extensions, curls, braids, you name it. I'm hoping to get a salon job at one of the hotels downtown."

"Nice!" The music gripped me again.

Precious Jesus, I am ready
to surrender every care.

"I missed you terribly, Drew. But like Psalms says, 'God puts the lonely in families,' doesn't he?"

I was stunned at the recognition. "Yes, yes he does."

"All those women inside were like children to me. I sometimes joked that after you were adopted, I had to take more prisoners."

I squeezed her hand again. The pine forest thickened as we approached the Apalachicola River. We crossed the Big River, flowing brown and constant to the Gulf. It was low, its bottomland forests thirsty above sandy banks.

A smile wreathed Mum's face. "I do believe the Lord had a plan B for me—and now he's giving me back my Plan A."

"Yes, he is." I nodded and beat out the timing of the music.

Come and join us, in the river,
Come find life beyond compare,
He is calling, He is waiting;
Jesus longs to meet you there.

We passed a few semis and RVs, and turned south in Marianna on Route 276, then south and west again on 167. Several miles later, we dipped through undulating highway. "Look Mum, these hills were formed wave action, back when this was the Gulf Coast."

Her jaw dropped and her face lit up.

We rolled to a stop at Highway 231, and I looked both ways, glimpsing the Midgets bar, out the passenger window.

"Drew, once I would have asked you to take me in for a drink."

"I know, Mum. Once, I would have. But I've learned the hard way. A DUI arrest. Had to call my adoptive parents from jail. They got me into a twelve-step program—and helped me keep my job with the state."

"You're a stepper too, Drew?" Her eyebrows rose.

"Yup, binge drinking, my costliest lesson ever. I paid a lawyer who help clear my record, though. That's probably thanks to your prayers, too."

We turned north on Highway 231 and took the first left onto Scott Road. The pavement ended and the Prius skidded along a red sand road, swerving as I hit the brakes at the Econfina Creek sign. We bumped over a sandy berm, left by years of road-plowing, and pulled into the parking area beside a blue van.

We took a moment to study the kiosk map. It showed the Florida National Scenic Trail running south along the creek on Northwest Florida Water Management District conservation land.

"This is Panama City's major drinking water supply."

"You know so much." She hugged me tight.

I pointed to a photo of volunteers building a footbridge. "I know those guys; helped them clear trail and build bridges."

Mum tilted her face up. "You've done so much."

I led her along a sandy trail through grasslands dotted with newly planted longleaf pine "candles." The path dipped toward an oak and magnolia forest, and I showed her the orange dollar-sized blazes we'd painted on tree trunks along the trail. "If you ever worry you've left the trail, just stop and look back."

She stopped with me, and turned around.

"We painted orange blazes on both sides so you can look back and know you're still on the right heading."

"How comforting, Drew."

She stumbled and I caught her.

"It's been like that for me these eight years. Whenever I trip up, I just have to look back and see how God led me."

Sunlight danced through glittering leaves for a mile or so, and we reached the creek, a rushing rapid, flowing in the ravine beneath us.

We paused and headed up a short rise and down into a mucky dip where the volunteers had laid boards with shingles for grips. Two large turkeys flushed from a roost over the path, their huge variegated wings spreading as they flew up the creek.

We hiked up another hill and down another dip. We slid into a stream and three quail flew up, twittering, at our feet. Water trickled in the gully and flowed in rivulets over the ravine into the creek.

"Wow, how I've missed life outside the fence," Mum said.

We scaled the next rise, and voices rose and fell through the forest. We picked up our pace as the path opened and widened along the creek. There, around a bend were several women and children crossing a sturdy footbridge. A tall woman in purple scrubs ambled behind two school children and a pig-tailed pre-schooler in yellow tee-shirt. Leading the way was a petite woman with corn-rowed poof carrying a bobbing baby in a backpack. She turned at the bridge to wait for the others.

Something seemed familiar about her. "Mum, look up ahead. Is that Cinnamon?" Or was it just a school girl in jeans and sweatshirt carrying a baby doll?

"Yes, Drew!" Lexis quickened her pace. "Cinny!" She called, waving.

Cinnamon turned and shrieked. "Lexis, Drew! How did you find this place?"

"How did you?" We rushed together and collided in shouts and hugs.

50
Healing Rises

Still Cinnamon, still grateful.

Lexis and Drew fell in behind us along Econfina Creek,
and Tony jumped higher in the backpack, calling *Mama, mama.*

Lexis cooed in Tony's face, and he grabbed her nose 'til
she yelped. She had played with the kids many Sundays at Rocky
Comfort Visitor's Park and they loved her like their own grandma.
We *were* family.

Lexis bubbled with energy. "Drew picked me up from work
release in a ghost car that moves without making a sound."

Annie grabbed her hand. "What, Nana?"

"It practically drives itself too."

"Like a ghost?" Annie asked.

"Yes, Drew was driving it like magic. And I learned to use
his cell phone—and sent my first text message, too."

"Like magic." Annie nodded. She knew.

We reached the bridge, and Ruby pointed to the clear,
tannin-stained water flowing over a sandy bottom. "It looks like
co-cola."

Drew led her and Denny down over some roots to the
water, crouching and scooping some up to drink.

Ruby gasped and Denny hollered. Annie skidded down the
root ladder with Kita close behind.

Drew smacked his lips. "Yes, it's clean water. In fact, it's
what runs from the taps in Panama City. It's stained by leaves—
just like tea."

I slowed to wait for the kids scrambling up the bank, and
Lexis caught up with me. "Did you hear that Reese's human
trafficking case was scheduled for a hearing?"

"Whew, sure took long enough. May it go well." I shifted Tony back to center, but he crawled up again, peering over my shoulder at Lexis. "Do you know if Mindy ever got out?"

"Yes, and her charges were dropped. She got her job back too."

We reached the other side of the creek, and the path wound downhill. The stream gurgled over the creek bank and we reached a sandy beach on a large bend in the creek. We paused to let the stragglers catch up. Tony squealed and waved.

"Look Ma." Annie pointed to a large tree lying across the creek. "It's a bridge."

"Yes, that's how people used to cross the creek before we built all those foot bridges." Drew got down on her level. "Would that be fun?"

She danced around on the sand, bobbing her head. Drew grabbed her hand and teetered halfway across, then back. There was only jungle on the other side.

We headed back to the path, brushing palmetto fronds, beating a hollow, woody percussion with our knees. A faint gushing, grew louder, and we rounded another bend. I turned to Drew directly behind me. "How did you know about this special place?"

"Oh, don't you know?" Drew's brown eyes twinkled. "I discovered them as a Conquistador, centuries ago."

"Yeah, right."

"In fact, it was with my stepdad, Day, while hiking the trail several years ago. I've been working with the trail volunteers, ever since."

I tripped over a log and Drew grabbed Tony before he tipped out head first. He heaved the heavy log off the path.

Around another bend, a gushing spout rushed over the bank and into the creek. I stopped and filled my longing heart. *Dex, oh Dex.*

Lexis gasped. "Oh Cinny! Are these the falls your brother took you to?"

"Yes." I turned and faced my family, reaching for Annie's hand. "These are my healing falls."

Drew lifted Tony off my back and took off Tony's shoes, bouncing his round feet on the sand

I shucked my shoes, and helped Annie with hers. Drew unlaced his hiking boots and the others kicked theirs off, too.

Lexis lifted Tony, brushing his feet. "Does this child have a godfather?"

"What's a godfather?" It sounded like a murdering crime boss.

"Not like the movie." Lexis laughed. "It's someone who takes a spiritual interest in your child, remembers his birthday, and comes to visit, Christmas, Easter, holidays and weekends. Someone who supports his growth and development."

That's exactly what my kids needed, especially with their fathers gone. "Yes, please, Drew! Will you be Annie's godfather, too?"

Annie took my hand, then reached for Drew's, and pulled her legs up, swinging between us.

"Why sure, I've always wanted children, lots of them."

Lexis grinned. "And you have your sister's kids too. You'll be busy."

Nikita lined the children's shoes along the bank. "And mine, too, if you like." Her smile spread across russet cheeks.

We skidded down the slope into chilly water. The children shrieked and splashed in the current. It pushed us sideways and we grabbed them, climbing over logs. We gathered at the foot of the twelve-foot falls, Annie clinging to me, and Tony hanging onto Drew's neck.

"Watch this." I knelt in the roiling water, beneath the powerful falls, its splash washing grit from my face. Eyes closed, I sifted through the sand, and felt a sharp stone. What I pulled up was a carved arrowhead.

Drew gasped. "Cinny, that's priceless!"

"This hole beneath the falls is what Dex called a honey pot. He found a dugong bone for me last time."

Drew bent down, still clutching Tony, and swished, too, pulling up a smooth round rock, worn by the sands of time. He handed it to Denny. "A memory stone so you always remember this day."

I gave my arrowhead to Annie. "Put it in your pocket. Your grandpa's people made it hundreds of years ago."

"Nice," Lexis said. "So you're Native American, too?"

"Yes, this is our sacred land."

Annie rubbed and tasted the bleached, furrowed arrowhead.

"It's okay, you can lick it—that's clean dirt." I scooped her up in wet arms and faced the others. "It's time."

"Time for what?" Drew read my vibes.

"Time we start a community transition program where parents can serve time with their kids."

"Great idea, Cinny!" Nikita swept her hand through the air and the powerful waterfall. "Ouch, needles! We can start it at our new home."

Drew grinned. "Any idea what we'll call it?"

"Healing Falls!" Lexis sang out from behind the flowing curtain, holding out her hands. Drew and I each grabbed one, and pulled in Kita and the kids. We huddled, concealed behind the shimmering curtain.

Gazing through the sparkling water, its splash washing our feet, the falls seemed to reverse themselves and flow backwards.

Healing rises.

Acknowledgements

The many women inside who inspired me deserve the highest honor and affection for inviting me into their lives. They showed more faith and hope than most people on the outside. Often, the good shepherd carried them through deep valleys; they lost custody of their children, and the law enforced legalized suffering. They endured painful separations, and pursued their sons and daughters against all odds. Some gave up babies for adoption against their wills, taking paltry payouts. Their greatest joy was reuniting with children, and building back trust. Families and communities ached too, and I yearned for solutions. I envisioned building nurseries in prisons, and discovered that some have them.

I thank Celebrate Recovery Inside, the prison staff who invited us in, and volunteers who accompanied me year after year: Barbara Ward, Kate Brady, Melanee Davidson, Connie Collins, Liz White, Gaby Hawkes, LaFaye Kiely, Lisa Hamby, Kristina Holman-Mohr and others.

I'm indebted to my Tallahassee writing group who responded to early drafts: Nina Sichel, Betsy Kellenberger, and our perennial host, Lynn Peterson. Other readers, too, gave valuable feedback, Annie Layer, John Frantz and self-publishing phenom, Babette De Jongh. I thank those who encouraged me along the way, Michael Morris, Ralph Friesen and my launch team in several nations.

Tracy Leigh Foutz, your edgy, narrative cover has already touched a mother separated from her children. And my other colleagues at Florida Health, thanks for many inspired moments, especially artist Tiffany Huba Bonilla for early cover designs.

My husband Philip Kuhns advised me financially, and my father, sisters (Hope, Charity, Grace), and children, waited and hoped. Thank you, Anthony, Tom, Stefan and Sarah.

About the Author

Faith Eidse was inspired to write *Healing Falls* by her own twelve-step process, and taking the program into women's prisons of northwest Florida—state, federal and work release center. She resonated with the suffering and resilience of inmates, especially mothers separated from their children.

(Faith Eidse photo)

She, too, was separated from family during revolution as a global nomad born in Congo, and raised among worlds, in Congo/Zaire, Canada and the U.S. She co-edited a Hachette title, *Unrooted Childhoods*, now a Princeton University textbook, and *Writing Out of Limbo* (Cambridge Scholars Publishing, 2011). She won a Florida Historical Society award for the oral history, *Voices of the Apalachicola* (University Press of Florida, 2006), while working at Northwest Florida Water Management District, and has published an oral history of her linguist-medical missionary parents, *Light the World* (Friesen Press, 2012). It includes portions of a Kingsbury Award-winning memoir chapter on her leprosy treatment, penned while earning a Ph.D. in Creative Writing from Florida State University. She is adjunct English professor at Barry University, and senior editor at the Florida Department of Health. Her "How to Write" series is video-conferenced statewide.

If you enjoyed this novel, please leave a review at https://www.amazon.com/Faith-Eidse/e/B00IWT66YA